# Naked

## By

## Jim Shields

ISBN: 9798671879360

PublishNation

www.publishnation.co.uk

# Contents

Very special thanks to

Eileen Watt who showed me the way and Annette who encouraged me all the way.

# A Journey in Faith

It was a rough crossing. The mutinous black seas lashed the boat, relentlessly tossing it about like a cork in a turbulent stream. Sitting alone, wrapped in a black-and-white habit, the Cross and Passion nun furiously fingered her beads. The head-on wind increased to gale force and mountainous waves played with the boat, hurling it around like an orca toying with a doomed seal. Beleaguered, the nun clung to the railing, thankful her stomach was empty. Clutching her rosary beads, she prayed the sorrowful mysteries: the Agony in the Garden, the Scourging at the Pillar, the Crowning with Thorns, the Carrying of the Cross, and the Crucifixion.

In her desperation, she wasn't praying. She was petitioning her Lord of the Cross to rescue her from drowning, like a child pleading for a good exam grade. Sister Clare couldn't swim. It hadn't crossed her mind that nobody could swim in the stormy sea battering the boat. In her anguish, with eyelids welded together, she felt a presence beside her.

"Don't be afraid," a voice in her head whispered, "you of little faith."

Abruptly transported, she was in the boat with Him on the Sea of Galilee, when He rebuked the wind and calmed the sea.

"Are you still afraid? Have you still no faith?" the voice in her head asked.

Bolstered, her demon fears driven out, she opened her eyes, loosened her grip on the beads, and furtively glanced around. She was alone. A gentle stillness settled on her.

She had always wanted to be a teacher. Though she loved her profession, she felt called to something else, something more. At first, it was just a gentle rousing that gaining momentum, acquired powerful energy of its own. Eventually, after much prayer and thought, she surrendered to the call. It was one evening, just before Christmas, when she unceremoniously announced to her unsuspecting parents in

Glasgow that she was going to be a nun. Her father, aghast, said,

"You're what? You're going into a nunnery?" Her mother, she thought for a brief moment, rejoiced, before incredulity showed on her face.

She read her thoughts.

*My wee Mary Ann a nun. Sure it's only like yesterday her hair was in pigtails. Absurd, her that's so fond of boys and dancing. I won't relish being thought of as the mother of a nun, or the neighbours saying, "Well for you, missus, with a daughter a nun to pray for you."*

In the days that followed that announcement her father frequently posed the question,

"Are you sure you know what you're doing? You'll be giving up a lot you know." An only child, she knew what he meant.

"Very sure," she always responded.

When she looked back at it she quietly smiled. She was christened Mary Ann. Clare was her chosen name when she became a novice. They had travelled by tram across Glasgow, the three of them, that day. She sat beside her mother. Nothing much was said. The tram lurched forward, transporting them into different futures. All the things she had been told to bring with her, fitted with room to spare, into the small case she was grasping.

In the convent, they were ushered into a small reception room by Mother Josephine, the sister responsible for the well-being of all the novices. Putting them at ease, Mother Josephine candidly engaged her parents in conversation. She was open and authentic. As the moment of parting neared, and the conversation lulled, Mother Josephine tactfully excused herself and Mary Ann. With her case in hand, she was taken to her cell.

It was a small, bare space. Her postulant habit lay folded on the bed waiting for her. Alone, she suddenly felt claustrophobic. The cell walls were closing in on her. She wanted to scream but fought against it. She had chosen the cloister rather than the secular world, she reminded herself.

2

Composure restored, she put on the long black postulant habit with its white collar. A short black cape and a shoulder-length veil completed the transition.

She looked around for a mirror. There was none.

*How do I look? How will others see me?* she thought. It was a moment of transformation. With Mother Josephine, she rejoined her parents, said her goodbyes, and freed them to go their separate way.

That was a long time ago. Now she was being sent on a mission to establish Saint Comgall's Cross and Passion Convent to nurture the education of Catholic girls in the parish of Larne.

Lost in thought, she wasn't conscious that the boat had docked. It was the disembarking passengers shuffling past who signalled that the moment had come for her to set foot in Ireland. It was then she realised that this was the first time she had travelled beyond the boundaries of her native Glasgow. Making her way from the harbour to the terraced house that was to be her convent home, she cut quite a figure in her black-and-white habit and headdress of coif and wimple. Quickly the natives grew accustomed to the cohort of penguins dwelling among them.

An increase in the number of nuns in the sisterhood, of which she was now Mother Superior, meant that they needed more spacious secluded accommodation. When a suitable property presented itself Sister Clare snapped it up and moved the convent into it. Throughout the next decade, she busied herself managing the growth of the convent and servicing the needs of the parish. She was an astute, accomplished, and decisive leader.

But the most exciting, exhilarating, and challenging experience of her religious life lay in wait for her. The community acquired Drumalis Mansion and Estate, and for three years she oversaw its adaptation to transform it into a convent and retreat house. When it was fit for purpose the Sisters took up residence.

*It was a long time ago, a different time and a different world in many respects*, she thought, sitting alone in her favourite spot in Drumalis on a balmy summer's evening, gazing over the tranquil sea, stretching to merge with the sky. She was blissfully unaware of how the stigmatic disadvantages of her working-class background had somehow been surmounted.

An act of God, perhaps. Who knows? Her aptitude for science and music was recognised in school, encouraged, and supported. One day the headmistress took her aside, she thought for a telling-off. Instead, rather sternly, she said,

"Your education is easily carried by you, child. It doesn't weigh much on your back. You have God-given talents. Be sure to put them to good use."

She felt a slow-burning fuse of ambition ignite somewhere within her consciousness. She could have a future. It was up to her. It was her moment of aspiration.

Diligently she applied herself to her studies and matriculated, and later graduated with an honours degree in physics. It was quite an achievement then, for a woman, especially a woman from a working-class background. But that was not all. She didn't neglect her music. Mary Ann was an accomplished musician.

She got a job she grew to love, teaching physics and maths in a college close to home. Most weekends she went dancing with friends. It was great fun. Boyfriends … she had boyfriends. There would have been something wrong with her if she hadn't. Quite a few, actually, when she thought about it, but none found the cradle of her heart.

Two Cross and Passion sisters taught in the same college as Mary Ann. The college principal was one of them. Her daily contact with the sisters, her involvement in parish pastoral care, and her participation in retreats, missions, and other activities organised by the Cross and Passion Convent offered Mary Ann more than a glimpse into their way of life, their vocation. They were teachers too, but with a higher purpose, it seemed.

She found their way of life more appealing, more desirable. Tentatively, inquisitively at first, she asked her nun colleagues about their way of life. Actually, on reflection, she was telling them more about her than they were telling her about themselves. She was exposing her inner self, often without encouragement.

Mary Ann persisted and offered herself as a candidate for admission to the Cross and Passion Order. She had taken her first firm step on a journey of faith. Once her request was approved, she became an aspirant. The process of discernment had commenced. A journey of discovery into what religious life embraced had begun.

It was a slow, gentle journey that let her experience community life in stages at first hand. It was a two-way process. She would get to know the community and they would get to know her. At first, she spent Saturday afternoons participating in the routine work of the convent. The sisters referred to the convent as 'the house', which seemed to her entirely appropriate, as it was their home. Later she stayed overnight at weekends and immersed herself more fully in the life of the community.

Her induction lasted a full year, during which the dawning of her unfolding began. She felt the magnetic pull of Jesus and sought unity with him in discipleship. The year had passed quickly. For Mary Ann, it was the moment of decision on her journey in faith: to disengage or to take the next step. To deepen her commitment and test her vocation she decided to join the community as a postulant.

The day she entered the Cross and Passion community is one she would never forget. How could she? The tense, awkward, silent tram journey across Glasgow with her parents, alone in her cell putting on the postulant habit, vainly looking for a mirror, greeting her parents dressed as a nun, the solemn induction at mid-morning prayer, and finally the presentation of the postulant crucifix from the Mother Superior. Afterwards, at the parting, she didn't shed any tears. She was happy. Alone in her cell that night she nervously fingered the postulant crucifix, touching and retouching the wounded body of Jesus. She couldn't extract the nails that pierced his body but she firmly resolved to shoulder his cross.

Life as a postulant for Mary Ann was the same as for the professed sisters. Each day began with early morning prayers, followed by spiritual exercises that unified the pattern of communal life. The Cross and Passion Order, which had been established with a mission to teach, was a natural habitat for her. She was able to continue teaching. But now, with distancing from the world and all its distractions, her contemplative vocation added new aspects to her work. Amid all the activities in the convent, there were moments of recreation when she cheerily entertained her sisters playing tunes on the piano she had once danced to, and occasionally voicing a song. She loved the Divine Office, which was sung many times during the day in Gregorian chant.

In the rhythm of the academic year Mary Ann's time as a postulant flashed past. Decision time had arrived again: another milestone on her journey in faith. The next stage towards becoming a professed nun was to enter the noviciate. That would mean signing up to two years of study, focused on the meaning of religious life, with particular emphasis on the vows of chastity, poverty, obedience, and devotion to the Passion of Jesus.

She considered the vows in reverse order. Putting her shoulder to the cross of Jesus was already a commitment. Jesus, her saviour, who she would be obedient to unto death, was a model she could follow. Poverty didn't challenge her working-class background. But chastity troubled her. It wasn't the vow. She aspired to give all her love to God and through God to all people. It was her father's remark,

"You don't know what you'll be missing." She knew exactly what she would be missing: a family of her own. There was no doubt in her mind about that. Most women aspired to motherhood. But as an only child, she would sever her father's branch of the family tree if she became a nun. End his lineage. She understood his feelings. Her thoughts swung back and forth like a thurible on the end of a chain in the hands of a priest sending petitions disguised as incense heavenwards.

Sometimes, as her thoughts twitched, the thurible in motion wobbled, disturbing the upward-petitioning flow of incense. Slowly her thoughts stilled. She made her decision.

On becoming a novice Mary Ann received her religious name. Now she was known as Sister Clare. She wore the habit of a Cross and Passion nun without the distinctive sign worn over the heart. Her black veil was replaced by a white one. She continued with her teaching duties, which she revelled in, but now there was a change in focus and emphasis. She rose early every morning for private prayer, followed by morning prayers, which were part of the daily liturgy, then Mass, mid-morning prayer and breakfast. And that was only for starters.

Her college duties did not impinge on her religious studies and her development towards becoming a professed nun. She loved the silence in the convent, the easy way her sisters went about their work and play, the gentleness in the tone and intonation of their speech. There was lots of recreation time when her musical talents were put to good use. Her workload was heavy but, in pleasant company, easily borne. The evenings ended with the night prayers at 9 p.m., which invited silence until the dawning of another day. As time passed her unfolding continued unabated. She was becoming in faith more childlike, trusting, uncomplicated, and innocent.

Her two years as a novice, separated from the humdrum activities of the world and all its distractions, formed the foundation for a religious life of sacrifice, atonement, holiness, and devotion to the Passion of Jesus. As a junior professed sister, she renewed her vows temporarily to allow her time to consider the next step on the path she had chosen to become a professed Cross and Passion nun. She joyfully received the sign of the Cross and Passion congregation: the black veil to replace the white one, and the wedding ring symbolising her maturing love for Jesus.

Knowing her mind, Sister Clare did not deliberate long. After many years of preparation, she willingly pronounced her perpetual vows and became a professed Sister of the Cross and Passion congregation, consecrating herself to Jesus forever.

The sound of doors opening stirred her. Retreatants in ones and twos and more tumbled out into the cool evening air, talking and laughing. Sister Clare turned and looked, a hint of a smile shaping her untarnished lips. She said,

"I could see and hear them, but they couldn't see me."

Sister Clare had long passed away. Passed on, perhaps, but never gone.

"When you visit Drumalis," she continued, "sit in my favourite spot. Face the sea, close your eyes, and embrace the silence of seascape. You might sense my presence. You might experience the surprise of your unfolding."

# Atonement

Julia came from a well-regarded family and was proud of her rural background. She had an easy way about her that belied a backbone of steel burnished on home farm labour. Her melodic voice had a distinctive lilt. She was good company. Blessed with an infectious laugh she made friends easily. Her first year at university, after the initial settling-in period, passed quickly and uneventfully. Julia had many friends at university but no boyfriends as such, meaning that she had many boys who were friends, but not an intimate boyfriend. Romance had yet to touch Julia. She was pure in thought, word, and deed.

In her first week at university, she sought out the chaplaincy, noted the times of the services, and thereafter attended Mass every Sunday as well as on designated holy days. She got to know Father Owens, one of the chaplains, particularly well. He was a middle-aged man from a neighbouring parish, who was kind and always available whenever needed. Julia liked him. He reminded her of the parish priest at home. He persuaded Julia to become a Minister of the Word. She would read the assigned readings at Mass for the congregation to hear the word of God. It was a duty that demanded commitment, conviction and preparation. Later, when encouraged to become a Eucharistic Minister, she declined, because she genuinely felt unworthy of the honour of dispensing Holy Communion. As was custom and practice in her upbringing and moulding in religious ritual, she went to confession every month without fail, keeping the First Friday Devotions, which included attending Mass, receiving Holy Communion, and periods of meditation. These devotions were something most of her contemporaries had long abandoned. She religiously confessed her sinless sins: the careless word, the forgotten night prayers, a selfish thought – or neglecting to phone her mother at the weekend – comprehensively described the extent of her veniality.

During her first year at university, she had difficulty for a little while, as lots of first-year students do: coping with the new-found freedoms, being treated as an adult, experiencing lectures for the first time, and just the newness of it all. But, with diligence, commitment, and hard graft, she coped. Firm in the faith and the morals of her upbringing, the year passed quickly. With her many new friends, Julia enjoyed a very full and active social life participating in sports and many other activities. She was thriving on it.

Then one Sunday in September at the beginning of Michaelmas term Father Owens announced at Mass that a new chaplain had been appointed to replace him. His parish and university pastoral duties had become too much for him. The new chaplain, Father Fitzgerald, would take up his appointment with immediate effect. Father Owens added that he was sure that they would all give Father Fitzgerald a big welcome and every support in his new ministry.

After Mass Father Owens said his goodbyes, wished everyone well over a cup of tea, gave them his blessing and left with a hint of a tear in his eye. Julia, like her friends at Mass, wondered what the new chaplain would be like for a moment or two until more pressing matters like coursework submission deadlines claimed her attention.

A couple of days later, Julia was hurrying along the central mall in the main university building between lectures. As she approached the chaplaincy she noticed a new name on the list of designated chaplains. Father Fitzgerald had replaced the name of Father Owens. She paused to look, then continued on her way. When the door of the chaplaincy burst open in front of her, she was abruptly brought face to face with a young man dressed as a priest leaving in a hurry. With eyes cast down, he narrowly avoided colliding with her. Standing practically face to face, he apologised for his clumsiness and with a twinkle in his bright blue eyes, introduced himself.

That was her first encounter with the new chaplain, Father Fitzgerald. At first sight, he was young, tall, athletic, and ruggedly handsome, with short-cropped jet-black hair and piercing bright blue eyes. When he spoke he had a bit of a brogue, which made for easy listening. As they briefly exchanged pleasantries an image of Father Fitzgerald formed in Julia's mind. She liked him. She could trust him. With her first impressions of him logged, she hurried off to her next lecture.

It was a busy week for Julia, who was always fastidious about her studies, meeting the deadlines for her coursework and writing up lab reports. It was only when checking her dairy that she realised she was on the rota for reading at Mass on Sunday with the new chaplain, the celebrant. While checking her missal to prepare for the readings, she read about St Paul's problem with the thorn in his flesh.

Julia arrived in the chaplaincy early, to ensure that the Gospel lectionary on the lectern was open at the passages she had prepared to read. A few fellow students already there were chatting to Father Fitzgerald, not yet dressed in his vestments. Other students and staff drifted in as the time for Mass approached. Before Mass Father Fitzgerald introduced himself to the assembled group of worshippers, outlining what he had been doing since ordination and what he would try to offer by way of pastoral care.

Then he prepared for Mass but did not wear the full array of vestments, as Father Owens had always done. His robing for Mass was minimalistic and his homily was short, direct, and to the point, leaving everyone present something to think about in the week ahead, and ending with the assurance that he would always be available when and if needed. After Mass, there was much chatting over tea and coffee. Julia didn't engage with Father Fitzgerald, other than referring to their previous brief encounter. He was busy getting to know everyone who was there. Unnoticed, she slipped away.

The first Friday of the month was approaching. During her upbringing, Julia had cultivated a devotion to the Sacred Heart of Jesus that consisted of going to confession, attending Mass, receiving Holy Communion, and a period of meditation once a month. This practice was known as the First Friday Devotion. She didn't need to put it in her diary. Custom and practice in her rearing had habituated her. Old habits never die. With Father Owens, confession was always very formal and ritualistic conducted via a Chinese wall in the form of a screen divider. In the chaplaincy, confession could be by appointment if preferred, or at set times for confessors to present themselves and avail of the sacrament. As she had always done, month by month, Julia prepared for confession by way of a thorough examination of conscience.

Properly prepared, she presented herself at the chaplaincy at the set time. She was not usually the only confessor there, but on this occasion she was. When Father Fitzgerald asked if she wanted confession Julia nodded her assent.

Putting on a purple stole, he gestured to two chairs that had been arranged facing each other and waited until she was seated before taking the other chair. Julia felt very ill at ease. Father Fitzgerald sensed her discomfort and smiled.

"Take it easy and slow. This is how we do it now. And don't worry. We won't be interrupted. The sign outside beside the door is red," he said.

Julia somehow stuttered through her litany of sinless misdemeanours until she had cleansed her soul of any imagined minuscule stain of sin. Father Fitzgerald listened without interruption, let her talk, and, when she had finished, asked about her family, how often she was in touch with them, how were they doing, about her siblings, her holiday plans, and more. The formality of confession had been transformed into a conversation within the boundaries of pastoral care. Julia left the chaplaincy relieved of any feeling of sinfulness and with her faith in a loving God reinforced. In truth, in her heart, she welcomed the open conversational, informal approach to seeking forgiveness and ultimately redemption.

*It's how I would talk to Jesus*, she thought.

And so the confessional encounters continued over time, increasing in frequency from once a month in Michaelmas term to once a fortnight in Hilary term, then to once a week in Trinity term. It could only become more frequent than that by appointment. Julia's friendly weekly conversational confessions continued until, just before Christmas, the pattern changed.

With the Christmas break fast approaching, term exams in full swing and festivities arranged, no one noticed the change in

Julia. Her close friends, as they exchanged Christmas gifts and greetings, didn't perceive that she was much quieter than usual and didn't laugh as much as she used to.

After Christmas, with everyone back on campus settling down to business as usual again, it was a little while before the change in Julia's demeanour became apparent. She wasn't her normal bright, outgoing, and fun-loving self. She was withdrawn, almost self-absorbed. She didn't resume the weekly pattern of confession she had pursued previously and, for the first time in her life, missed Mass.

It was only when she failed to read at Mass as rostered that concern registered with Father Fitzgerald. His discreet enquiries alerted him to the changes in her behaviour and he wondered if something had happened at home to make her so withdrawn, quiet, and, by all accounts, sad.

*Julia*, he thought, *the one with the infectious laugh, who is held in such high esteem by all her friends.* It was his duty, he knew, to seek her out and find out why she had distanced herself from her friends and what, if anything was troubling her.

He was pacing the chaplaincy, pondering how best to do what he had to do, when, glancing out the window, he saw her wandering forlornly around the playing fields. He stopped pondering, checked his diary, cancelled all his appointments, and hurried out to meet her. Wednesday afternoon always in term time, was set aside for sports. Teams and spectators were gathering for football, hockey, and other sports, but Julia plodded on, totally unaware of what was happening around her.

She didn't see him approaching, didn't know he was beside her until he spoke in his soft, engaging brogue. She didn't acknowledge him, just kept on walking as he gently escorted her away from the playing fields towards a river walk that bounded the campus. By the side of a pool in the river, where the music of the running water quietened, there was a bench. When they sat down he breached the silence between them, and with concern colouring, his voice asked Julia what was troubling her. For a little while, the only audible sounds were made by the river water, washing the stones in its way, and the birds pitching love songs to one another. Then, as she slowly turned to face him, he caught a glimmer of something in her eyes. Something beyond sorrow something akin to sad surprise. Then her eyes dulled and the glimpse he thought was hope disappeared.

He liked Julia. If truth be told, he was very fond of her. She was good company. He enjoyed her bright, breezy, and joyful unconscious self and her happy laugh. Now, sitting beside her, he thought,

*She is but a shadow of the person I knew. An empty shell. What on earth,* he wondered, *has happened to this girl, who was once so full of life?*

Emboldened by desperation he asked, then implored and finally demanded that she tell him what was troubling her. Julia abruptly stood up and walked away along the river path. He followed in silence. After rounding a bend in the path he could see there was a small breakwater across the river that made the water cascading over it turbulent, changing the pattern of flow until, further down the river, the water free of turbulence, calmed. Gazing at it, he wondered if it was a metaphor for what Julia was experiencing.

Against this backcloth, Julia turned her ashen face to his, for a brief moment her old self, and blurted out that she had fallen in love with someone she knew, who could never love her the way she loved him. Father Fitzgerald looked at her intently. Inwardly he relaxed, thinking,

*Is that what all this is about?*

"Julia, we all fall in love. All the time," he said, somewhat relieved. "And we all fall out of love all the time too. It happens to everyone. It's all part of growing up, maturing."

He was careful not to say,

"You'll get over it," but, unaware that he had slipped into his confessional persona, he did ask if the person she had fallen in love with knew of her feelings, where and how they met, and how often they met.

Julia rounded on him vehemently and, with bitterness in her voice, told him that the person she loved didn't know of her feelings, they didn't meet socially, and that the person she

14

loved so dearly was wedded to another, a wedding promise that he would not and could not break.

"That is my dilemma," she shouted. "My agony forced on me without my desiring any of it. Not through my fault. Not through my most grievous fault. I haven't done anything by word, deed, or omission."

In her voice, he could hear her anger, desperation, and disdain. Reaching out he took hold of her hands. She was trembling.

"Julia, feelings are neither right nor wrong. It's what we do with them that matters, and ..."

"Do you think I'm that stupid?" she retorted.

Undeterred, he carried on in his gentle and concerned priestly way and reminded her how they had first met, literally bumping into each other. Her mouth creased into a tight-lipped attempt at a smile that looked more like a grimace at the thought. He continued, reminding her of his first Mass in the chaplaincy, when she read the lesson about St Paul's thorn in the flesh, and asking her if she remembered. Julia nodded. Careful not to lecture, he repeated the story of how St Paul had some unknown problem that he asked God to rid him of. Three times he asked, and each time he was told that God's grace was enough for him. He saw that Julia was listening to him.

"Let's go to the chaplaincy and discuss St Paul's thorn in the flesh, why he was afflicted, and how he dealt with it. It might help us. What do you think?" Inside, in familiar surroundings, he made coffee, didn't switch on the external red engaged signal, and settled down with Julia to talk. He read St Paul's letter slowly a couple of times before attempting to engage Julia in conversation. In the process, he began seriously to question his competency but carried on.

It was a difficult conversation. Julia could not understand why a loving God would give anyone a thorn in their flesh and, if not give, inflict it on someone to torment them. He tried to explain, as best he could, that human nature was prone to weaknesses of one sort and another that had to be guarded against, and that no one was immune. Gently probing, he asked if she had prayed against it.

"Have I prayed? Have I prayed? My soul is a bogland of prayer. My knees are sore from kneeling in front of the cross. My chapped, swollen lips refuse to form any more prayers. I have emptied myself in prayer, to no avail. I didn't seek this love. It has taken hold of me without my bidding."

He responded,

"St Paul felt exactly the same, but he didn't give up. He embraced his weakness, not by self-denigrating or despairing or giving up because he was not perfect, but by accepting himself for what he was: imperfect.

That, Julia," he continued, "is where we find humility in ourselves. In our weakness, we open out to Christ and let him touch us. Weakness can make you strong. Focus on it, conquer it, and when you have conquered it find a new weakness and overcome that too. Then suddenly you are on an upward spiral of continuous self-enhancement."

The thought forced her to try a smile but failed miserably. Then someone entered the chaplaincy. The moment was lost.

"I'll see you at Mass on Sunday, won't I, Julia? Pray against it. I'll be praying with you."

With those words in her ears, she left. At Mass, the following two Sundays the barbed thorn in her flesh sharpened and pierced further into her heart and soul. She could not remove it. It was too deeply embedded.

After Mass, she didn't linger and was gone before he disrobed. He had tried to catch her eye, hoping she would stay with the others for tea and a chat, desperately wanting to know how she was feeling, but she had chosen to avoid him.

Then suddenly it seemed the campus emptied. The middle of Trinity term always heralded the arrival of summer. He enquired after Julia, to be told that she had gone home for the summer, taking her project work with her. That she was keeping up with her studies eased his anxiety and concern.

He was alone in the chaplaincy when he took the call from the vice chancellor's office which brusquely informed him that a student in his pastoral care had tragically died. He was told her name was Julia Johnston. Overwhelming cold disbelief shivered through him, searching for hope. He didn't know how to respond but managed to mutter something and the call ended. His caller, he could tell, didn't know the person he was referring to, but that didn't surprise him. Shocked, he cradled the phone, sat down confusion and despondency enveloping him.

Julia had gone swimming in a quarry pool often used by her and friends. On this occasion, she had gone alone and had drowned. She was gone, passed away, lost. He would never see her again alive. He had failed her, as had all the prayers on her behalf that he had mouthed. As the news spread those who knew Julia filtered into the chaplaincy. Father Fitzgerald was there to greet them. They prayed together for Julia and her family. Their shared grief was so crushing that he had to go outside to find relief.

He found a private place and wept, while painstakingly searching his soul. When he gathered himself together he went back inside, listened to the conversations circulating the room, obtained what information he could about Julia's funeral arrangements, looked up her home address, and announced that he was going to visit her family and there was room in his car for anyone free to accompany him.

A little later he set off with three of Julia's friends for company. He was glad of their presence. On the way, not much was said. They sat deep in their private thoughts, remembering Julia as they had each known her.

Outside the house, people were standing about in twos and threes, talking. Seeing his clerical collar they parted, letting him through to the house into the arms of Julia's distraught mother. She clung to him with a ferocity that took his breath away. By contrast, Julia's father shook his hand and said nothing in his manly grief.

Julia was laid out in a back room. The curtains were drawn, shutting out the summer daylight. The candles in the room guttered with the movement of people coming and going. In repose, she looked angelic. Her lips were silent, and her gentle face nestled in her lustrous hair. Scourged by unrequited love, now so still, she seemed at peace. Her kind, appealing eyes would never again see in this world. He knelt and silently prayed,

"Julia, go in peace. You were forgiven all your sinless sins. I am the sinner. I failed you, but Christ welcomes you into paradise." He couldn't hide the tears in his eyes.

He assisted Julia's parish priest at her funeral Mass, and after the interment spent time with her mother and father. Julia was an only child. It was hard for them. The death of a child is difficult for parents to cope with; it doesn't make sense, it isn't in the scheme of things. As they talked, mostly Julia's mother talked. Her father said little. He just listened, while his private priestly thoughts moved like a slide show through his memories of Julia and the beautiful person she was.

When he was leaving, Julia's mother embraced him at the front door.

"Julia, you know, loved you," she said, looking him straight in the eyes.

"What?" he frowned.

Her eyes registered astonishment. In that moment of revelation, the truth engulfed them. From the pocket of her cardigan, she extracted a piece of neatly folded paper.

"Julia left this," she said and went back inside.

Standing alone, tentatively he unfolded the page and read the neatly handwritten words:

Love came upon me,
Like soft warm mizzling rain.
Unprepared I feebly resisted,
And I surrendered to its persuasive charms.
Often you spoke of love,
Pure love, genuine love.
How was I to know?
The soft warm mizzling rain,
Now is a piercing shower of cold sleet,
Chilling my heart.
Autumn has come upon me now.
Like trees shedding their autumnal colours,

I too am readying to go,
Knowing that when true love finds me,
It will be pure, genuine love.


He crunched the page tightly in his fist and, with his hands in his pockets and his face inscrutable, he trudged disconsolately away.

That night, alone in his room, before the crucifix pinned on the wall, he knelt and prayed. He was still on his knees in prayer when the day dawned, still a priest under the shadow of the cross.

When they found him three days later, prostrated before the crucified Christ on the wall, his jet-black hair was pure white.

# An Innocuous Remark

Their neighbours had a barbecue last week. His wife Maureen, not to be outdone, insisted they have one too, even though only the two of them were there to enjoy it. Their seven children had long flown the coop.

It was fast approaching seven o'clock in the evening when he finished his barbecue preparations for the next day. An air of calmness had settled over the twilit garden in anticipation of nightfall. His one wilful thought, as he left the garden, was that tomorrow there would be a gentle breeze blowing in the right direction to waft the tantalising smell of barbecuing lamb cutlets all afternoon towards their neighbours.

Saturday evenings were for him special. Their contract with the telephone company included free weekend calls to anywhere in the country. They always made full use of it. But who to call first? It was always a tough decision, but over time a rota system had self-seeded. He dialled the 031 code for Edinburgh, wondering who would answer this time: his daughter, her husband, or one of his four grandchildren.

His daughter's bright and breezy voice greeted him.

"Hi, Dad, how are you?"

They chatted about this and that for a while, all the usual stuff, with his ear acutely tuned, as was hers, for any hint that might suggest that something was not all as it should be. All seemed well. He was about to pass the handset to her mother when his daughter casually mentioned that her second eldest child, Matt, would be heading off on a school excursion to Germany in a few weeks.

As she spoke his hold on the handset slowly tightened and squeezed until he was gripping it like a vice. Anxiety spread through him, his breathing quickened, and his heart pounded against his ribcage. He couldn't help it, couldn't control it. He just hoped she wouldn't sense his trepidation. But his daughter carried on, oblivious of his mounting dread, telling him Matt would be going to Bavaria and staying in the neighbourhood of

Würzburg and outlining the itinerary for the trip. He said nothing, not because he hadn't anything to say, but because the dread in his heart rendered him speechless.

When enthused about something, his daughter didn't know when to stop talking. On this occasion, he was glad she didn't stop. The longer she talked the more time he had to recover his composure. As she talked his mind was elsewhere. His throat, desert-dry tight, felt like it was being throttled. He tried to swallow but retched instead, inviting her question,

"Are you all right, Dad?"

"Yes, I'm fine. It's just a slight throat infection that's doing the rounds over here. Nothing to worry about. The doctor gave me something for it," he lied, covering up his discomfort and anxiety.

Somehow he managed to sound enthusiastic about Matt's trip to Germany. He asked a few pertinent questions to allay any lingering concerns she might have about his well-being, then told her it sounded like a great trip, how fortunate Matt was, and how he wished he was going too. They chatted for a while about other things before he passed the handset to her mother. Only when he had released his grip on the phone did he notice the white knuckles on the fingers of his right hand. Fortunately, Maureen didn't notice.

With his wife and daughter engaged in conversation, he retreated to the lounge, dimmed the lights, found his favourite armchair, sat down, and tried to compose himself and piece together his fragile, fragmented thoughts.

*She must have forgotten. She couldn't have forgotten. Could she?*

The thought minced and grated through his mind. He didn't know. He would never know because he would never pose the question in case she had forgotten. No, it might have slipped his daughter's mind, but she wouldn't have forgotten her brother Harry. Surely not. She had her own family to look after. Maybe it just slipped her mind, as things do. But it didn't slip his. Never, ever.

21

*There's enough pain shovelled around in this life*, he thought, *without my adding to it by mentioning Harry, especially now Matt is going to Germany.*

His daughter's innocuous remark forced his mind to drill back through six decades to that Monday morning in July when Maureen delivered the first of their seven wonderful children. It was a day that every parent, with all the glorious wonders of new life that was in it, could never forget. How easily, effortlessly memories of that day and more flooded back from the reservoir of feelings sheltering deep within him. He knew exactly where he was, what he was doing, who he was with, what the weather was like that day when the telephone call came that told him of their firstborn's arrival into a new world, outside the sheltered womb. He was a father. It was a time when fathers didn't have the privilege of being present at the birth of their children. Immediately, abandoning everything, he presented himself in haste, a bunch of cut flowers hand, the proud father, at the door of the maternity ward, unsure of himself and what to do.

It had been a long birthing process, but he was too happy, young, and immature to notice his exhausted, fatigued wife. He saw only his son sporting a mat of blonde hair, cradled lovingly in his mother's arms. The joy in his heart was boundless. Life, new life … it was awesome. He was ecstatic.

Later, when making his way home, he remembered thinking as a child might think, if a child could ever think, about the responsibilities of fatherhood and all that that entailed. Moments that are carved into the recesses of memory: baptism, the first day at school, the birth of siblings, the making of friends, the eleven-plus exams, the transfer to grammar school, the cost of uniforms, the successes on the sports field, the joy when he was accepted into university, as well as all the other everyday bits and pieces that characterised his growing up, scrolled across the monitor of his mind in gloriously vivid, vibrant colours.

Their firstborn was christened Henry in the same church, at the same font, as he had been. His parents and Maureen's parents, who had all now passed away, were there, dressed in their Sunday best. It was a wonderful occasion.

Henry was a name given to all the firstborn males in Maureen's family. Her father's name was Henry, although only Maureen's mother used the formal form. Everyone else called him Harry. What's in a working-class name, anyway? So it was with his son Henry. He became known by the familiar form as he progressed through school and college to university.

His first day at school was something never to be forgotten. With his uniform on and photographs taken before leaving the house ... that was the moment when Harry decided that he didn't want to go to school. Maureen, applying her maternal craft, diverted Harry's attention and made school seem like an exciting, interesting place. It saved the day. Harry had taken the first step on the educational ladder.

Six more children followed Harry safely into the family fold, three girls and three boys. It wasn't easy, he remembered, and money was tight. But, working together, they managed to make ends meet. Harry was the first of their brood to face the challenge of the eleven-plus examination hurdle to determine his fitness for a college education. But with good teaching, an aptitude for learning, and parental encouragement, Harry made it to college.

The progress from college to university for Harry, however, was anything but straightforward. At the beginning of his final college year, he suffered from nasal congestion. At first, it was thought that it might just be hay fever or something like that. All the usual home remedies were tried but to no avail. The seriousness of his condition was brought to the fore the day he was sent home from college because of concerns about his well-being. His doctor's diagnosis was nasal polyps, which were explained as small growths in the nasal passages that obstructed the flow of air. Harry's breathing difficulties wouldn't be remedied until the polyps were reduced in size or surgically removed.

Non-invasive treatment was successful. The polyps were reduced in size, but his breathing problems persisted. Endoscopy revealed a growth deep within Harry's nasal cavity.

The word 'growth' immediately suggested cancer. Fortunately, a biopsy confirmed that the growth was benign. But it would have to be removed. After several consultations, during which the difficulties in removing the growth were explained, it was decided that the best approach would be to surgically remove the growth orally. But, during this surgical procedure, Harry spasmed. The procedure was terminated.

After further consideration, another surgical procedure that would necessitate the removal of some facial bone structure, where the growth was located, was proposed. He remembered how it all sounded so routine. The reassuring words of the surgeon to Harry,

"It'll be just like going to the dentist."

Acknowledging to himself that he had felt reassured too, he almost smiled. But all he could manage was a grimace.

The operation, performed four months before Harry's final-year exams thankfully was a success. The benign growth obstructing his nasal passage was completely removed. After two weeks of post-operative care in hospital, Harry was discharged. To look at him, it would have been impossible to tell that he had recently undergone serious surgery. At home, his recovery continued. He rapidly regained his physical strength, while at the same time earnestly applying himself to his A-level catch-up studies. Harry, in his stoic way, sat his exams, achieved good grades and gained admission to his first-choice university.

Maureen was still chatting on the phone to their daughter as all these thoughts filtered and bubbled through his mind like coffee in a percolator. What did he know about anything then? Water under the bridge now, wasn't it? Some currents run deep and things long submerged can be forced by something innocuous to resurface, screaming, from the secret places in the mind.

The currents of thought that had resurfaced cascaded through his mind faster than any supercomputer could have processed them. He was tense, he could feel it. His breathing had quickened again and he was gasping. He needed to get a

24

grip of himself otherwise, he would hyperventilate, and Maureen, who was still, thankfully, on the phone, would notice. He tummy-breathed slowly, inhaling and exhaling, quelling his racing thoughts and pulling the handbrake on them before he fell completely to pieces. If that happened now it would be a disaster.

He calmed down. His grandson Harry was going to Germany, to Bavaria, around the Würzburg area, on a school trip, he reminded himself, deliberately diverting his thoughts.

He had been there several times. The first time was in the late 1950s on holiday, one of those cheap-as-chips bus tour packaged holidays. The ones where you sleep sitting all night on the bus, with little spending money in your pocket, and can convince yourself that you enjoyed it. Endurance was only a vague concept then.

Somewhere, in the attic just above his head, were lots of photographs of that holiday, nowadays seldom looked at. Boxed up and stashed away with other memories. Bunged in, he thought, with the rest of their accumulated baggage, for others to root through, ruminate over, search, undervalue, and discard when he and Maureen dropped off their respective perches. Maybe he should do something about it. That thought didn't trouble him for very long.

Würzburg, he remembered, a hint of a smile ghosting his lips was the starting point for the famous Romantic Road tour that was part of the holiday via Rothenberg and Hohenschwangau, all the way to the Alps.

It was aptly named the Romantic Road, he thought. It was on that tour he met the girl he would marry. He noticed her when he was visiting the Marienkapelle in Würzburg before joining the tour. She was visiting it too and, as fate would have it, she joined the same tour as him. They were the youngest among the group, both unaccompanied, free and easy. He was in the line behind her, queuing up to get ticked off the tour guide's list. That's how he knew her name was Maureen, discovered where she came from and heard for the first time the gentle softness in her voice. Her hair was dark and curly, just

25

shoulder-length. She wore no bracelets, chains, or lockets. Her only adornment was a pair of small diamond stud earrings. She was dressed simply, suitably, and sensibly for the long coach journey. The longer he eyed her, the more alluring she became. He sat several seats behind her on the first leg of the bus tour, observing her friendly, open engagement with those around her. During the various stops for food and excursions as people mingled, they became acquainted. Then they became travel companions and as the tour progressed their relationship matured into something more.

Love at first sight, perhaps? It was when visiting the Basilica of Saint Mangs in Füssen that he felt something between them change. In hindsight, it was a moment of significance, life-changing for both of them.

They had celebrated their golden wedding anniversary nearly seven years ago. Fifty years was, for some of their friends, he acknowledged, much more than a lifetime. It would be a long time after that tour before he and Maureen would visit Würzburg again. His daughter's casual mention of Harry's school trip brought that occasion vividly into focus.

While dredging the recesses of his mind, Maureen's conversation with their daughter ended. She was in the lounge, speaking to him. Through his mind fog, he heard her say she was tired and would go on up to bed and asking him if he would like something to drink. It all seemed to him to be happening in slow motion. Afraid to speak, he signalled a "No thanks," with a shake of his head and held up the book he was pretending to read, suggesting he would read for a little while. It was well past nine o'clock when he poured himself a whisky and settled down not to read, but to think. Doors long closed in his mind had been sprung wide open. He wouldn't be able to close them now even if he had wanted to. The house was quiet.

While sipping his drink, the Saturday morning he drove Harry across the country to register for his first term at university surfaced fresh in his mind. Freshers' week started the following Monday.

Everyone at home had risen early that morning, readying themselves for Harry's exodus. It was his big day, a family event. He was the first from either side of the family to 'darken the door of a university', which is how his grandmother would have described it if she had been still above ground to witness the occasion. When he had walked into the bathroom that morning Harry was standing at the washbasin with his face lathered with soap and a razor in his hand, looking at himself in the mirror and seeing his father's quizzical face behind him.

*How on earth has he grown up so quickly? How has he fast-forwarded so much before my unseeing eyes?* He didn't know then and didn't know now, but somehow his growing up had reeled right through him at high speed. He comforted himself with the thought that for Harry to fully grow, he had to leave home and come back. It would be the making of him, he believed. His anxiety then was about whether or not they had prepared him enough for the journey.

When morning had edged towards midday, all the goodbyes and best wishes had been exchanged. It was a very emotional moment. The three-year-old hatchback, full to the gunnels with Harry's gear, including the ever-present guitar, which couldn't be left at home, was cranked up. Then father and son set off on an estimated six-hour journey, at first along narrow hedgerow lined roads, through familiar landscapes, on their way into the unfamiliar. During the long drive, he resisted the temptation to impart fatherly advice on how to behave as an adult. But he did share with Harry the advice his mother had given him, which was,

"Be careful of the company you keep." Very sound advice which, on reflection, to his cost, he had on occasions chosen not to heed. But back then, he reminded himself as he took another deep sip of his honey-coloured whisky, the world was a very different place.

Eventually, they arrived at Harry's hall of residence. His allotted room looked no bigger than the closet they stored their outdoor gear in at home, but he kept his mouth shut. Somehow they managed to cram all Harry's gear into his new abode, explored the campus, and found somewhere to eat. He was in no hurry to leave, but he could sense Harry's restlessness growing. He was eager to explore his new surroundings.

A little later, well-rested and braced for the parting, he took his leave with a hug, wished Harry well, and reminded him again to look after himself. He had slackened his hold on his son, freeing him to explore and experience unhindered a wider world. Exiting the campus he paused and looked back for a farewell wave. All he saw was Harry's broad shoulders and a final bob of his hair, which was now black, disappearing into a stream of fellow students as he strode confidently away into his future.

He didn't expect the pain of separation. The searing intensity of it was almost unbearable. He felt like a wounded, throbbing wisdom tooth would feel, waiting for the dentist's drill.

In the car, he sat and wept. As he saw it at that moment, he had left his son to live in a wardrobe. What was he thinking? In his heart he knew he was coping with letting Harry go, setting him free, but it didn't come easily to him. Once he was safely back home, he reported that all was well with Harry. He was well settled in, had taken to university like a duck to water.

The next two years passed quickly, uneventfully, or so it seemed, looking back. There must have been many things that as a family they had to deal with that seemed very important at the time, but nothing surfaced in his thoughts.

*Perfect memories, if they exist at all, are as elusive as soap in a bath. They just keep slipping and sliding away*, he thought. Perhaps his memory had become self-serving. There must have been many things that hadn't registered with him on the family-scale of importance.

"I was too busy working to give them sufficient attention, perhaps," he chided himself.

The third year of Harry's four-year thick sandwich programme was to be spent working in industry, with the placements organised by the course placement tutor.

Towards the end of his second year Harry, with some considerable excitement, disclosed that his placement year would be in Germany, working for a company located very close to Würzburg. Harry had studied German at O level, so on his next holiday, he retrieved all his O level German notes from the attic and spent a lot of time revising. In conversation, he told Harry that he was familiar with the Würzburg area, divulging that he had met his mother on a coach tour along the famous Romantic Road that stretched from Würzburg to the distant Alps. The Romantic Road story became the subject of much inquisitive chat and good-natured leg-pulling around the dinner table.

With his second year at university behind him and his summer vacation at an end, it was time for Harry to take up his placement in Germany. He recycled in his thoughts the morning he and Maureen had driven Harry to the airport with crystal clarity. All the necessary arrangements had been made, his accommodation had been booked, and all the addresses and phone numbers had been noted. Likewise, his health insurance had been confirmed and a bank account had been opened in Harry's name in Germany. Everything he could think of was done, including providing enough Deutschmarks to tide Harry over until the cash transfers between his UK and German bank functioned satisfactorily.

Harry would be met on arrival by a representative from his employer and he would ring them to confirm, hopefully, that all was well with him. And so it was. Once or twice in the coming months, he needed a few extra Deutschmarks over and above what had been budgeted for.

*Why be young and miserable for the sake of a few Deutschmarks?* he thought at the time *when you should be enjoying the most exciting time of your life.*

Harry's homecoming at Christmas was much anticipated by his siblings. Their expectations had been seeded with tales of Würzburg's Christmas markets and all the available goodies.

29

At the airport, the arrivals board indicated that the Würzburg flight had landed. It wasn't long until Harry entered the arrivals hall, pushing a luggage trolley in front of him laden to overflowing with various bits of baggage, where he was greeted with embraces and hugs from his parents. They shepherded him to the same old hatchback and whisked him off home.

He remembered thinking that Harry was looking good, that Germany had been good for him. They all watched eagle-eyed as Harry laid out his wrapped Christmas gifts underneath the Christmas tree one by one. When he had finished his tantalising little drama he stood well back and watched as they scrutinised the colourful array of packages, none of which had name tags attached. Harry liked to tease and play guessing games.

Over the Christmas period, Harry told them everything (well, almost everything) that he had experienced in Germany and Würzburg in particular. He elaborated on what it had to offer the young and the not so young. He regaled them with many tales and misadventures, especially when he had overconfidently stretched his knowledge of the German language way beyond its O level limits. They celebrated Christmas as they always did, at Midnight Mass, heralding the dawning of Christmas Day, and then at home afterwards, sharing and opening gifts.

Too soon the new year passed into history. The holiday was over. It was time for Harry to return to Germany. He could tell. Harry was getting restless. Looking forward to it would have been an apt but insufficient description. Harry was excited. On this occasion, on his own, he took Harry to the airport, said goodbye, and saw him on his way. It wasn't easy for him to say goodbye to Harry. But he was happy because Harry was happy, and showed it.

He recalled later telling Maureen that he had never seen Harry looking so good physically. He had grown tall, filled out into manhood, and was now really broad-shouldered. He was neatly dressed in sky blue designer jeans, black casual shoes, an open-necked white shirt, and a smart leather jacket. His curly black hair was cut short but not too short. He looked the part as he turned and waved goodbye, then disappeared from sight airside.

He didn't know why, but he went to the observers' lounge. Something took him and held him there until Harry's Lufthansa flight had taken off and disappeared out of sight into the clouds. How silly he had felt, waving to the tail end of an aeroplane, but that's what he did.

Three weeks after Harry's departure for Germany he boarded an early morning flight to Geneva with two colleagues for business meetings. Everything went smoothly in Geneva. The negotiations, as expected were tough, but in the end, he was satisfied with the results. On the flight home two days later he and his colleagues were in good spirits, tired but happy with the work they had done and what had been achieved. As always, he was glad to be going home.

Homeward-bound flights always seemed to him to be longer than the outward-bound ones. Desire always his impatient companion.

His companions had long since left the airport and he was standing alone in the airport car park, now full of vehicles, trying to remember where he had parked his car a couple of days ago when the car park had been practically empty.

"This is happening to me more frequently. I must be getting old. Next time I'll note down where I parked the blessed thing," he promised himself. But he always said that and never did. Eventually, after searching around where he thought he had parked, he located his car by intermittently using his electronic car door key, loaded up his bags and baggage, and paid the ridiculously high car parking charge, thankful that his employer was picking up the tab.

He was finally on the last leg of his journey home. It would be close to midnight when he got there. Maureen would be waiting up. She always did. The younger children would be in bed, with another day at school to look forward to. He looked forward to hearing all their bits and pieces at breakfast in the morning. Tomorrow would be just another day at the office for him too. That's what he thought.

On turning right, making ready to swing into his driveway (he knew Maureen would have the gates and the garage doors open for him), he noticed a car parked outside the house. He saw it, couldn't miss seeing it, didn't recognise it, made nothing of it, and swung past it into the driveway.

He was home. The garage door was closed. That was unusual, but nothing untoward. He parked, left the engine running, opened the garage door, drove in, silenced the car, gathered up all his stuff, including his duty-free, locked the garage door, and, with a spring in his step, headed for the front door, key at the ready. He was delighted to be home. It was awkward trying to open the door with his carry-on bag in his left hand and his duty-free bits and bobs and his door key in his right hand, but he managed it.

As the door eased open he crossed the threshold into the dimly lit entrance hall. Immediately an uneasy feeling engulfed him. Something was not right. The ambience was all wrong. It was not welcoming. It was ominously heavy, foreboding.

Something was very wrong. All his senses had gone to red alert, signalling caution, danger. With his lightness of heart displaced by dread, he peered deep into the gloomy hall. When his eyes adjusted to the dim light he saw them, shadowy figures huddled together under the archway at the far end of the hallway. Maureen was bent double, ashen-faced, with the children gathered around her, a montage of anguished humanity. Everything he was carrying crashed to the floor. Maureen was shielding the children, or were they propping her up? He couldn't tell. Standing frozen, immobile, just inside the threshold, leaving the front door lying wide open, he was desperately trying to make sense of it. What had he walked into?

"What's wrong?" he managed to utter, not once but several times. But this extracted no response. Then in desperation, he yelled, "What's wrong?"

"Harry's dead. Harry's dead," Maureen screamed back at him, a bone-chilling, piercing scream. Stupefied, his mind searched for meaning, clarity, comprehension. He grabbed on to the door for support as he felt the floor slipping away beneath him, but he knew he had to stay on his feet. He couldn't go down.

"What did she say? Don't be ridiculous," a voice in his head shrieked. "It doesn't make sense. Tell me that again." With his face buried in his hands, he quietly demanded,

"Tell me that again."

Then she let him have it. Full frontal screaming, howling,

"Harry's dead," like an animal in agony. How long they stood riveted to the floor he didn't know. It was, he remembered, like a scene from an old black-and-white movie. Then, as if stung by his immobility, Maureen screamed at him again.

"Harry's dead. Harry's dead." Her red-rimmed pained eyes appealed to him to do something.

"Do what? What are you saying? What do you want me to do?" He silently, helplessly, pathetically mouthed, "What are you saying?"

They stood staring at him in shock, a little bundle of suffering humanity, expecting him somehow to make their nightmare go away. They stood calcified like useless biblical pillars of salt. Maureen, her mouth wide open, was staring, her eyes weirdly sightless, and the traumatised children were clinging to her like limpets.

Behind them, something moved. A shadow, perhaps. The shadow took form, revealing their parish priest. Much was said that night, most of which he could form no useful recollection. Neither could he recall within any certainty what happened the rest of the night.

His memory convinced him that he had sought the darkest place in the house, the linen cupboard, and had gone in there, closed the door, and stayed in the pitch-blackness until he could somehow grapple with the enormity of what had, like a bullet train, smashed into him when he walked in through the door.

The children were at some point returned to their beds. The parish priest left. He had an early Mass in the morning. Maureen apologised for keeping him so late. In the eye of their

33

catastrophic storm, she was still somehow able to be considerate of others.

Then they were alone. Silence settled over the desolate, dismal home. When the blackness of night surrendered to the light of day they were still sitting huddled together. Maureen slowly, painfully, in her own time, in her own way, recounted again the events of the previous evening.

When he was homeward-bound she had responded to the beckoning of the telephone, thinking it would be him. It was about eight o'clock in the evening. She was unprepared as if ever anyone could be prepared for the bomb the caller was about unwittingly to detonate. Harry's professor introduced himself to Maureen and proceeded to offer his condolences on Harry's tragic death.

"His what? What's he talking about? Can't be right. He's made a horrible mistake," she thought naturally, instinctively incapable of harbouring the notion. Sensing his confusion at her reaction, and not wishing to compound his error, she advised him that he must have a wrong number. And with that ended the conversation.

About two hours later the phone rang again. Answering it she recognised the voice. It was Harry's professor. This time he asked to speak to her husband. When told that her husband was on his way home this evening from a trip abroad he apologised profoundly for being the bearer of bad news. He thought that Maureen already knew that Harry had been killed in a road traffic accident in Germany. He muddled his apologies and condolences until she screamed back down the phone at him,

"Nonsense. It's not possible. It can't possibly be." She couldn't remember how the call ended, but it did. And she was home alone with her children, who were, when the call ended, clustered around her, bewildered.

When she eventually somehow gathered herself together, she did what came naturally to her. She rang their parish priest, apologised for disturbing him so late, and asked him to please come to the house. He must have heard the pain and desperation in her voice because Maureen said he was at the door almost before she had put the phone down. When she told the priest what had happened she was in such a state that the poor man knelt before her and clasped her hands in silent prayer. It was the only language that made any sense. Their lives were forever shattered. A little later he arrived home, unaware of the disaster he would confront.

The professor's telephone call was all they had to go on, nothing more. No one else had contacted them. It could be a misunderstanding, an absurd mistake. There was a glimmer of hope, a straw to cling on to, and they clung on to it with all their combined might.

They were trying to gather their thoughts and decide what to do when their front doorbell rang. Maureen opened the door to the chief inspector of the local police. Harry's professor, reacting to Maureen's response to his phone call, had contacted the local police to find out what they knew if anything about what had happened to Harry. The chief inspector informed them that they had no knowledge of anything concerning Harry, despite having made preliminary enquiries, but assured them that he would use all available channels to find out what he could and get back to them if and when he had any information.

Time passed slowly, raising their hopes that it was all a dreadful mistake. There were mistakes, a catalogue of mistakes, but not in substance. Harry was dead. Someone in Germany had misread or misunderstood something, misinformed someone, contacted the wrong people, wasn't diligent enough, didn't care, was bereft of compassion ... All this caused delays, unnecessary confusion, distress, and chaos when only efficiency and empathy were needed. Harry was just another case number processed by administrators, prisoners of routine, devoid of feeling. Eventually the whole administrative cock-up was exposed. People were disciplined and notes were added to their files. Not that it mattered much to him and his family, but the timeline of events then became clear.

Harry and some German friends were going to see a band they liked in a neighbouring town. Harry was in the back of their car, seat belt on when it was struck by another car joining the autobahn. He took the full force of the collision. The driver of the other vehicle, an off-duty American soldier, had three children in his car. He recalled feeling relieved that none of them was injured. Of the eight people involved in the accident, Harry was the only fatality.

It happened on a Saturday afternoon in February decades ago. Harry was rushed to the hospital and was pronounced dead early on Sunday morning. The Sunday morning, he had flown to Switzerland, Harry was lying dead in a hospital morgue in Germany. Three full days had elapsed after the accident before the professor phoned. Little wonder the poor man assumed Maureen and he knew what had happened to Harry.

Two weeks after the accident Harry's remains were flown home from Germany. Then followed the trauma of his funeral and dealing with his affairs. He didn't know how they got through it, but somehow, with the support of many people, they did or appeared to. It took a long time for him to come to terms with what had happened, to get his head around it, to think, to take stock, and to decide what to do. If there was anything he could do.

To survive he immersed himself in work, but he couldn't hide. His mind had shut down sufficiently to let him function, without fully absorbing the magnitude of what had happened. And then slowly, over time, it released bits of information fragment by fragment, when he was able to cope with it and survive. That process took years. But when the thoughts galloping around in his head calmed and settled a little, some months after Harry's tragic death, he did what he would have done had the accident happened at home.

German lawyers were engaged to represent Harry in any judicial proceedings. Several months passed. Then they were informed that the criminal proceedings of the careless killing against the off-duty American soldier had been halted by order of the prosecution attorney's office at the state court of Würzburg. They had handed the case for further prosecution to the permanent US military administration. A legal review of the case conducted by the office of staff advocate of the 3rd

Infantry Division did not find sufficient evidence of the soldier's failure to exercise due care at the intersection. The case was closed.

But that was not the end of the matter. When the German traffic police furnished their report on the accident it was determined that there was probable cause to believe that the off-duty soldier had acted negligently. As a result of his negligent failure to yield right of way, the off-duty soldier received nonjudicial punishment. His commanding officer found him guilty and ordered him to forfeit a week's pay, a small price to pay for killing someone. Not even a slap on the wrist. More of a pat, a caress.

Nonjudicial punishment under the US Uniform Code of Military Justice, he discovered, was administered informally. There was no hearing. As such, Harry wasn't represented. His family weren't informed, nor did they even know it had occurred. That was it. All done and dusted: game, set, and match, while he and his family were consumed by grief.

He consulted his German lawyers, sought the assistance of the British embassy in Bonn, obtained the German traffic police accident report, and acquired a record of the nonjudicial proceedings against the off-duty soldier. But that was it. There was nothing else he could do. The matter was closed. For some perhaps, but never for him.

Pragmatic as ever, he had learned to survive, to live with the past, and to deal with it. But the past has a habit of not going away. It lingers, dormant, waiting for something to bring it back to life.

Time had moved on. It was getting late, and his memories lingered like half-forgotten pals from yesteryear. He fingered his glass. Another large one for the night shift, perhaps? Better not. No point in being maudlin. His thoughts would turn to slush. All this rumination had been unwittingly provoked by his daughter happily telling him about his grandson's upcoming school trip to Germany in a phone conversation. Was it just coincidence that he and Maureen would be in Edinburgh on Harry's next birthday? Perhaps. They knew the precise moment he came into this world. His mother had kept the maternity cot tag. He and Maureen would celebrate his birthday with him as always at morning Mass.

Readying for bed, at peace with himself, he just hoped for a good day tomorrow, with a gentle breeze in the right direction for the benefit of the neighbours. That thought encouraged the hint of a mischievous smile. Just then the telephone rang. He looked at the longcase clock standing at the far side of the room. Its big face told him it was nearly midnight.

Who on earth could that be? he thought. Anxiously he picked up the phone.

It was their daughter Lily in Queensland, Australia, with the best part of a new day ahead of her. It transpired that about the time he had been talking to her sister in Edinburgh, Lily was giving birth to her first child, a boy, and she was going to call him Henry. They knew she was due, but her timing was impeccable. She hadn't forgotten.

Coincidence. Perhaps. But life is full of surprises.

Overjoyed, he rushed phone in hand to share the news with Maureen.

# Children

You are our conception,
We waited for you
To leave the mother womb,
Enter our world.
We nursed you through infancy,
Nourished you through childhood,
Guided your adolescence,
Saw you grow.

Mentored you to maturity,
Fuelled your imagination,
Rejoiced in your being,
Gave you wings to fly.

Freed you to go solo,
Anywhere your imagination knew.
All hopes and aspirations
Fulfilled in you.

# Landscape of Love

Willie Brady was five feet six inches tall and fifty-seven years of age. Past his prime, you might have thought, at your first encounter with him. He was an easy-going sort of character, single-minded when needed to be, and unmarried by choice. Not that he hadn't felt the magnetic pull of love. The youngest of six children, his female siblings ensured that Willie, from when he was able to walk and talk, gained an acute awareness of the opposite sex, in transition as it were, through the early ages of Shakespearian man. Of course, Willie hadn't read Shakespeare's play *As You Like It*, but as a child, he was exposed first hand to the ages of woman. Something Shakespeare neglected to articulate.

This story begins with Willie in the schoolboy stage of Shakespeare's schema of man's development. His formal schooling started at the ripe old age of five. And miraculously, two years later, on his seventh birthday, he had, by all the conventions of modern society and religious culture, attained the age of reason. Essentially it was assumed that he knew the difference between right and wrong, but only in a childish way.

Willie was anything but Shakespeare's model of a schoolboy. He was not a whining, whinging boy. Quite the opposite. He was a happy little boy with bright azure blue eyes, a shock of curly blonde hair, and a happy, smiling face. He ran to school every morning. Couldn't get there quick enough. Loved school and his teacher, Miss Brown. He was bright, curious, inquisitive, and observant beyond his years. He didn't miss much. Some might have thought that he was a bit old-fashioned or that he'd been here before. Be that as it may, there was a loveable boyish innocence about him.

His sister Winnie, often described by his mother and others as 'a bit of a tomboy', was two years older than Willie. He hadn't the faintest idea what a tomboy was. In Willie's mind, Tom was a boy's name, so he wondered if Winnie was a boy in disguise. Now at Willie's age, the age of reason, he hadn't any

40

notion of what exactly a girl was either. The pair of them played together, climbed trees, bathed in the sea, rode bicycles, and got up to all sorts of mischief. They had great fun in the long, warm, sunny summers of their shared childhood.

Willie's sister Noreen, two years older than Winnie, didn't often join in their fun and games. She seemed to Willie a bit more self-contained, if not self-absorbed, and preferred the company of her girlfriends. To his inexpert and inexperienced childish eye, she dressed differently and was somehow just different. It was very confusing, but in his imitable way of sussing it all out, Willie figured she was just getting ready to go to the big school after the summer holidays. He thought no more about it.

Bridget, Willie's third sibling in the hierarchy of the family sisterhood, was to Willie's keen eye a different kettle of fish altogether. She dressed differently, walked differently, put things in her ears, and looked at herself in the mirror a lot. Sometimes she wore shoes with big heels. He observed her walking in them strutting like a turkey, he thought. One day, when she had gone out of the house, Willie put on her shoes and tried to strut like her. He fell flat on his wee face. Fortunately, he suffered no visible injury. But then a child's pride feels little pain.

Gradually Willie became aware that something strange came over Bridget every month. When it first registered with him it was difficult to tell, but for a few days, she would be a completely different person: anxious, irritable, and unbearable. Confused at first, Willie quickly learned that whatever it was that came over her, it would be wise for him to keep out of her way. Of course, he didn't know Bridget's hormones were going crazy. He wouldn't experience anything like that until his voice broke and hair started to grow on his face and in other places.

Willie saw but was too young to understand, the growth, both physical and emotional, that Bridget had to cope with. All he felt was that the distance between him and her was growing. He didn't like it. Bridget, for her part, knew exactly what was happening, as physically and emotionally she stretched towards maturity. She was getting a beginner's introduction to biology in school, but she couldn't conceal the transitional side effects of maturation all the time.

Eileen, Bridget's older sister, was preparing for her O level exams. One of the subjects she was taking was biology, so she was well informed of everything that was happening to her biologically and emotionally. To Willie's childish eye she was more mature than Bridget. She could be moody now and then, all right, but was less stressed. She fascinated Willie with her constant preening. She was always looking at herself in the mirror, patting herself here and there, especially the lumpy chesty bits, looking at her body shape, front and back and sideways, up and down and all around. It was a never-ending dance of self-appraisal.

Willie was so intrigued with what Eileen was doing that, following her example, he examined himself in front of the bathroom mirror. With the door locked, of course. As soon as he had tossed his shirt carelessly on the floor and stood on the bathroom stool, he examined himself with his fingertips all over, searching for any signs of the kind of growth his sisters, it seemed, desired. Disappointed at not finding anything, he put his shirt back on and left the bathroom somewhat perplexed.

One day Eileen was weighing herself on the bathroom scales. Willie knew she weighed herself every morning and evening.

"Eileen, have you put on weight?" he innocently asked in passing. Erupting like a volcano, she spewed vitriol at him like a red-hot machine gun.

That incident taught him to keep his wee mouth shut. Listen, observe, don't speak, and know your place. Later, when she had calmed down, she searched him out and apologised for the way she had unleashed her bad temper on him. They were friends again. All was well. Peace and harmony temporarily restored. Willie felt Eileen treated him differently after that encounter. She was cuddlier and motherly. She had friends she would bring to the house. Willie would watch and take note in his own childish way of them too.

His eldest sister Fiona was studying for her A-level examinations. She had her heart set on going to university to study medicine and become a doctor. Her desire, unknown to her, fired Willie's imagination. To him, she was very grown-up, knew what she wanted to be, and even wanted to learn to drive their father's car. She was always very particular about how she dressed, especially when she was going out anywhere. She had lots of friends, including boyfriends. There was one in particular who would call at the house for her. Willie didn't like the look of him but didn't know why.

Fiona took great care with her appearance, regularly visiting the hairdresser and beautician to have her hair, nails, and other stuff done that Willie didn't know anything about, other than what he heard his sisters discussing. It was confusing. Sometimes her fingernails and toenails had funny-looking coloured patterns on them. His sisters said they were false, not real, but Willie couldn't understand that because he knew his fingernails grew all the time they were part of him. He knew that for sure, from nibbling on them.

Willie noticed that Fiona spent most of her time during the week with her nose in books, studying, appearing only when Mother called the family together at mealtimes. At the weekends she was out a lot with friends. From this observation, Willie concluded that the older you got the less time you spent with your family. He didn't know what to make of that, but it saddened him a little.

So Willie, at the grand old age of reason, surrounded by five females – six, actually, including his mother – was moulded and shaped. His mother, as mothers do, spent all her long days nurturing them, as well as his father. It was a process of a continuous giving of self that did not pass Willie's keen eye unnoticed.

His father, a figure hidden in the undergrowth of family life in this story, taught Willie much in his own distinctive, oblique way. When female hormones were on the loose, rampaging around the house, he would take a back seat, hold his tongue, keep his distance, and let his wife deal with it. He communicated his thoughts by way of a look, a glance, an imperceptible nod of his head, or a flick of a finger. He was the quintessential quiet man about the house, who knew his place in a houseful of females and when to stay in it. At heart, he was a survivor.

Then came the day when everyone was out of the house somewhere, except for Willie and his mother. She had just finished hanging lines of washing out to dry in a fresh breeze when she had to pop out on some errand. The sky was overcast. Fearing the worst, she asked Willie to bring in the washing if it rained. Now, remember, Willie had only just reached the magical age of reason. He didn't yet know the differences between boys and girls. He was on a learning curve that would change shape dramatically when the rain came. His mother's request about the washing, if it rained, was more in hope than expectation. But, being the obedient child he was, at the first spit of rain, Willie was out like a dog after a bone to bring in the washing.

He unpegged garment after garment. His wee arms were aching. When he reached the underwear department, his journey of discovery found wings. It was the first time in his young life that he had seen girls' underwear up close, never mind touching it. It was all shapes and sizes: frilly, very small, and there were also concave cuplike objects with straps and fastenings. Perplexed, he wondered what his sisters hid in the cups. Embarrassed and confused, he grabbed the individual items by the handful, wrenched them off the clothesline in case someone should see him and wonder what he was doing, dumped them into the basket with the rest of the washing, and hurried back inside the house. In the kitchen he stood looking at the washing basket, puzzled. His father's handkerchiefs were bigger than some of his sisters' underwear he had just taken off the washing line. He was still puzzling over that when his mother rushed in.

"Good boy, Willie. Well done. I'm glad you got it all in dry for me," she said, seeing the washing in the kitchen. Willie responded with a kind of confused shrug, which for once his mother didn't notice. He was thinking,

*Handkerchiefs, knickers, and other strange things.*

That was then. Willie's learning curve would increase exponentially when he began to experience hormonal influences on his progress through adolescence. But somehow in the mysterious scheme of life he and his sisters negotiated their transitional phases towards maturity unimpaired, happy in themselves and with each other, and moved on. But that's another story.

In Shakespeare's ages of man Willie was still in the schoolboy phase when, like his sisters before him, he followed Fiona's footsteps to university. She was the first child of either of his parents' families to make that journey in life. It was quite an achievement, involving much sacrifice and encouragement by their working-class parents, to ensure that all their children if they were academically able, had a university education. This fact was not lost on Willie.

He would often recall his father, a carpenter by trade, standing out in the backyard of a summer's evening, up to his ankles in pinewood shavings, planing away at a piece of wood. Poetry in motion. Stooped at his trestle workbench, his braces stretched to near breaking point over his shoulders as he pushed the plane with ease along the timber he was working. The back of his shirt stained with the sweat of his labour. Rivulets of pinewood shavings curled up over the plane as he worked and fell away, to be collected later as bedding for the neighbour's dogs. Occasionally he paused to test the sharpness of the plane's blade with his forefinger before continuing the music of wood planing.

As Willie watched his father working, the aroma of freshly cut pinewood invaded his senses, making him determined to repay his parent's faith in him. In Shakespeare's scheme of things, he was still very much a schoolboy. The next stage, the love phase, lay dormant, deep within him, for the moment.

Willie put his innate curiosity to good use in pursuit of knowledge. His first term at university was a whirlwind of activity and engagement that took some time to get used to. But in the end, he took to it like a duck to water. Christmas at home

45

with all the family, a welcome relief from a hectic first term, was celebrated quietly, except that Willie was now an uncle to nephews and nieces, courtesy of his married sisters. It was a while before he realised that on their maternal side he was the only uncle his nephews and nieces would have. He felt kind of awkward about it at first, but that was before he had to think about Christmas presents in addition to birthdays and more. Uniqueness, he discovered, incurred lots of hidden costs.

All too soon Willie was back at university, immersed in his studies. He didn't socialise much. Not because he was unsociable. He was quite the opposite. He just didn't have the time, his nose to the grindstone and all that stuff. There were a couple of girls in Willie's year, fellow students, who he shared coffee with now and then. He was still in his boyhood phase, while they were several phases ahead in their ages of woman. Absorbed in his studies, Willie didn't notice.

Keen to ease the financial burden on his parents and determined to leave university without a huge debt, he found summer employment with a clothing manufacturing company based conveniently close to home. His summer job could be described as a gofer, an errand boy, except that it had a designation. Willie was a PMA, a production manager's assistant. He was made up. But of course, he knew in essence that he was a factory floorwalker, seeing, hearing, and reporting anything untoward back to his boss, and very occasionally dealing with issues that were within his competence. He was a fetcher, carrier, and general dogsbody, but that didn't matter to Willie. He loved it. He observed with both eyes wide open, listened with both ears cocked, and quickly learned the power of silence. He was getting paid and gaining invaluable work experience while engaging with a predominantly female workforce. Willie couldn't have asked for anything more. Reared in a female-dominated home, Willie walked the factory floor undaunted, from the patternmaking department through the cutting, sewing, pressing, finishing, and dispatching departments.

Slowly his floorwalking opened his mind's eye. A perception formed that females came in all shapes and sizes, way beyond the boundaries of physicality. There were subtle differences in behaviour he noticed too. In different departments, girls eyed him up and down as he strutted his stuff, concealing a smile. Here and there was the occasional crude remark, which he chose to treat as complimentary. In the sewing department, the older women mothered and sheltered him from the flirting and teasing of some of the girls. In the finishing department, everything was much more sophisticated.

Then abruptly it seemed summer was over and it was time to return to college. Willie, having made a good impression, left his summer job on a high note. He was offered a job for the following summer if he wanted it. Wanted it? He didn't need to be asked twice.

Back in college as a second-year student familiar with the routine, he quickly settled to his studies. With some time in hand he was able to socialise a little more, and in the process got to know his female classmates better. Like the first year, the second year was a blur. He was a floorwalker on his summer job again, self-assured, confident, and competent. He had filled out physically. He wasn't tall, but solidly built, and was not unaware of the attention the young women in the factory were giving him. In the canteen he got to know some of them quite well, but, whatever magnetic attraction they might have been generating, Willie didn't react. He remained, in Shakespeare's scheme of human life, the eternal schoolboy. As before, when his summer vacation employment ended, he was rewarded again with the offer of summer employment for the following year. His acceptance this time was optional because he hoped to graduate and find employment to further his chosen career.

Willie's first year at university had, it seemed to him, quickly merged into Year Two. Now he was entering the business end, Year Three, at the end of which his results would be make or break for him. His single-mindedness kicked in with a vengeance. There would be no distractions of any kind allowed. It would be head down and nose to the grindstone all the way to get the job done, hopefully to his satisfaction.

Willie's reward for his single-minded determination was a first-class honours degree, the only one awarded in his year. It was a proud moment for Willie and his family when the chancellor of the university doffed his cap to confer the award.

Willie didn't take up the offer of further employment with the clothing factory. Employment was not a problem. He was snapped up by one of the largest engineering companies in the country and set to work as part of a team on a major bridge-building project.

On his journey through university Willie remained steadfastly in the schoolboy phase of Shakespeare's ages of man. It may seem a little surprising, but it shouldn't. He had no choice in the matter. There wasn't a button he could press to initiate the transition. It would be a natural progression. Many young men remain schoolboys for a long time before entering the Shakespearean love phase. Willie, after all, was reared in a house full of women – dominated by women it might be said. He was used to females. They were the warp and weft of the fabric of his life. They had shaped him. His voice had broken, he was shaving his face, hair had grown in his oxters and but that was the total hormonal influence on Willie, as far as any knowledgeable observer could discern. He showed no romantic interest in the fairer sex. Some might have thought him a bit odd, but Willie was just being himself.

On impulse on one of his rare Saturdays off work, he popped into the local library in search of a book he had long meant to read. Entering the library he passed a librarian at her workstation. Willie paid her little heed and went on about his business. At the first rack of books, he stopped abruptly without reason, turned, and stared at the back of the young woman he had just walked past. Perplexed, he pondered what he was doing and why he was doing it.

Then he moved into concealment behind the rack and stood staring at her through the gap between the books and the bookshelves. Momentarily he felt ridiculous but was transfixed. He couldn't take his eyes off her. Her long black hair draped languidly over her shoulders down her back on to the backrest of her chair. She was wearing a short-sleeved white blouse or shirt, over which she had a black pinafore-type garment with broad shoulder straps. It was the broad straps on narrow shoulders that caught Willie's eye. All this he took in at a glance.

Intrigued, he manoeuvred quietly and unobtrusively in and around the book rack, angling to get a better look at her, all the while neglecting to question why he was doing it. As he continued his manoeuvring he viewed her in profile, left and right, up and down, and all around as best he could, but realised he wouldn't be able to get a head-on look at her unless he stood in front of her. Eventually, his foolishness forced him to desist and go in search of what he came in for in the first place. But even though he searched thoroughly he couldn't find the book he wanted.

Disappointed, he sought help from a librarian. The only person on duty was the young woman who had attracted his attention when he came in. As he diffidently approached her, she was sitting with her head bowed at her workstation, engrossed in her work. When Willie sheepishly presented himself it seemed to him that she raised her head in slow motion to look him in the eyes.

It was like the unveiling of a priceless portrait. He gazed into two velvety deep brown eyes, framed under a pair of bushy black eyebrows. Her satin-textured beige-coloured skin glowed with well-being, and when she smiled her brilliant white teeth illuminated her face. The only jewellery she wore was a little fine gold chain around her neck. Her appealing lips moved, forming words of greeting that, momentarily, Willie didn't hear. In that instant of first encounter, Willie crashed headlong out of boyhood into the Shakespearean love phase.

After a pause that seemed like an eternity, Willie found voice to tell her what he was searching for but couldn't find. She didn't say anything. Willie watched mesmerised, as her fine-boned fingers made music on her keyboard. In the end, her electronic search was fruitless too, but she offered to request what he wanted. Willie was up for that. He would welcome any opportunity to see her again. She checked his contact details against what was on the library's database, including his phone number, and placed the request. Reluctantly, as far as Willie was concerned, they parted company. She went back to work and he left the library in something of a daze, but inexplicably happy.

That night in bed he tossed and turned. Couldn't sleep. It wasn't a hot, humid, clammy night. The girl in the library was the yeast fermenting his thoughts. It was like an out-of-body experience. Something had infused the very marrow of his being. For the first time beyond family boundaries, Willie had encountered the full force of love's fierce and unyielding magnetic attraction.

As the next day was Sunday, he went to church as usual. But instead of spending the day reading, as was his wont, he went hill walking to try and clear his head. He walked for hours, mulling over the images that had invaded, taken possession, and fertilised his mind the night before. He ventured off the well-trodden path, raising the occasional hare and lark as he went. His step was light, free, and easy. Ignoring the dewy grass, he wandered blithely on. In his heart, it was as if spring had come early and all of nature was answering its call. Perhaps it was the majesty of the landscape he was experiencing. It didn't matter. He returned home feeling the better for it.

Absorbed in his work on Monday, the events of the weekend didn't surface until he was readied for home in the evening. He couldn't resist the lure of the library. He had to see if she was there. He didn't even know her name. She wasn't there. Nor was she there any night that week when he checked, leaving him with the thought that perhaps she only worked days.

On Saturday afternoon, a week after his encounter with the girl in the library, as he thought of her, Willie returned, on the pretext of looking for the book he had requested. She wasn't at the workstation where he had seen her before. His pulsing heart paused in his breast. Had she been transferred? In bad humour, he was gathering his frayed thoughts, when suddenly he saw her standing way back in the far reaches of the library, by a coffee machine. Slowly, shyly, with his heart pounding, he edged towards her.

As he approached she turned and looked up at him, and smiled in recognition. After returning her smile he explained that he had just called to see if his book was in. She beamed back at him, her bright eyes dancing, and told him that it had just come in this morning, adding that if he gave her a minute she would get it for him.

*If I gave her a minute*, he thought as she poured her coffee. *A minute well spent.* Coffee in hand, she led him back to her workstation and without ceremony reached down, picked up his book, and passed it to him. Their fingers touched, a sacred moment of first touch that Willie would feel for the rest of his life. After thanking her, he managed somehow to invite her, if she was free, for a coffee after work. To his great surprise and relief, she was free. His thumping heart sang like a blackbird greeting the rising sun.

Over coffee, the seed of acquaintance germinated, and in the weeks and months that followed grew into friendship and more. They met frequently, took long walks together, and explored places of mutual interest in the process getting to know each other. Her name was Desiree. She had been born in the Seychelles, her mother's homeland. Her mother's name was Eldora and her father's name was Raphael. He was French. Desiree, an only child, was much amused when she learned that he had five sisters. As they became more intimate, he would call her by her familiar name, Dessi. Content in their own company, they didn't socialise much. They had similar interests in music, theatre, and other pastimes. Literature was initially problematic. Willie had little interest in fiction, whereas Dessi was a fiction devotee.

The engineering firm where Willie worked organised a midsummer charity ball every year, which all employees were encouraged to support. Blissfully unaware of what was involved, Willie invited Desiree to accompany him to the ball. It was to be held in the grand hall of the city hall, a place that she had never been to before. For the gentlemen, it was a black-tie event, but the only black-tie Willie had was the one he

51

occasionally wore to funerals. He had to hire the dinner jacket, trousers, and shirt as well as the black bow tie. He felt like a penguin out of water when he put it on, and even worse when he discovered his shirt cuffs didn't button. He needed cufflinks.

On the evening of the ball, he called for Desiree at her home. Her mother showed him into a reception room, which in Willie's neighbourhood of terraced houses would have been grandly called a parlour. He waited nervously for Desiree. When she walked into the room he was stunned. She was wearing a full-length long-sleeved white kimono with a red flower pattern, left open at the front. She looked fabulous.

In the city hall, Desiree left her kimono with the cloakroom attendant and took Willie's arm to enter the grand hall. The hall was full of men in black tie and bejewelled ladies with sculpted hair set as firm as concrete by the liberal use of hairspray. Heads turned to look at them, causing Willie to wonder why everyone was looking at him ... before realising that they weren't looking at him. They were looking at Desiree. She was wearing a simple round-necked long black gown that flowed with the contours of her body when she moved. Her only concession to adornment was the fine gold chain around her neck. Her long black hair was not concreted in place. It ebbed and flowed with every move she made. After the moment – which seemed like an eternity – passed, they found their table among Willie's co-workers, spouses, and partners.

After the preliminaries and the banquet, all was readied for the dancing. The band tuned up and couples eagerly took to the floor. They danced as the huge glitter ball rotated above their heads, spearing shafts of reflected light into the far recesses of the great hall.

Willie couldn't dance. He was too embarrassed. After sitting out while everyone at their table danced, he eventually revealed to Desiree his inadequacy. Not in the least daunted, Desiree laughed.

"Come on, I'll show you how. I'll lead, you follow," she said, taking his arm. That's exactly what they did all night. They waltzed, foxtrotted, and quickstepped the night away. At first, though, Willie was uneasy, unsure. He had never embraced Desiree before. He didn't know what to do with his arms, his hands ... She was so delicate in his mind's eye that he was afraid of bruising her.

He needn't have worried. On the dance floor, Desiree took firm hold of him and danced merrily around the floor to their heart's content. It was way past the midnight hour when he and Desiree parted. They stood outside her house at the garden gate and made small talk for a while before exchanging their goodnights. They didn't embrace. They didn't kiss.

Through the next year, their relationship deepened. To everyone who knew them, they were a couple, an item, loving. But not yet lovers, in that their lips had not yet brushed each other. It was as if a kiss, however fleeting, would in some way tarnish their relationship. Perhaps it was simply that Willie, reared with five older sisters, didn't know how or when to make the first move. He wasn't by nature an icebreaker. There was, however, nothing glacial about Desiree. The warm blood flowing in her veins could melt ice, but she chose to let Willie find his way, in his own time.

One thing Willie did do was take dance lessons and, hard though it may be to believe, he was a natural at it. There was rhythm in his blood and bones. Where it came from he didn't know. He and Desiree took to dancing like children would take to a playground. They became regulars on the dance hall circuit around the country. It was great fun. They made many friends and often car-shared when going to dances.

They were standing at a cliff edge gazing out over the ocean as it battered the rocks below, thinking their own thoughts. They hadn't talked much on their walk. Willie, sensing Desiree was troubled, said nothing and waited for her to unburden herself.

She spoke in a whisper. He could barely hear her over the noise of the waves crashing on the rocks far below. Softly, gently, almost apologetically, she told him that her mother had been diagnosed with a terminal illness and wanted to go home to die in the Seychelles and be laid to rest with her family. The

53

bottom line was that she had to go with her parents. Her father needed her too. Willie's mind and lips formed words that he couldn't speak. He listened as Desiree explained it was her duty. She could not do otherwise, just as he would not be able to abandon his elderly parents now that all his sisters were away from home.

That much Willie understood. How long they stood in silence, staring to were ocean and sky merged, Willie would never know. He felt as if his heart and soul had been siphoned out of him. Emptied. Eventually, without another word spoken, they turned their backs on the bleak, false unity of ocean and sky, and walked away homewards into a setting sun.

*A metaphor for my life and love*, Willie thought, before discarding the selfish, wilful intrusion.

They walked in silence all the way back to Desiree's home, a sacred silence that defied violation. Outside they stood face to face, coping as best they could with their feelings. Desiree's bright brown eyes had lost their sparkle. They were dull, and her face had lost its glow, but in Willie's hurting heart she was more beautiful than ever. No pulse of joy pounded in Willie's heart. He was lost in a desolate forest of feelings at the bottom of a pit of blackness.

At this moment of parting, Willie reached forward took Desiree's hand and gently kissed it. Desiree turned away with tears in her eyes and ran up the path into her house without looking back. Willie watched her go. Once she was inside Willie wandered home numbed. He didn't acknowledge the folk he met on his way. Nor was he aware of crossing the streets busy with traffic, without looking.

In the weeks and months that followed they carried on meeting as usual, including going dancing with their friends. But to Willie, it wasn't quite the same. The ballrooms of romance they frequented had lost their allure and the country music they danced to now seemed to be saturated with heartbreak and sadness. Sometimes the poignancy of the setting, the music, and his tangled emotions would almost reduce him to tears, but he persevered.

Willie helped Desiree settle her parents' affairs and to dispose of the items and artefacts they didn't want to take with them to the Seychelles. It was when the family home was sold that Willie finally accepted that Desiree was leaving. He was losing the love of his life.

Early on the morning of their departure, he drove them to the airport, knowing that each revolution of the wheels under his feet was taking Desiree further and further away from him, perhaps forever. He compressed his lips into a grimace, didn't engage in small talk, and drove on into an uncertain future.

At the airport, preliminaries negotiated, they approached the departures gate, which for Willie was the end of the line. He could go no further. As Desiree lingered with Willie, her parents carried on through. It was the gate of no return, perhaps, and they both knew it. Slowly, gently, imperceptibly, they moved closer together. She melted into his loving embrace. Their lips brushed, settled, tasted, lingered, and pressed together with more than a suggestion of passion. In that moment of his first kiss, Willie's love for Desiree was cemented forever. Reluctantly they disengaged. Desiree melted away. When he raised his head she was gone.

Like a little boy lost he lingered, in the forlorn hope he might catch a glimpse of her. On his way out of the airport, he paused, thought about going to the viewing deck to watch her flight depart, but decided against it. He'd had all he could handle for one day.

On automatic pilot, Willie made his way home, garaged his car, went inside, pulled the blinds to shut out the day, and sat in the half-light until the gloom of night engulfed him. He moped around the rest of the weekend, not knowing what to do with himself, swilling coffee until it became distasteful. He was glad when Monday morning dawned and work beckoned. It was a distraction.

All week he buried himself in work, going at it day and night until he was on the point of exhaustion. His friends, aware that Desiree had taken her parents back to the Seychelles, encouraged him to ease up and get out more. To no avail. He was rescued from his torpor by Desiree's girlfriends, the ones they took with them when going dancing. They needed him. Without him, they had no means of transport. Reluctantly he agreed.

In the end, it was his salvation. When they arrived at the first dance he took them to he didn't want to go into the hall, but they dragged him in because the band was already playing. He was hardly through the door when an elderly lady swept him into her arms and waltzed away with him. Willie, a very good dancer, hadn't lost the knack. He was danced by one lady after another all night, with a queue jostling for the last dance. In the car on the way home he felt tired but the better for it, while his passengers planned their next outing with him included.

Willie and Desiree exchanged letters and cards frequently, keeping each other in touch with everything that was going on in their lives. Desiree's mother's condition continued to deteriorate but, like so many terminally ill people, she confounded her physicians. She clung to life for twenty-eight months.

*It's always the way*, he thought. *There aren't too many people willing to kiss goodbye to this so-called valley of tears.* In time their exchange of letters and cards dwindled to a mere trickle. Desiree discouraged Willie from flying out to attend her mother's funeral.

*There's no point*, she wrote. Willie didn't insist. Later he learned that Desiree's father was not in the best of health.

*She has enough to cope with*, he thought, *without me intruding.*

Time passed. Willie continued going dancing with his friends.

"Which ballroom of romance are we heading for tonight, ladies?" he would ask after he had picked them all up, and off they would go. It didn't matter which dance hall they frequented. Willie was popular with the ladies because he could dance. Dance properly, that is. At first, a bit of jealousy and resentment surfaced among the local lads, which could have got rather ugly, until they realised that Willie wasn't interested in their womenfolk. He was only there for the dancing, nothing more. Willie was careful when around women. His sisters had taught him that.

Then after a period of silence, he heard from Desiree that her father had passed away. As with her mother, she dissuaded him from attending the funeral.

*No need. Too much trouble for you,* she wrote. Their relationship had changed over time. It had made his heart grow fonder, but now he wasn't sure about Desiree's. His uncertainties were confirmed when he learned in a rather circuitous way, as one often hears unwelcome news, that Desiree had married. So devastated was Willie that at first, he refused to believe it. More was revealed morsel by morsel, in the months that followed.

After her mother had passed away Desiree attended a bereavement counselling group meeting. As it turned out, there were only three people at the meeting. Everything was explained to her and she was paired with a therapist who best matched to her perceived needs. His name was David. He was a psychologist by profession, who was offering pro bono services as a bereavement counsellor. He was young, softly spoken, and attentive. A schedule of six consultations was arranged in local authority premises designated for the purpose, with the option of further consultations if deemed necessary.

As their meetings progressed David got to know a lot about Desiree. She relaxed in his company and spoke openly about herself, revealing the love she had had to leave behind when she took her mother home to die. As the consultations progressed she divulged more about her family, her father, and their assets. As Desiree's trust in David grew, her dependence on him also increased. Towards the end of their scheduled consultations, they would meet for coffee and a chat, and when the consultations finished Desiree invited David to visit her at home. They had become very friendly.

Desiree's father's health began to deteriorate. He suffered lapses of memory and would stumble and fall as if intoxicated. His doctors tried every test they could think of but could not arrest his failing health. Her father just faded away. David handled all the funeral arrangements and other things on

57

Desiree's behalf. She couldn't cope. Folk thought she was fortunate to have David around to help her.

A respectful period after her father's passing, Desiree and David married. David took care of all the arrangements, including the guest list, from which some friends who had been thought close to Desiree were surprisingly omitted. There was no honeymoon. David thought it unnecessary. He moved in with Desiree, after disposing of his property.

Desiree's parents had bought the substantial property when they moved back to the Seychelles. It had four bedrooms, three reception rooms, and a swimming pool overlooking the bay down below. The previous owner, looking for a quick sale, accepted their cash offer. It was big enough to accommodate David's practice. He could work from home and be close at hand if Desiree needed him.

Life it seemed settled. But little things, which generally went unnoticed, changed bit by bit. Girlfriends were not encouraged to visit, as they used to, certainly not unannounced, and most definitely when David was not at home. Desiree's social activities dwindled and eventually petered out. Telephone calls were acknowledged by the answering machine and seldom returned. With time Desiree had become increasingly isolated.

After her father had passed away, David, with Desiree's authority, had dealt with all the probate issues, convincing her in the process that it would be less complicated for both of them if they switched their bank accounts to new joint accounts. Desiree, increasingly dependent on David, trustingly agreed. It took several months for all the necessary formalities to be completed, but when they were David and Desiree celebrated quietly at home.

A few weeks later David casually suggested that perhaps they should declutter. There was too much stuff about the house that was never used and which wasn't to their taste. Over time, Desiree's mother and father had accumulated quite a collection of silver, art, collectables, and memorabilia. It was all too much for Desiree to be cleaning and looking after, David insisted. It would be much better if it was all put safely away into storage so that they could make a fresh start, making their home completely their own and shaping it to their liking.

It took a little while to convince Desiree, but David's persistence eroded her sandstone block of resistance. At the end of the decluttering process, their home was minimalistic in every respect. One day when David was out Desiree wandered around her home distraught. Afraid of offending David, she hid her feelings, but her health was deteriorating.

David, who was not unaware of Desiree's deteriorating health, suggested to Desiree one evening that he should give up his private practice so that he could devote himself to be with her full time. Desiree, overcome with emotion, clung to him like a limpet to a rock. Although she had been buffeted and battered in the turbulent sea of life, she felt safe and secure in his loving embrace.

As their lives settled into a routine of slow walks around the garden, with David cooking for Desiree, reading to her, and attending to her every need, Desiree calmed down and placidly followed where David led. At bedtime, David would prepare Desiree's nightcap to help her sleep.

A little time after his retirement David introduced to Desiree the notion that perhaps they should downsize – find something smaller, more manageable, and more secluded. Desiree, by now dependent on David for practically everything, was easily persuaded. They sold up, bought a smaller place, and carried on with living. Their routine reset.

One Friday evening, a month after they had settled into their new abode, David brought Desiree her usual nightcap. He lay beside her on the bed reading aloud until sleep closed her eyes.

It was Saturday evening after seven o'clock when Desiree's eyes opened again. She was confused and disorientated. She called out for David. Then she tried to get out of bed but couldn't. She fell back on the bed and sleep overwhelmed her again.

Desiree was found by a passer-by on Sunday afternoon, walking along the road outside her house in her nightwear. She was incoherent and didn't know where she was or what she was doing. David was nowhere to be found. She was taken to the hospital and admitted for observation. Blood samples showed that she had ingested diazepam and marijuana. After a few days in hospital, Desiree was able to recount what had happened on Friday evening. David, in the meantime, could not be found. He had disappeared.

Desiree was later to discover that not only had David disappeared, but that their joint bank accounts had also been cleaned out and that all the silver, art, and collectables she thought were in storage were gone too. She was broken, devastated, and almost destitute. After protracted legal gymnastics, she secured the outright ownership of the property she occupied.

She was alone, deserted, impoverished in every way, miserable, and in poor health. Her friends, who she had been isolated from, rallied around, doing everything they could to help, but in her mind the stigma of abandonment clung to her like a millstone, dragging her further down day by day.

All the while the search for David continued and widened way beyond the Seychelles, but he had, it seemed disappeared off the face of the earth. Investigations into David's background revealed that he wasn't a psychologist. He didn't have any qualifications. He was a charlatan, a con man. When he volunteered his services at the clinic due diligence was lacking. None of these revelations helped Desiree. They just made her feel even more miserable and let-down.

Six months after David had absconded with Desiree's assets, leaving her ruined, she received a letter. Her only living relative, Elizabeth, a first cousin, had written inviting Desiree to come and live with her, now that her mother and father had passed away. Desiree considered Elizabeth's invitation, mulled it over in her head, and talked it over with the few friends she thought she could trust.

*If I could ever trust anyone again*, she thought. After due deliberation, she accepted Elizabeth's invitation.

Desiree was back some six weeks before word of her return filtered through to Willie. He didn't know what to do. He was uncertain, unsure, and conflicted. He knew where her cousin lived but he couldn't just present himself at their front door unannounced. It wasn't in his nature. For several weeks, under the cover of darkness, he walked past their house, occasionally glimpsing shadows behind the curtained windows.

It was months before he set eyes on Desiree. He had just parked in a supermarket car park and was about to get out of his car when a taxi drove in and parked in a parking space two rows directly in front of him. The rear doors of the taxi swung open and two women with walking aids slowly emerged. It was a moment or two before Willie realised that one of the women was Desiree and that the other had to be her cousin. He wasn't close enough to distinguish their features in detail but he could tell when they moved off towards the supermarket entrance that physically both were impaired, hence their walking sticks for balance and support. As the taxi pulled away and they entered the supermarket he wondered what to do.

*Should I follow them in? Why would I do that? What if by chance I meet them?* He was confused. In the end, he decided to find a space that afforded an unobstructed view of the supermarket entrance, where he could park, wait and watch.

He waited over an hour before they emerged, each with their walking stick in one hand and their shopping in the other. Willie, wearing sunglasses, with the windscreen visor pulled down, observed them closely. Desiree's cousin looked to be much older than her, but it was hard to tell because it seemed to Willie that Desiree had aged almost beyond recognition.

Her black hair, streaked with ribbons of white, didn't caress her shoulders and lacked lustre. Her face had a haggard look. The light had gone out of her eyes. She looked old, worn-out, beaten, and defeated. He couldn't believe what he was seeing. As he sat watching his eyes moistened, forcing him to reach for a tissue. The taxi that had dropped them returned, picked them up, and sped them out of Willie's sight. It truth he was glad. He couldn't have taken much more. He wasn't fit to go shopping. He went home.

Willie sat quietly in his room, thinking. Outside the sun was shining out of the heavens. It was a glorious afternoon. Everything in nature seemed to be in harmony, but he wasn't at peace with himself. His incoherent thoughts were all over the place. Never in his worst nightmares could he have dreamt of seeing Desiree as he had seen her today. She was nothing like the indelible image imprinted in his mind and lodged in his heart. Life had extracted the very essence from her, it seemed to him. Emptied her.

*Why?* he wondered. *Why pick on her?* He argued and debated with himself without coming to any resolution, then realised that if he continued he would probably become depressed. And then he would be no use to anybody, least of all Desiree.

As he pulled himself out of his whirlpool of agitating thoughts he decided that the best course of action was for him to keep a discreet, watching brief. Desiree knew where he lived. She had his address. He hadn't moved house since she had sent her last card, several years ago. If she needed to contact him she knew how. He wasn't being obstinate. His pride hadn't been dented. His mother always used to say,

"Pride feels no pain, Willie." That thought made him smile. He relaxed. It was just that he didn't want to intrude, bring her more trouble. In his heart, even after all the years of separation, Willie knew he still loved Desiree.

*Best for now to keep my distance*, he thought.

Time slipped inexorably by. Elizabeth's health deteriorated until she eventually succumbed to the Grim Reaper and passed over. In keeping with her wishes, the funeral was private, without ceremony. She was cremated and her ashes were scattered over the rose beds in their back garden.

Desiree was living alone again. Not abandoned or deserted, just left behind. Willie felt compelled to do something. But what? Desiree, who was by now almost a recluse, had become more fragile. A care package was arranged to enable her to stay at home. The carers visited three times daily: morning, afternoon, and evening. Willie, the silent observer, saw the frequent comings and goings but was unable to force his legs to take him to her front door. He told himself that she probably wasn't able to answer the door, and he wouldn't know what to say to her anyhow if he did. He didn't want to be a surprise. Or, worse, a shock.

With time the state of Desiree's mental and physical health warranted her being taken into care. It wasn't safe for her to be living on her own. She needed more care than the care assistants attending her could provide. Willie continued his routine walks past her empty house and watched it slowly acquire the dilapidated appearance of something abandoned.

*Just like Desiree*, he thought. Willie wondered if Desiree had put all her affairs in order. He reassured himself that she must have while reminding himself in the process that it was none of his business. Another thought nagged at Willie. He knew from keeping an eye when she was living at home that Desiree didn't have visitors. She didn't have any friends. His follow-up thought was that she wouldn't have anyone visit her in the care home. The thought troubled Willie.

He chose an afternoon to visit Desiree when all the bustle of lunchtime had ceased and there was some semblance of serenity. Willie found Desiree sitting asleep in a big armchair. He took a seat and sat quietly beside her. She was wearing a long dressing-gown, belted at the waist. She looked thin, wasted, and wearied. As she dozed her lips moved agitatedly as if in argument with each other. He couldn't believe how life had been so unkind, so cruel, to the girl he loved.

He was wiping his wet eyes when Desiree opened hers and looked quizzically at him. It seemed to Willie that her dull eyes brightened a little in recognition, before they slowly folded, closed, and faded away from him again. Willie sat for an hour and more waiting for her eyes to reopen before he reluctantly took his leave. He wondered if she had been medicated but thought it best not to ask. While walking home upset and at odds with himself, the world at large, and God, he forced himself to think positively. He focused his thoughts on what he could do for Desiree. By the time he got home, he had settled his mind. It was easy. He would be there for her every day if possible if she would let him.

And so began the process of Willie and Desiree getting to know each other all over again. It was a slow process. Desiree was nervy, tense, unsure, reluctant, and frightened, but slowly and surely her trust in Willie grew. She opened up, little by little, as a mistreated kitten would when it, at last, felt the soft, gentle caress of love. Willie didn't ask any questions or pry into her affairs. He kept the conversation light and impersonal, letting Desiree lead where she wanted to go. Gradually her whole demeanour changed. She brightened and was alert, and at times mischievous. Her improvement did not go unnoticed by the care home staff. But it was not all plain sailing. There were days when she would relapse and be difficult, deliberately awkward, uncommunicative, and sullen. But over time these relapses became less frequent.

With his constancy, their affection for each other slowly resurfaced. Willie would bring Desiree little gifts, little packets of scented wipes and things he thought she would use. Then one day with a mischievous look in her eye Desiree said,

"Willie there's something you could do for me."

Willie willingly responded,

"Certainly. What is it?"

"I could do with some new knickers," Desiree said, watching Willie's face change colour.

"Right," was all Willie could say as his mind reeled back to the day as a child he took washing off the clothesline for his mother when it started to rain. That was the first and last time he had ever laid a finger on any women's underwear.

Next day he ventured into Marks and Spencer on the high street but baulked at the entrance to the lingerie department and went instead into menswear, searched among the boxer pants in the underwear section for what he thought would be the right size for Desiree, and chose a selection in black and grey colours. There was nothing flamboyant about Willie. When he presented his packaged underwear to Desiree she didn't open it in his presence.

*To spare my blushes*, Willie thought.

Slowly Desiree recounted the story of her life after their parting so many years ago. Willie, dutifully listening, encouraged Desiree to unburden herself. He was visiting her daily by this time. Then one day Desiree asked,

64

"Willie, would you get me some new underwear, please? But not the sort you got me before."

"What sort would you like?" Willie queried.

"Use your imagination, Willie," Desiree said and left it at that.

His imagination couldn't do it for Willie. It couldn't fly that high. Back in Marks and Spencer, he forced himself to enter the lingerie department, hoping he would not bump into anyone he knew. It was his Father Ted moment, jouking around the aisles of lady's lingerie searching for suitable underwear for Desiree. At one point he had almost convinced himself that she was asking him to get her underwear just to embarrass him, but he banished that thought before it set firm.

Selections eventually made, he presented himself at the checkout counter. With his face as red as an overripe tomato, he stood in front of a young lady as she meticulously examined each piece of underwear, holding the items up one by one to the light in full view of everyone before wrapping them individually, first in tissue paper, then completing the task with beautiful wrapping paper and presenting them to him in an M&S bag with the words,

"That's a lovely gift for some lucky girl." Willie, mortified and scarlet-faced, didn't know where to look as he fumbled for his credit card. With his purchase complete, he ran out of the store on to the high street, glad to be in the fresh air.

The following afternoon Willie presented Desiree with the bulging M&S bag. Unlike on the previous occasion, she chose to open it in the care home's common room in full view of the residents and visitors. Willie's face coloured pink, red, and crimson as Desiree held his purchases up at arm's length one by one. Black, white, frilly, lacy, dainty, and tiny … She held each one up before her eyes, carefully examined them, and occasionally glanced through the lacy ones at Willie. As she lowered the last garment and held it daintily between the forefinger and thumb of each hand underneath her chin, Desiree looked him in the eyes and said with a serious face,

"Willie, people will think you have a girlfriend."

65

She held her serious expression as best she could before smiling her gentle smile. Willie's face relaxed and its natural colour returned as she said,

"And they would be right."

# Mother Father Son

It was a market and seaport town built in the middle of the nineteenth century. The sum of its parts, the Old Town and the New Town together, didn't add up to very much. It was challenged in every way by its time and its setting. The Old Town, known locally as the head of the town, was knitted together by a network of rough boreens and unsightly narrow alleyways.

The town had about five hundred inhabited dwellings, housing a population of approximately three thousand souls. Many of the dwellings accommodated between two and five cohabiting families, some of them, by all accounts, big families. Employment for those fortunate enough to find it was in cotton – weaving and sailcloth making. Other jobs existed in rope making, flour milling, tanning, farm labouring, and general labouring.

But the town was prospering and tourism was booming. All was well. A golf club was founded in 1894, but not with the working class in mind. In 1908 a bowls and tennis club for 'gentlefolk' came into being. Which begs the question: who exactly were the gentlefolk? Lots of gentlefolk lived in the Old Town, but they wouldn't have had much use for a golf club or tennis racket, other than for swatting flies and vermin.

William was born into this landscape. His parents lived in a terrace of whitewashed single-storey thatch-roofed cottages on Quay Lane. As the name suggests, it led to the harbour, before the new quays were built and Quay Lane was renamed Quay Street, a name that today hints back to its past and the emigrant families who used it in search of a better life in other lands.

William's mother died in childbirth. Growing up, he would carry no memory of her. He never had and never would possess any kind of image of her. It was an essential part of him that would be forever missing. But more misfortune was to come his way. He was five years of age when his father was killed at the quayside, not a hundred yards from their home. He was unloading timber from a boat when a sling snapped letting baulks of timber crash down on top of him. He was killed instantly.

William, an orphan, had no extended family. As was the custom at the time, he was subsumed into his next-door neighbour's family as one of their own. Suddenly he discovered brothers and sisters. That was how working-class communities supported each other. A neighbour's trouble was the community's trouble. Neighbourliness meant something.

He wasn't legally adopted. There was no formality. The next-door neighbours simply took him in and treated him as part of their family. There was nothing unusual about it. No one passed any remarks. The neighbours were Catholics. William's parents had been Presbyterians but that didn't matter much, either. When William was of school-going age, they consulted with the minister of the Presbyterian church, which William's father had infrequently attended, and William became a fully-fledged Presbyterian. On Sundays, he would be taken by one of his adoptive family to attend service and then collected afterwards, until he was old enough to go to church on his own.

As he journeyed through adolescence, William, in turn, adopted his new family, and when he felt like it would go to Mass with his foster father. He never felt he had to. It was his choice. At the age of eighteen, unbeknown to anyone, he became a Catholic. Many years later, when asked why he converted to Catholicism, he said,

"Because I was taught how to be a Christian by my adoptive family."

William wasn't tall. He stretched to about five feet six inches was of slim build but was sinewy, strong, and supple. He was too tall to be a jockey, yet he had the jaunty walk of a jockey: the roll of the shoulders and the sway of the hips. Tough as old boots, he could tame the wildest of horses. That's how he earned the tag 'the horsey man'. He always had a rakish air about him as he went about his business. As he matured he changed little in stature or demeanour.

Agnes, the youngest of five children, was born in the townland of Killyglen and Cairncastle. She, with her brothers and sisters, was reared in a Presbyterian household. Her parents farmed a smallholding. Life was far from easy. It was hard work, day in, day out, just to survive. Each child had to contribute something to the running of the homestead as soon as they were able. There was no room for passengers. The family worked long hours and ate what they produced. Nothing was wasted.

Their home was a small stone-walled cottage with a thatched roof, without amenities. Oil lamps were for lighting and cooking was done over an open peat fire. To get to anywhere they walked. As a child, Agnes walked the three miles to and from the national school every day, hail, rain, or snow. Her basic education was the three Rs: reading, writing, and arithmetic. She learned to write using chalk on a slate.

After school, like her siblings, she had chores to get done before the light faded and the darkness of the night hemmed them in. One of her first chores was to fetch the drinking water from the well at the bottom of the paddock. But before she had reached the age of twelve Agnes could milk the few cows they kept as competently as her father and brothers.

Agnes's home was about five miles up out of the town. On Saturday summer evenings, when all the week's toil was laid to rest, folk would gather at the Killyglen and Cairncastle crossroads for a bit of a hooley. In was on one such fine summer evening that Agnes spotted an unfamiliar face among the gathering. In that moment of first sight, she surveyed the young man from head to toe with the eye of a sparrowhawk. In a few crucial seconds, she would decide whether or not he was what she was looking for.

Later in the evening, as the sun was going down, he asked her to partner him in an eight-hand reel. Face to face, Agnes looked into his piercing sky blue eyes and, without her speaking a word, their fate was settled. Love, the uninvited intruder, beckoned. Smitten, they embarked into an uncertain future.

Agnes and William had found each other. But they were unaware of the ominous backcloth that threatened their nascent love. The English Reformation led to institutional anti-Catholicism in Britain and Ireland. Irish Catholics were forbidden to purchase land, to vote, to hold political office, to live close to towns, to obtain an education, or to enter a profession. Nor were they permitted to take part in many of the areas of life necessary for a person to be somebody in society. But, by the beginning of the nineteenth century, Catholics could sit in parliament, following the Roman Catholic Relief Act of 1829. Agnes and William, given their basic education, continued their courtship, blithely ignorant of anything that could affect their budding relationship.

But ominous clouds were gathering in the social, religious, and political backcloths encompassing Agnes and William. The cumulating issues of sectarianism and home rule threatened the prospects of their shared future together. But love brightens any clouded sky.

Unaware of the gathering storm clouds brewing around them, the lovers journeyed blindly towards marriage, making plans, and thinking about where to live. In Ulster, intermarriage was then a rare occurrence. A Presbyterian girl converting to Catholicism to marry was practically unheard of. She would be labelled a turncoat. But Agnes didn't know that. That revelation would arrive later in various forms. Thankfully Agnes reared in a rural community, was spared the treatment meted out to urban-dwelling turncoats. Her family, although far from being overjoyed at the prospect of her becoming a Catholic, were eventually reconciled to her will.

Agnes and William married in 1896. Simply but immaculately dressed, she stood tall, proud, beautiful, and serene beside William. She was in every way a colleen, but not the stereotypical young Irish woman with red hair, a fiery attitude, and a soft Irish accent. Her long black hair swept back over her head, braided by her mother with tender love and care, hung elegantly in plaits behind her ears. Her brown eyes shone like beacons in the night, proclaiming her inner happiness. Her rosy cheeks radiated joy. She was broad of shoulder and narrow of hip, as she stood calmly responding to the priest's prompting in broad Ulster-Scots,

"Ah, dea."

After their wedding, Agnes and William made their way to their new home in shared accommodation on Pound Street to begin life together, for better or for worse. They lived there for over a year before moving to the Mill Brae, where they would spend the rest of their lives together.

William and Agnes's first son Samuel, who would be better known by his familiar name, Sammy, was the third of their fifteen children. He was born in 1898. The Mill Brae, which was part of the Old Town network, consisted of a string of single-storey thatch-roofed whitewashed terraced houses. These unsightly, unattractive, and poor-looking dwellings determinedly climbed up a rough, steep track, over which farm animals wandered at will. It was a working-class slum.

From the top of the Mill Brae, young Sammy and his pals could have looked towards Islandmagee on a clear day to see gentlemen golfers at play on the fairways and greens of the new golf club. But as children, they couldn't see that far just yet. It would be some time before they would look at life through a different prism.

Sammy's schooling in the North End National School, tucked in beside the Catholic church on Agnew's Lane, was basic. He could read and write, but he was working-class, without a whispering hope of social mobility. His place in society was forever fixed. His schooling never opened his mind to the belief that he could be anything he wanted to be. It was more indoctrination than education. Liberation of the mind was not for his class. That aspiration was the birthright of others, further up the social scale. Sammy, like most working-class children, left school at an early age, burdened with low self-esteem and bereft of ambition.

From the age of twelve, he found employment wherever he could, as best he could, in a society and a world that were rapidly changing around him. With his background and education he understood little of what was happening politically, economically, socially, or locally (never mind nationally or internationally), other than that life for him and his family was tough. When he left school he was living at home in a small two-bedroom single-storey whitewashed house, with nine siblings and his parents. Things were tough, all right, and they were about to get tougher. Yet, strange as it may seem, the town was prospering. Which begs the question: who was prospering, and at whose expense?

Seismic change was in the wind. As Sammy moved inexorably through childhood into adolescence, the earth was moving beneath his feet. The home rule debate in Ireland simmered. In the year 1912, when he was approaching the age of fourteen, the Ulster Covenant was signed by nearly five hundred thousand people in Belfast City Hall, with the intent of opposing home rule in Ireland by any means. Mutiny was in the air folk breathed.

What young Sammy made of it all is anybody's guess. He was, after all, only fourteen years of age. The home rule debate intensified, climaxing when the SS *Clyde Valley* sailed into port, laden with armaments for the Ulster Volunteer Force to use in opposition to home rule. What must the atmosphere in the prosperous town have been like then?

Further afield, war clouds were accumulating. The assassination of Archduke Franz Ferdinand of Austria in June 1914 triggered a diplomatic crisis that would ensnare Great Britain and Ireland in a world war. What was young Sammy to make of all this? Had he ever heard of Archduke Franz Ferdinand, Serbia, or Sarajevo? Could he have found these places on a map, if he had one and could have read it?

Does it matter? Yes, it matters because, at the outbreak of World War I, Sammy one month short of his sixteenth birthday, with ten sisters and three brothers, unknown to his parents enlisted in the British army.

He was posted for training to Dublin. Sammy, a sixteen-year-old teenager, had grown to his full height. He was broad-shouldered, compact, and stocky. His blonde hair was cut short, his eyebrows were black, and he had piercing blue eyes and a smile that would melt ice. It was said he took after his mother. He certainly had her disposition and was gentle, kind, and easy-going.

But why would a working-class Catholic boy, given the overbearing backcloth of sectarianism, join the British army to fight in the Great War, as it was later labelled? Why would he enlist in the Royal Irish Rifles? Was it because his future prospects in his home town were so poor? After all, by all accounts, it was prospering.

Had the political landscape in Ulster changed so much that perhaps he felt alienated? Did the anti-Catholic atmosphere pervading the town force him to find a way out? Was the king's shilling a sufficient inducement? Perhaps it was the lure of excitement, the manliness of it all, or simply boredom. Did he just want something better than life at home? Or had a latent aspiration to better himself stirred him into action?

It is difficult to know what Sammy's motivation was. It certainly wasn't a career choice. Perhaps he just wanted out of the mire he was in. Imagine the feelings of his mother, father, and siblings when they discovered what he had done. His distraught mother lamented for days on end over her firstborn son.

Spurred into action, his father wrote to the military authorities on 3 March 1915:

*Dear Sir,*

*It would satisfy my wife and family if you could see your way to release our son Samuel, of the Royal Ulster Rifles, on account of his youth. He was only sixteen years of age on his last birthday and he went away without asking us or letting us know. I think it is hardly fair to me or his mother. I hope you will see your way to send him home as soon as possible – provided he is able to come, as I believe he was in hospital for a few days recently.*

*Hoping you will oblige,*
*Yours sincerely,*
*William and Agnes Shields*

The letter failed to generate a response, but Sammy's father persevered and wrote again to military headquarters on 31 March 1915:

*Dear Sir,*

*I respectfully beg to forward this line on application to have my son Samuel discharged if it is possible. I presume it is not fair for him nor for me that he should be asked to remain in the army when he is not of age. I ask you for a reply stating with reasons, what course of action you are going to take in this matter as I fail to see any obstacle to him obtaining his discharge. His mother and I understand that a man, a private in the army, must be at least eighteen years of age. So why should I not have a claim to have him discharged at an early date, knowing him not to be eligible to join the army according to his age? I have already forwarded his birth certificate to serve as evidence of my statement.*

*I ask you kindly to let me know what your intention is and let me know on which date you will give him his discharge.*

*If you would be so kind as to let me know what you intend doing.*

*Yours sincerely,*

*William Shields*

In the end, perseverance paid off. Samuel, aged sixteen years and seven months, was discharged from the army for having made *a misstatement of his age on enlistment.*

There was much relief when Sammy was returned home. All seemed well for a while, but he wasn't settled. Shortly after his seventeenth birthday, Sammy informed his parents of his intention to re-enlist in the Royal Irish Rifles. His intent generated fractious argument, debate, and pleading within the family for him to change his mind. His mother told him,

"I don't want my son to kill other mothers' sons." What mother would?

"I didn't bring you into this world to become a killer," she shouted at him one day when frustration got the better of her. In the end, all his mother's and siblings' attempts at persuasion were to no avail. Sammy's resolve was set as firm as concrete.

74

Just as firm as his mother's when she decided to marry his father, much against her family's wishes. Sammy re-enlisted in the Royal Irish Rifles and trained for war.

This story could end here, but it doesn't.

For reasons beyond comprehension, Sammy's father followed him. William volunteered to serve in the Great War and followed in his son's footsteps. Why he volunteered remains a tantalising conundrum. Did he mistakenly think he could in some way afford Sammy protection? Surely not. A notion circulated in the family later that William's wife, Agnes, was so fed up with producing children for him that she encouraged him to go. The expression 'Give me a break,' floats easily to mind. Sammy's father, as it turned out, served in one of the support units servicing the front-line troops, where his horsemanship was put to good use. Perhaps William didn't volunteer. He might have been conscripted. It doesn't matter. All that matters is that he was there. He served.

A family tale often told was of a time that father and son met by chance, in a cafe in a village somewhere behind the front lines. William offered his son Sammy a soft drink by way of greeting and refreshment. But Sammy, having matured somewhat since their last meeting, treated his father to something a little stronger. They spent a very pleasant afternoon together, after which, arms interlocked, they emptied their glasses of Calvados. Over time this story has become family folklore.

Sammy was wounded on 1 July 1916 at the Battle of the Somme. When fit he was returned to front-line service. Seriously wounded a second time his war was ended. Miraculously, both father and son survived WWI. Sammy was hospitalised in Manchester for many months before being discharged from hospital and the army. His home town, although still prospering, it seemed, offered little by way of prospect for him. This survivor of the Battle of the Somme, who was twice wounded, sought a future in England where he settled, married, and raised a family.

His father came home too. Unscathed and full of vigour, he sired two more children and, by all accounts, lived a full and fruitful life. William was eighty-one when he passed away. Hard-hatted men dressed in mourning black lined the streets to escort his remains to the Catholic church, such was the respect for William and his family.

Almost to the day, a year later, William's wife Agnes passed away. Although she was a convert to Catholicism, after taking Communion on her deathbed, Agnes asked her parish priest if it would be all right if she could be buried with her ain folk. In the 1950s the cemetery in the town was segregated, with Catholics interred in one area and Protestants in another. The parish priest, a man of God blessed with great wisdom, put her mind at rest. Agnes was interred in a grave in the Protestant part of the cemetery while William, over the wall, as it were, interred a year earlier, lay in wait for her in the Catholic part.

Maybe Agnes had had enough of William, or perhaps, deep within every soul, there is a longing always to be with your 'ain folk'. Today Agnes in her grave is not alone. Two of their children rest with her and, keeping their relationship in equilibrium, two of their children rest with William too. May they rest in peace. Now you are at liberty to make of that what you will.

But what of Sammy? He and his family came back to his home town frequently for summer holidays and stayed with his parents. After his parents went to ground, as a family they visited less frequently. Sammy, however, without fail, returned every year at the beginning of July.

Although he wasn't a tall man, Sammy had a soldier's bearing. He always wore a belted long gabardine coat and a fedora hat, set well back on his head. He was a soldier looking at you from top to bottom.

Back home for 1 July, as regular as clockwork, he would leave the house on the Mill Brae well-dressed in the morning and return well-oiled, as they say, sometime in the evening. But never eight sheets to the wind. He was never difficult or carnaptious. He was easy-going, like his mother. Sammy never said much in the house but always quietly listened, absorbing everything. Occasionally when a conversation was taking a particular bent he would say,

"Never put your hand out further than you'll be able to pull it back."

Or, when someone was beyond help, he would say,

"Never pour water on a drowned mouse." But he was a compassionate person. Perhaps what he had experienced in the war had shaped him.

On one occasion, after he had returned from his July 1 afternoon outing, he was alone in the house with one of his nephews from down the road. Sammy was sitting upright in his favourite fireside armchair, adjusting and readjusting his black-framed eyeglasses. He always maintained, even when sitting, a soldier's posture, with his back straight and his shoulders four-square.

He was idly gazing out through the living room window across the fields beyond. His mind was far away, lost in thought. Perhaps he was in the trench mud before the whistle blew and he had to go over the top. Who could guess where his mind was? He was wearing an open-necked shirt, over which loosely hung an unbuttoned patterned cardigan. His trousers, of a dark worsted corduroy material, nestled on top of spotlessly clean brown leather shoes. His old army belt held up his trousers. He seemed at peace with himself, on a faraway quiet island of thought.

Then the shrill voice of his nephew, who he had forgotten was in the room, opened up with a barrage of questions. Sammy instantly roused from his thoughts looked at his nephew. He held his silence. But his eleven-year-old nephew, without seemingly pausing for breath, went on about the war, the fighting, the machine guns, the tanks, and much more.

"Were you wounded, Uncle Sammy?" his nephew blurted out. Sammy ignored the question, not just once. But his nephew persisted until he relented, and with a nod of his head replied,

"Twice, son." He always used the word 'son' when talking to younger men. There's a familiarity in the sound of it on the ear, something friendly. But the inquisitive boy was like a dog with a bone. He wouldn't let go. Finally, in exasperation, Sammy pulled up his shirt, exposing the ugly scarred flesh in his side and revealing were a machine gun bullet had ripped away a huge chunk of flesh and muscle. It looked like a gored cabbage.

"Go on, son. Put your fist into it and feel what it's like." The boy hesitated. "It's not as bad as it looks, son. Go on, do it," he encouraged. "It won't bite you."

His nephew fisted his little hand and gently buried it in the hole in his uncle's side. It was a cathartic moment for both of them. Then Sammy, looking his young nephew in the eye, repeated his mantra,

"Never put your hand out further than you'll be able to pull it back."

Instantly the boy's hand snapped back. A smile brightened Sammy's face. It would take the boy a year or two to grasp the real meaning of what his uncle had said to him that day.

But the curiosity of the young is incorrigible. Sammy's nephew wanted to know where his uncle went every day, especially on 1 July. To find out was simple enough. He had to play detective and follow him, and that's what he did. He followed his uncle discreetly, as only a child could, down, through, and around the streets and lanes of the Old Town, and watched as he entered the Royal British Legion Club. He didn't know anything about the Royal British Legion, didn't even know it existed. Why should he?

The boy waited and waited and was wondering what to do with himself when he heard the sounds of marching bands somewhere down in the town. He went to have a look and saw a parade heading south on Main Street, away from the cenotaph and towards him. Knowing they would do a circuit of the town, he headed up to the high street to position himself to watch as they paraded on their return. He was standing waiting for the parade when his uncle, who was swaying slightly, he thought, in the breeze, headed towards him. On seeing his nephew, his uncle took his little hand and with the eye of a trained rifleman, surveyed the approaching sash-wearing paraders. Some of them, who were wearing medals, attracted his nephew's attention, provoking a question.

"Uncle Sammy, you were in the army. You have medals. Why aren't you parading?"

"I don't have to, son. I was there. They know nothing about it. Come on, let's go up home," Sammy said, and with that, they left the paraders to their parading and made their way to Mill Brae.

The parade they had witnessed was the annual commemorative parade for the Battle of the Somme. Sammy, who had been wounded on the first day of the Battle of the Somme, didn't need to parade. He had experienced the real thing at close quarters. But for his nephew the puzzle of Sammy's behaviour, year in, year out, was never really solved, understood, and appreciated until many years later, when an exhibition celebrating the centenary of WWI was staged in the town library in 2016. Among the photographs prominent in the exhibition was one of Rifleman Samuel Shields, with a footnote that read,

*Rifleman Samuel Shields of the Royal Irish Rifles, who has been wounded for the second time, the first being on 1 July 1916. He is the son of Mrs Shields of Mill Brae and his father, Pte William Shields, who is also serving. Rfm. Shields was wounded in his left side on 2 September last and is now in hospital in Manchester.*

In their Mill Brae home, the evidence of William's and Sammy's military service had places of honour. Sammy, on his last trip home, took everything related to their service to king and country, including medals and citations, back to his home in England. As time passed memories faded, such that their service in the Great War became a family rumour. The photograph made prominent in the town library exhibition of 2016 converted rumour to fact, for all to see.

But there was more. The exhibition listed the names of the soldiers killed or wounded in action from the town on the first day of the Battle of the Somme. Many of the one hundred and twenty-five soldiers listed came from the Old Town area: Mill

Brae, Meetinghouse Street, Mill Street, Blacks Lane, Ferris Lane, Mission Lane, Pound Street, and Carson Street. It would seem perfectly reasonable to infer that Sammy chose to be home every year on the first day of July to be with his comrades, especially those from the Old Town, who he had gone over the top with on 1 July 1916.

This story could end here, but to end here would be an injustice to Sammy, to his father, and to all the Catholics who served in the 36th (Ulster) Division – the Pals Brigade, as it was known. For over a hundred years they have been airbrushed out of history. To such an extent that some folk believed, it is said, that the German soldiers only shot those British coming over the top who were wearing orange sashes at the Battle of the Somme.

The playwright Frank McGuinness redressed the historical imbalance in his iconic play, *Observe the Sons of Ulster Marching Towards the Somme*. The lead word in the title of the play invites the audience to *observe* that McGuinness, in his cast of eight soldiers, had included one with Catholic origins.

In praise of the men of the 36th (Ulster) Division it was said,

'Whether town dweller or country lad, volunteer or regular, officer or other rank, Catholic or Protestant, the sons of Ulster knew a comradeship and a trust in adversity that should be a lesson to us all.'

Perhaps that reveals the real reason why Sammy always came home for 1 July every year.

But what societal lessons were learned from the sacrifices of so many? When William and Agnes married in 1896 the cumulus clouds of sectarianism darkened their bright skies and opposition to home rule for Ireland was simmering. Now, a century and more later, sectarianism lingers and home rule is still an issue. Perhaps the lesson is that there is no tying up of old soldiers' tongues. You may wonder what Agnes, William, and Sammy would make of it all.

They lived for a dream, born at a Killyglen and Cairncastle crossroads hooley, one summer Saturday evening a long time ago.

# Naked Windows

Imperfect memory sketches
In bold primary colours.
Images of the neighbourhood
That shaped me.

With its resonating personality
And an embedded incongruity,
The Old Town, a
Twentieth-century community.

Families lived cheek by jowl
Not walled in,
But constrained by heritage,
Inconsequentially clustered together.

In keeping with the season,
Orange arches stood proud.
Tri-coloured kerbstones lined
Every pedestrian way.

Flags flown from windows
From homes celebration-readied.
Naked windows obstinately flagless,
In silent abjuration.

From our naked windows
Morning, noon, and night
In plain sight Baxter's
Graffitied gable wall.

Bids welcome to all
Except pope and papists.
In language ambiguity-free,
Loud and rancorous.

Year in, year out,
Day in, day out,
Vilified, ridiculed, belittled,
Humiliated on a wall.

Granddad, world war veteran
Quietly living below the radar, said,
"Ignore it, son.
"Pass no remarks."


His firstborn son Sammy
Wore the uniform too.
Wounded at the Somme
And once more.

Took me by the hand
To walk, shoulders squared.
Upright, straight, and tall,
Head held high.
Eyes half-shut,
Adolescence came and went
Without direction, aimlessly drifting,
Ambivalent and inarticulate.

How could I know
     My future-blithely unaware
     In another enclave, waited.
     Close at hand?

Happenstance our meeting place
A moment of first sight.
Cupid's little seed sown, An awakening begun.

A future clearly manifesting, Love's transforming grace
shaping,
     Journey in life beginning,

Pilgrims together binding.

Was it all predestined,
Mapped out for me?
Womb's implanted little seedling, Life to be.

Neighbourhood streets shaped me
Graffitied walls toughened me,
True love rescued me.

# One Day in July

She came out of the womb bawling, the youngest of five children, in 1945. Her home was a mid-terrace house fronted by a small walled garden. The rear garden was accessed by a network of alleys connecting the backs of other neighbouring terraced houses. She was familiar with the labyrinth of alleys. It was her playground.

When her schooling began, she noticed that her friends went to different schools. Barbara was enrolled in Saint Mary's School, a Catholic school for girls, which was staffed by nuns. Her brothers were enrolled in the McKenna Memorial School, a boys' school. The boys were not taught by nuns. Barbara's childish querying of her parents as to why she didn't go to the same school as her friends was difficult for them to explain to a child.

"It's just the way it is, dear," they said and left it at that. It was an early introduction to the differences that Barbara would learn to cope with.

From an early age, she could distinguish the seasons of the year. She slowly came to understand that there were seasonal events and celebrations, which at first seemed inclusive but were anything but. The celebration that climaxed in July was one in particular. It was a celebration, preceded by months of beaverish activity: gathering combustible material for bonfires, hanging flags, stringing street bunting, painting kerbs, and raising arches.

At first, as any child would, Barbara joined in the chaotic activity of celebration until a curtain of understanding slowly lifted far enough for her to realise that some celebrations were exclusive. Her parents didn't join in, didn't hang out flags from their windows as their neighbours did. She noticed that her school friends' homes were also conspicuously flagless. Barbara was well able to read when she first noticed the graffitied gable wall of a house she had walked past many times. It captured her attention. She stopped, read what was written on the wall, reread it, and began to think about her place in the neighbourhood, her home town, and her country of birth.

To find space to comprehend, she would occasionally avoid some friends by slipping out through her back garden into the labyrinth of alleyways steering clear in the process, of the demoralising graffitied gable wall. Her adolescence was peppered and punctuated with strained friendships and stilted conversations. She felt at times like a tolerated outsider in her neighbourhood, a sponge soaking up society's vitriol, somehow to emerge unaffected, untarnished. She was to learn that loving her neighbour could be difficult.

But July gave way, as it always did, to August. The year moved through summer into autumn, and winter heralded Christmas, the season of goodwill towards all. Christmas greetings exchanged, Christmas trees illuminated, and Christmas messages loudly carolled. Normality reset. But she learned to keep a tight lip, to say nothing, to never mention religion, to acquiesce, and to be wary of coiled tongues.


Fast-forward forty years. The historical event-fuelled Troubles had ended with the signing of the Good Friday agreement.

Barbara was employed as a regional carer with social services. She liked her job, which essentially entailed visiting people on the social services register, assessing their needs, and reporting any changes in the circumstances of her clients. Her client load was town-based, so she could walk weather permitting, to all her clients, varying her route to suit her mood. She liked walking, and townscapes were as interesting to Barbara as landscapes. She noted the gardens fronting the dwellings she passed, the balconied apartments festooned with geranium-filled window boxes, the hanging baskets, the trimmed hedges, the bird feeders, the coloured facades, the door furniture, the width of the streets, and the things that characterised the different neighbourhoods. Her eagle eye sent its laser into back gardens too, revealing much.

On the first Monday of July, Barbara left home in good time for morning Mass. Her day's work already planned. She liked to begin her day, every day, that way if she could.

The first destination on her list was Queens Street, but although she had lived all her life in the town, she had no idea where it was. Primed with her husband's directions, Barbara made her way to the Bank Road. After walking past its insignificant entrance several times she discovered Queen Street. It wasn't really a street. It was a steep, narrow lane leading down to a row of two-storey dwellings that were squeezed in between the backyards of the houses looming above on the Bank Road and the adjacent railway. Stepping gingerly down the lane, Barbara felt like Alice heading into Wonderland.

At the bottom, she paused and looked around. The little terrace of houses had no front or rear gardens. The dwellings had tiny backyards, with nothing at the front other than a wire-netted six-foot-high fence between them and the railway. The narrow lane abutted each dwelling at a threshold that was just three inches high.

Barbara took a deep breath, checked her notes, confirmed the number of the house she sought, and sallied forth to undertake her first visit of the day. Because July was the month when loyalist cultural celebrations climaxed, streets all over the town were strung with tri-coloured bunting, flags hung from celebrating homes, and street arches proudly marked territories. Queens Street was no exception. Each house was marked with a flag.

The solid front door she approached was stained a deep mahogany colour. The brass door furniture glinted in the morning sun. The door swung open to the second rap of the door knocker, indicating that someone was expected.

The woman standing there smiling a welcome was a tall, elderly lady with a mop of unruly curly white hair held back from her face with hair clips. Her deep blue eyes, framed under jet-black bushy eyebrows, keenly surveyed Barbara. Everything about her was friendly and natural. With Barbara seated her client Janet ignored her refusal and disappeared into the adjoining kitchen to make tea. But she soon reappeared, holding a laden tea tray. She had prepared for her visitor.

Sitting facing the only window in the room, Barbara looked out through the wire-netted fence across the railway tracks to the marshalling yard beyond. There wasn't much to see, but at least there was some activity that might temporarily relieve boredom. Barbara noted, as she was trained to do, that the room was neat and tidy. It wasn't bare or overstuffed with things. It had what was needed for everyday living and everything was in its place. An unlit fire was set in the grate of the neat Devon fireplace.

*The fire is probably lit at night*, Barbara thought, as there was no sign of any other form of heating. She didn't see a television in the room, but there was a radio in the shelved recess by the fireplace. The twin-shelved recess on the other side of the Devon fireplace was filled with books. The room decor was simple. The walls and ceiling were painted white, the skirting boards were stained dark oak, and the floor was covered with patterned linoleum. The small room had personality. It was fresh, clean, and tidy.

As Janet poured the tea, a train lumbered past, easing its way to the station, rattling the windows and startling Barbara. Without pausing or looking up Janet said,

"Don't annoy yourself. That's only the nine-thirty arrival from Belfast. Sure I can tell the time by them, night and day."

"I suppose you get used to it," Barbara offered sympathetically.

"At times it's company on a slow day, you know," Janet responded, offering Barbara a choice of biscuit. With the noise of the train receding they settled to tea and conversation.

*Sharing tea is a gentle, universal icebreaker*, Barbara thought. *The preparation, the care and attention, the presentation, the ritual, all just for me, this simple ceremony? Welcome to my home.*

Barbara led the conversation, asking how Janet was doing, if she visited the market often over by the station on Wednesdays, and also enquiring what her neighbours were like. It was just casual conversation, which allowed Barbara to unobtrusively gauge Janet's communication skills. There was no problem in that department. Janet was articulate and erudite. It was as Barbara would have expected, given the shelved recess full of books. As Janet talked, Barbara listened, her antennae acutely tuned for any nuances that might suggest perhaps that something was not as well with Janet as it seemed.

But she couldn't sense any reason for concern. She had scrutinised Janet's file over the weekend in preparation for this visit and, as they chatted, was reassured that Janet was well in herself. Preparing to take her leave, Barbara insisted on carrying the tea tray into the kitchen. It was tiny, but like the front room, it was neat, tidy, and clean, with its food cupboards well stocked. Barbara arranged a date and a different time for her next visit and said goodbye to Janet.

As she walked back along the potholed lane she talked into her mini-cassette recorder, noting for the record the details of her visit. Turning right and looking up towards the Bank Road, she was amazed how steep the incline was. Breathless, on the Bank Road pavement at the top of the lane, she made a note into her machine to walk Janet over to the market yard on her next visit. Even if Janet could manage the steep incline in summer, winter was a different matter altogether, she reckoned. Barbara doubted the council would be salting Queens Street in winter.

Barbara walked back towards the Glynn Road, paused for a moment before the Tullygarley graffitied park wall, looked at it, smiled, then strode on, leaving it to its past. It never occurred to her that anyone watching might have thought she admired the artistry and lauded the sentiment. After walking with purpose past the Bridge School and over the bridge under which the Inver River gurgled its way to the sea, she entered Riverdale, a redeveloped part of the Old Town.

She lingered for a moment at what was left of the Mourne Clothing Company building, now put to other commercial use. Her thoughts meandered through the network of lanes that once knitted together the Old Town and wove the patterns of everyday life in the neighbourhood. She thought about Cooper's Lane, where once a man who made barrels had worked, Mission Lane, where Reverend John Wesley had preached, Trow Lane, Black's Lane, Mill Lane, Ferris Lane, and more.

She knew this place well. School friends had lived there. It was a tight-knit industrious community, with its butchers, bakers, and candlestick makers. There were all kinds of shops selling goods, workshops making stuff, a saddler making leather goods, and a wee pet shop selling exotic birds, and other weird things. The smell of stale porter, slaughtered pigs, and oiled leather lingered and filled her nostrils. All that was missing was the sound of the factory horn.

Then she made her way past the one remaining block of multi-storey flats built in the late 1960s where Mill Street, once the arterial heart of the Old Town, climbed upwards to connect with Pound Street. She was making her way to her next client, who lived midway up the Mill Brae, in a red-brick two-storey two bedroom terraced house.

Barney Brady was a good-natured placid man, who seldom lost his temper unless seriously provoked. His wife had passed away several years ago, leaving Barney on his own. Mrs Brady had worried about him, but she needn't have. Barney was the sort of man who could live happily on a desert island. He wasn't introverted, though. He liked company and mixed readily and easily with others.

As she approached Barney's house she could see him at the door. Well, she couldn't actually see him. She saw the crescent of his belly protruding like a horn beyond the terrace facade and the plume of smoke from his pipe billowing out and filling the air, signalling his presence. Barney was leaning against the door frame. His fulsome belly was supported by a combination of belt and braces. The latter was strapped over his shoulders and buttoned front and rear to his corduroy trousers. His brightly coloured patterned lumberjack shirt, with three buttons undone at the neck, allowed his hairy chest to breathe.

Standing squinting down the stem of his pipe at her, a cloth cap pitched back on his head and a pipe in his hand, he was the quintessential pigeon fancier. As a child, she remembered men

89

gathered at the bottom of the Brae on Saturday mornings wondering if the birds were up yet, which meant,

"Have the pigeons been released?" Then, when the word was received that the birds were released, they would go their separate ways back to their lofts to begin the vigil, their eyes searching the sky, hoping they might clock the early one this time.

"You're late as usual, Barbara," he said, the pipe bouncing in his mouth as he spoke. "Ah suppose some things never change," he muttered, as he made way for her to squeeze past him. "The soup's warm, anyways. I'll toast you a bit of soda bread." It was a tight squeeze.

"Some things are too good to rush, Barney," she managed to say. A hint of avian odour lingered on Barney's clothes. She was glad he wasn't a fisherman.

The routine never changed with Barney. When her soup was consumed and she had a cup of tea in her hand, she sat as Barney regaled her with the goings-on around the area. The who was doing what to who, always prefixed with,

"Wait till I tell you this." He might be placid, but his mind was razor-sharp and his wit was keen.

The first time she visited Barney he invited her in.

"Would you like to see my birds?" he said. What a chat-up line. She couldn't refuse. He escorted her through the scullery and out of the small enclosed yard to the back of the house, where he and his fellow pigeon fanciers had built their lofts. There were quite a few of them dotted about the place, and a few aviaries as well. Up the wooden steps she climbed, behind Barney, into the loft. All the pigeons had names. He was so gentle handling them, checking them over, while explaining to her the different breeds of racing pigeon. Back in the house, he proceeded to tell her all about how he won the most prestigious race in pigeon racing, the old bird race from France.

"You see, lass, I had this great wee bird. A wee hen. She had won races for me before. But I was afraid to send her off to France. It's a brave bit away, you know, and she was very light."

As Barbara nodded sagely, Barney continued.

"But we were lucky, you see because a couple of weeks before the race she was sitting on eggs. Right?" Barney asked, making sure Barbara understood what he was imparting. "Well, you see, I took one of the eggs and blew it. Right?" But at this time of asking, Barney realised that Barbara hadn't a clue what he was talking about.

"OK, here's the way of it," Barney explained. "I took one of her eggs, pierced it both ends with a pin, and blew out the yolk and all so that I was left with an intact empty shell."

"But why did you do that, Barney?" Barbara naively asked. Barney roared with laughter. When he gathered himself together, he explained what he did.

"I waited two days before the race. Then I went out into the garden and found myself two wee thin worms. I sealed them inside the shell of the egg and put the egg back in the nest box with the eggs she was sitting on. When that wee hen felt them worms wriggling under her, she was fit to be tied. She won the race by a street. That was a great day, I can tell you," he explained when he eventually stopped laughing.

Barbara had to be careful with Barney. She liked him, he made her laugh, and she had known him a long time, but she had a job to do. Barney could now and then be a little forgetful, especially about taking his medication. He had contracted BFL, the dreaded bird fancier's lung disease. He wore a pigeon fancier's mask now when tending the birds, but he didn't race them any longer.

As they chatted and laughed she was, in one way and another, sussing out how Barney was doing. On the face of it, he was fine, but she had to ask to be sure about his medication. He was on steroids and occasionally needed oxygen. There were potential fire safety issues, but he didn't smoke in the house or the pigeon loft. Barbara figured that Mrs Brady had had something to do with that.

Barney, happy to put Barbara's mind at rest, got his medication and showed her what he had left and what he had taken. He also got out the little capsule container that stored the pills in sections marked with the different days of the week, which he used to remind himself to take the pills. Satisfied that

Barney was fine, Barbara prepared to take her leave. At the door, Barney asked,

"Do you remember the winter of 1963? There was some snow on the Brae that year."

"Do I remember?" Barbara laughed. "That was some winter, all right. Sure I was a teenager then. Oh, it was a great year. The schools were closed. Didn't we spend many days and nights sleighing down the Brae? It was great. Hasn't been anything like it since."

"And hopefully never will be again," Barney muttered. "Do you know the wife had to knit jackets for the pigeons? The poor souls were foundered." Barbara wasn't going to be caught by that one. When she gave him her incredulity look, Barney started laughing. She joined in, and on that happy note, they parted.

Looking across Magill's field, she could see the house she was born and reared in, on Lower Cairncastle Road. Her next client lived two doors below where she was reared.

"Nothing much has changed," she mused, gazing at the emerald green door through which she had taken her first infant steps into what she knew not. But to get there she had to pass the graffitied gable wall of childhood memory, negotiate her way past the huge pyramid-shaped bonfire stack at the foot of the Mill Brae, and walk under the triumphal arch and on the tri-painted kerbstones that marked the territory. It didn't intimidate or frighten her any longer. Barbara had come to understand that cultures, like off-the-peg clothes, could be ready-made and shaped to any purpose.

From the bottom of the Brae, she looked around the junction, observing and absorbing everything: the boys on sentry duty at the bonfire stack, Magill's dairy herd grazing in the field, and the atmosphere laden with expectancy. She was sure of one thing, though. Magill's dairy herd wouldn't witness the bonfire when it was lit on the eleventh night. On impulse, Barbara walked over to where she approximated the point of intersection to be, where the five roads converged. A weird feeling surged through her. She felt she was on holy ground.

"Your imagination's running riot. Get hold of yourself," she cautioned herself as she retraced her steps, hoping that no one she knew had seen her. Five was a significant number, perhaps even symbolic in Celtic mythology: the five great roads in Ireland, the five paths of law, the five provinces in ancient Ireland, the five great houses of Ireland, and the five wheels that Cuchulain had painted on his shield. Here, where she was born and reared, five roads converged, and she hadn't noticed that before.

Shaking her head, she went to visit Joe Rafferty, her next client. Joe, a tall and very stout well-built man in his late sixties, had a large, angular bald head and a sizeable forehead that suggested intellectual capability. His eyes possessed a permanent twinkle, hinting at a deep-rooted sense of humour. When he was enthusiastically in full flow his baritone voice resonated. So infectious and loud was his laughter that it was impossible to resist joining in the fun.

Joe, like a musical instrument, was a most agreeable companion at any time. He could sing a good song and tell stories and tall tales until the cows came home. His mind was as sound as a bell. Barbara enjoyed her visits with Joe, but she was concerned for him. Joe was once a tall, straight-backed man, but not any longer. He had over time acquired a pronounced stoop. With his walking stick in his hand for support, he opened the door to Barbara. As his condition deteriorated it would be two walking sticks, then a walking frame, until his mobility deserted him. For the present he was managing, it seemed.

Settled in his favourite chair, Joe was more himself and less hunched. Barbara made him tea, surveying the kitchen as she did so. Everything was neat and tidy. There was nothing on the floor for Joe to trip over and his fridge was well stocked with food. Joe sipped his tea as they talked. In his speech, Joe was clear, fluent, and sometimes quite eloquent. Joe had been a sailor.

"I sailed the seven seas seven times, like Sinbad," he would tell her, laughing loudly.

"It was a rough do, all right," was all he would say about his time as a merchant seaman in the war on the Russian Convoys.

He would tell her stories of his excursions up the Amazon, walking on the Great Wall of China, the Great Barrier Reef in Australia, and some of the goings-on when he and his mates went ashore in foreign ports. As they sat talking, Barbara seamlessly changed the subject, asking if he had visited any gardens abroad. She knew full well that Joe was very much into gardening. She discovered that his son now cut the grass at the front and tidied up various things for him out at the back. Joe had cultivated a great vegetable plot in the back garden. He'd taken pride in it, and in his roses too, but admitted he wasn't fit enough to do it any longer.

Barbara suggested they go and have a look. Joe was reluctant but wanted to please, so made the effort. Barbara's concern was Joe's mobility. In and around the house everything seemed OK. As she wandered around the garden, Joe stood wedged in the back door frame. The path down the garden was clear of obstruction. She thought for a moment about taking Joe's arm for a tour around the garden but then thought better of it.

While standing at the garden gate, she was for a moment back in her childhood, running and playing with friends around the backs, as they called the alleyways that knitted together a neighbourhood. In many ways it was like the Old Town, a community within a community, woven and shaped by alleyways … the backs. Lost in thought, Joe calling her interrupted her reverie.

Back in the house, she noticed that Joe had plugged the electric kettle into a socket by his seat and had placed some tea things on a little table between them.

"That's handy, Joe," she remarked.

"Aye. Saves me running in and out to the kitchen," Joe replied.

"So long as you're careful, Joe. Don't want you tripping and falling over."

"I'm not that daft, Barbara," Joe laughed. But Barbara wasn't laughing. As the conversation continued, she realised that Joe was spending most of his time in the one room, having gathered things around himself like the kettle and the tea-making things. It wouldn't have surprised her if he also had the electric toaster in there beside him at times too. Maybe even an electric fire. Something to look out for. It would be a fire hazard.

Joe had a downstairs shower and toilet. He only had to negotiate the stairs when going to bed. Barbara thought she'd better have a nosey, which she did when Joe went to the loo. She saw nothing that alarmed her. Joe was quite capable of living alone for the time being. He had loads of friends and his family were attentive, but the habit he was developing of gathering the tea-making things around him in his living room bothered Barbara. There was an article she had read about this kind of behaviour. She resolved to read it again. With their goodbyes exchanged and her notes recorded, Barbara headed back the way she had come.

At the bottom of the terrace, she stood on the footpath, paused, looked across at the bonfire, surveyed the five-road intersection again, and glanced at the gable wall. It took her a moment to realise that her face was smiling. She was happy to be back on the holy ground of her childhood.

Perhaps it was that feeling that turned her head to the mouth of the entrance to the network of alleyways – the backs – where she had enjoyed such fun and games with her friends. A glance at her watch told her she had enough time if she wanted to explore the avenues of her childhood's quiescent memory. So she set about exploring. Confronted with a choice at the first alleyway junction, she turned left and walked up the back of the terraced houses she had just left. Her rekindled childhood memory was of well-cared-for gardens full of summer blossom, lavender, lilac, roses, rosemary, and other plants of her childhood scenting the air, and of cultivated vegetable plots, people pottering, weeding, and talking on summer evenings and weekends.

But what she saw now beggared belief. What had once been well-tended gardens had been given up to garages of dubious DIY construction. Domestic oil storage tanks elevated on block-built plinths hovered ominously over the alley, while in one neglected garden an ancient motorbike raised aloft on makeshift supports hoped-for restoration. Only occasionally did a garden among the detritus of modernity offer a glimpse of past days and ways.

At the top of the alleyway, Barbara turned right. Her route was bounded by the college sports fields on her left and the back gardens of Rugby Terrace on her right. At first, looking straight ahead, she was confused. She didn't recognise the place. Slowly she pieced together what had happened. There had been a mini-land grab. The surface of the sports fields on her left was about one and a half metres above the level of the alleyway she was standing in. From the boundary fence, a bank had sloped down to the alleyway level at an angle of about forty-five degrees. Some enterprising opportunist had decided that the bank served no useful purpose, was a waste of space and had excavated the section of it adjacent to their property. The reclaimed space was then put to another use. Over time others had followed the lead.

Now, along the length of the alleyway abutting the sports fields, were oil storage tanks, sheds, parking spaces, secure storage spaces, and the occasional builder's mini yard. Barbara was dumbstruck. Walking along the alley, she recalled the ease with which she and her friends had gained entry to the sports fields, the freedom they'd enjoyed, and the games they had played in the innocence of growing up. It somehow seemed a lifetime ago. The back gardens were not as she remembered either. Now they were cluttered and unloved. But not all of them. Here and there she spotted a jewel. After leaving that part of the backs, she felt diminished and alien.

At the junction of the backs with Rugby Terrace, she felt a little uplifted. The once rough, unfinished road she had skipped on was now tarmacked. It looked good. Walking up Rugby Terrace, stretching her journey down memory lane, she stopped abruptly. The terrace of houses was pockmarked with ugly TV satellite dishes. Some of the small, neat front gardens had been removed. The whole facade looked like a pockmarked face with a gaping mouth missing some teeth. She was stunned. She noted grab bars by a couple of doors, suggesting mobility-impaired occupants, and the parked cars that wouldn't have been there when she was a child. People couldn't afford cars then. Life was slower-paced.

After turning to retrace her steps Barbara glanced across the road to where the allotment-sized gardens used to be. She remembered the lovingly tended plots, the harvested produce sold in Mehaffey's greengrocer's shop at the bottom of Carson Street, the shirt-sleeved men tilling the soil with robins at their feet in search of titbits, and the sounds of happy children playing. All that had disappeared. The supermarkets close at hand had rendered it redundant. The cultivated gardens had given way to an assortment of ramshackle sheds, garages, and man-made concrete islands for car parking.

What should have been a treasure of cherished memory was now forever sullied. Only the patient and silent surrounding trees spoke eloquently of former times. Her exploration had yielded disappointment. The lens of memory had raised her expectations, but snapshots of the here and now had impinged on her inward eye.

*Am I exaggerating, being too judgemental, too harsh, too nostalgic, in pursuit of a way of life long gone?* she wondered.

Wistfully she made her way to the Albert Street backs, intent on completing her journey. Three days of heavy rain had turned that alley into a quagmire, and she would have needed wellington boots to have given it a go.

*Perhaps another time*, she thought, knowing full well that there probably wouldn't be another time. The changed landscape had surprised, annoyed, disturbed, and challenged her memory with every step she had taken along the backs. Perhaps, on reflection, she had shone too severe a light on it.

Barbara hurried down Carson Street, walked under another arch, and turned left on to Pound Street as she made her way to Saint John's Place. Where Saint John's Place met Ronald Street, Barbara turned right into Elizabeth Avenue. Her destination was the mid-terrace house occupied by Sadie Barkley.

Barbara knew exactly what to expect. The front door was opened on her first knock. She was ushered in, sat down, and within minutes was presented with a mug of strong tea, liberally sweetened with sugar, accompanied by a full round of fresh-baked generously buttered toasted soda farl. Resistance was useless, she had learned. Best to acquiesce. She nibbled the soda farl. But she had come to enjoy these encounters, even though she always remained alert to the purpose of her visit.

Sadie lived alone. She came from a big family. All of who, except for her, were now gone to ground. When she was two years old she contracted polio and had been left severely mobility-challenged for the rest of her life. But she was a goer, one determined lady. She didn't walk. She hirpled with the aid of a stick, which she could wield in self-defence if needed. Her disability didn't confine her or hold her back. She was out and about every day, weather permitting. Barbara would often see her exiting Exchange Road on her way to morning Mass.

Sadie was full of chat. She knew more about what was going on in the town than Barbara. She had numerous friends, who all loved her fresh-baked soda farls. Content that all was well with Sadie, and refuelled with more tea, Barbara continued to her last appointment of the day.

Along Victoria Road, once the main thoroughfare in the town, and up the Old Glenarm Road, she walked to her neighbourhood destination, known locally as the Factory. Lost in thought, the flags, the tri-coloured bunting, and all the trappings of the July celebrations had faded from her consciousness. As she approached Lower Waterloo Road, the huge painted mural marking the entrance to Herbert Avenue reignited her awareness of self, place, and culture. In huge bold black letters, BOYNE SQUARE confronted her.

Barbara knew the area. There was no square. It was an old part of the town. But the thought had never troubled her mind before until now. The small terraced houses on Lower Waterloo Road looked across boringly at a sullen solid factory wall of red brick. Herbert Avenue didn't live up to its name. It was a narrow street that offered no privacy. The huge black label at its mouth was just another territorial marker, harking back to histories blemished by manipulation. Shirt sleeved men with nothing better to do leant in doorways smoking. Shaking her head bemused, she headed up Waterloo Road.

It was a wide thoroughfare that rose as it stretched towards the sea. The terraced houses on her left had bay windows and a parlour. Across the wide road, a well-constructed basalt stone building was pleasant on her eye. As she walked up the road, which was festooned with all trappings of celebration, to make her last visit of the day, the scent of the sea filled her nostrils. The taste of salty dulse crept about in her mouth. Every house except the one she was visiting brandished the Union flag. Some had two flags.

When she knocked on the door it was opened almost immediately by Peggy, with a warm and luminous embracing smile. Peggy, a petite woman, was nimble on her feet and blessed with a razor-sharp mind. Her hair was an auburn colour, short of shoulder-length and frizzy, with a mind of its own. Hazel eyes danced mischievously on a freckled face illumined with smiling lips. Peggy was another of Barbara's clients who wouldn't under any circumstances allow Barbara to do anything for her. It was a complete role reversal, and there were days when Barbara was glad of it. Barbara was always on the job, though, and, as they chatted, she sought any hint that all was not well with Peggy. There was none. She relaxed and let the conversation flow. Peggy talked a lot about her past her joys, sorrows, and regrets. With always a funny story on her tongue, she made Barbara laugh.

"You know what? My biggest regret in life is that I never had the opportunity to go to university," Peggy confided in Barbara.

Barbara wasn't surprised. Peggy was well-read, could hold her own in conversation in any company, and was surrounded in her home by loads of books, most of which Barbara had never read.

"Why was that, Peggy?" Barbara asked.

"Well, like most working-class parents, life was about survival, making ends meet. We all had to contribute something to the housekeeping, even as children. I suppose, even with all that to worry about, working-class parents lacked ambition for their children. What else could you expect when their schooling hadn't opened their eyes? But, you never know, I might get there yet," Peggy concluded. Barbara thought,

*Always the optimist. Always something to look forward to. That's you, Peggy.*

Engrossed in conversation, Barbara didn't notice Peggy's dancing eyes doing the quickstep, which should have alerted imminent mischief. Peggy, chatting away casually, said, knowing full well that Barbara came from a different tradition,

"I wasn't able to put my flag out this year, love. Would you mind hanging it out for me?"

Peggy watched with concealed amusement as Barbara's brow creased with confusion and anxiety. Barbara thought,

*A flag. What size of flag? How am I going to hang one of those big things out of her upstairs window by myself?*
Transparently her mind wrestled. Moments passed that felt like hours to Barbara. Then she said,

"Peggy, I'll try, but I'm not sure I'll be able to manage on my own. What do you hang it on?"

"Och, I'm sure you will, love, otherwise sure I wouldn't be asking you to do it. Billy next door has a ladder he'll lend you."

"What?" Barbara spluttered. "You expect me to climb up a ladder? Can't Billy do it?"

"No, he can't. You see, he has a wooden leg and he's not allowed to climb ladders, but he'll hold the ladder for you. It's a pity you're not wearing trousers, though," Peggy encouragingly offered.

"Well, at least I'm wearing my walking shoes. The best I can do is give it a try," Barbara said.

Then slowly, from behind her chair, Peggy produced a twelve-inch-high delph figure of a sashed orange man brandishing a Union flag that she had previously hidden there.

"If you'd just put him on the windowsill, Barbara, that would do nicely," Peggy continued, keeping her facial composure.

With the sashed orange man brandishing a flag placed on the windowsill as Peggy had directed, Barbara sat down and glanced at Peggy. Simultaneous laughter erupted and

100

reverberated around the house, eventually subsiding into irrepressible giggling. It was a wonderful ending to a long day, a day that lived long in Barbara's memory. With an embrace, which deepened the well of their affection, they parted.

From Peggy and Waterloo Road she made her way home down through Chaine Park and paused to take in the view. She thought about going across to Waterloo Bay to see if the curlew was there, but the tide was out. She loved the melancholy call of the curlew as it sought to roost. But she knew it wouldn't be there. A fresh salty onshore breeze caressed her face as she walked through the Town Park. Men were on the putting green, the tennis courts buzzed, and boys were playing football, while a couple of old men surrounded by onlookers slid huge chess pieces about on an enormous board with deliberation.

From the top of the zigzagging path that she had called the snake as a child, the panoramic view unfolded before her. Land, sea, and sky merged harmoniously. Released from her self-indulgence by the flashing lights of the Maidens Lighthouse, she snaked her way down on to the flagless promenade. The tide had ebbed and it made gentle music with the shingle, enticing her to hum a tune as she strolled homewards. Jagged iron stumps, protruding above the lapping waves, paid homage to the bathing boxes that had once enjoyed their support. No one swam in the sea there any longer. No need. The leisure centre, with its swimming pool, had put paid to that.

At Sandy Bay, she sat on a bench and thought of the seemingly endless summers she had spent with her children there. She recalled happy days as the Scotland-bound ferry nosed its way towards the North Channel. It was time for Barbara to leave too and to reconnect with reality. The western sky was tinged red, and her head was still in the clouds of memory.

On Main Street two weeks later she was asked,
"Did you hear about Peggy?"
"No. What is it?"
"She passed away last night in her sleep."

Later Barbara lit a candle in the chapel and knelt with her head bowed, silently praying and giving thanks for the privilege of knowing Peggy.

*The most sacred things in life,* Barbara thought, remembering Peggy, *are simple acts, like the sharing of tea and a kind word.*

"To greater service, I'll be going someday," Peggy had often said to Barbara. Of that Barbara had no doubt.

Unknown to Barbara, Peggy had substituted joy for regret. In her will, she gave her body to Queens University Belfast for medical research.

# A Worm Turns

Bob Fitzpatrick spent the morning in his south-facing garden, tending his beloved geraniums and other potted plants, strategically positioned around his herringbone brick-paved patio. Once the geraniums were deadheaded and the potted plants fed and watered, Bob started to tidy up the shrubs that filled the terraces elegantly before stepping down to greet the clear blue lake below. His little sailboat bobbed invitingly at its mooring on the timber jetty, like a puppy dog eager for fun. Bob had the small jetty specially built when their lakeside home was constructed some twenty years ago. It was a beautiful, well-chosen location. He loved it.

As the morning hurried towards midday Bob was so engrossed in his morning's chores that he didn't notice the occasional greyish fluffy clouds meandering overhead, staining the bright blue sky and occasionally blinding the sun. With his head completely hidden in the old wide-brimmed floppy hat he wore when gardening, Bob, immersed in his private thoughts, worked diligently, weeding and pruning.

As he moved slowly and methodically down through the terraces, the aroma of lavender saturated his senses. He loved the lavender. The fluffy overhead clouds merged, darkened, and thickened, changing the colour of the lake making it uninviting, more ominous. Wearied from bending and stooping, Bob paused and listened. When he heard the white noise of the gathering clouds he looked up at the sky, grunted his disappointment, stood, stretched to ease his arthritic backache, and decided that was enough gardening for the day. Putting the tools in the garden shed he thought about lunch while toying with the notion of spending his Saturday afternoon binge-watching television with a beer or two for company.

It was Saturday afternoon. There was bound to be something decent on TV, like Test cricket or a decent drama. That thought, coupled with the thought of beer, eased Bob's arthritic backache considerably. He locked up the garden shed and headed into the house.

Bob went straight to the bathroom to wash his hands. Patricia was a stickler for hand-washing and personal hygiene, especially after working in the garden. With a coarse nail brush and soap, he scrubbed his hands clean, like a surgeon meticulously preparing for open-heart surgery, removing any trace of his therapeutic morning spent tangling with the weeds. When his hands were scrubbed clean, especially under his fingernails, he dried them off on some paper towels before massaging a particularly viscous disinfectant into his dark brown skin, which Patricia swore by. Another ingrained, learned behaviour. Content that his hands were odour-free from the disinfectant, he headed for the kitchen to prepare lunch.

The kitchen was Patricia's pride and joy. She loved it and spent a lot of time in it cooking and baking. She was a cordon bleu cook. Bob could testify to that. It had a walk-in freezer that any high street convenience store would have been proud of. On occasion Bob used to look inside it to see what was in it: sides of beef, lamb, pork, and a piglet were nothing out of the ordinary. Occasionally there was a pig's head and other bits of animals that Bob would rather not have seen. But it was Patricia's domain. Best to let sleeping dogs lie. The kitchen also had a full-height floor-to-ceiling fridge to complement the freezer, but Bob just took it all in his stride. As long as Patricia was happy. That was all that mattered to him. A wide, purpose-built workbench that ran three-quarters the length of the kitchen, with a built-in sink, fitted with drawers and cupboards, dominated the kitchen. Her pride and joy was the six-ringed gas-fired Aga cooker on which, when she entertained, as she frequently did, every ring was aflame. It certainly was a sight to behold. On occasion Bob was her sous-chef, not that he was much help. More often than not he was just in the way, but he loved to see her at work in the kitchen, doing what she loved doing but more importantly doing it well. She would often chide Bob, telling him that all he was really good for in the kitchen was making a mess. But it was all in fun.

Earlier in the morning, he had taken two darnes of salmon out of the fridge to let them come to room temperature.

*Patricia would be proud of me*, he thought.

"Some things do eventually rub off on others. Persistence is key," he said, talking to himself. With all his bits and pieces readied, Bob set about cooking lunch. First, he heated a little vegetable oil and a dash of water in a large pan, to which he added two finely chopped cloves of garlic and a chilli. When the garlic and the chilli started to soften and colour he took the pan off the heat, passed its contents through a sieve, returned the pan to the heat with the garlic and chilli infused cooking liquor, and added the salmon darnes, skin down, to the pan. When four minutes had elapsed his timer told him it was time to turn the salmon darnes and add a couple of handfuls of chopped parsley and three cups of frozen peas to the pan. Then he turned the heat off under the pan, knowing that the residual heat would cook the salmon the way Patricia liked it. Then Bob set the breakfast bar for lunch.

He didn't set for two. He set for only one: knife and fork, condiments, a water jug, and a drinking glass and a roll of crusty bread. As soon as his darne of salmon, peas, and parsley were on a plate Bob sat down to lunch, occasionally ripping off pieces of crusty bread from the roll to add some crunch to his moist salmon. There was a confusion of anger, frustration, guilt, and anguish in the force used to rip the pieces of bread from the roll. The food Bob was eating was the same dish Patricia and he had for lunch every Saturday, sometimes with a glass of dry white wine. It was the only dish Patricia would let him cook in her kitchen.

Picking at his food, Bob's mind flooded back to the Saturday twenty-odd years ago when they married. They were seniors, a widow and a widower. The wedding service was a simple, private affair with a few close friends as witnesses. Patricia had lost her first husband to cancer after what was a long, debilitating illness. A nurse by profession, she had nursed her husband until he passed away at home. They had been happily married for thirty-seven years. The great sadness in their life was that they didn't have any children. If truth be told,

105

her husband couldn't have been better cared for. Bob knew that. He had witnessed their love and devotion. He and his wife Margaret were friends with Patricia and her husband. For many years Margaret and Patricia had worked together in the intensive care unit in the same hospital. Roughly three years after Patricia's husband went to ground Bob's wife Margaret followed him.

Bob, as usual, had risen early that fateful Saturday morning. Margaret, who was feeling a little tired, had decided to stay on in bed a little while longer. He went downstairs, freshened up, and went into the kitchen and made himself some coffee and toast. His coffee and toast consumed, he prepared a breakfast tray for Margaret: nothing elaborate, just some fruit juice, toast, and tea. Margaret didn't like tea in bed. Well, what she didn't really like was Bob having tea and toast in bed because she knew that there would be breadcrumbs everywhere. Nevertheless, Bob thought,
*It'll be a little surprise and a treat for Margaret.*
When he got to the bedroom, holding her breakfast tray and standing at the foot of the bed, he thought Margaret had fallen asleep again.
*Perhaps I should leave her*, he thought. Then for some reason thought better of it and decided to rouse her.
Margaret didn't immediately respond. Bob at first was puzzled, but not perturbed, and a moment or two elapsed before he realised that all was far from well. Something was seriously wrong. He felt for a pulse but couldn't find one. Margaret felt warm, but she was unresponsive. That was when his rudimentary first aid training kicked in, or part of it did. He spoke to her. She didn't respond. He opened her mouth and searched her airways as best he could. She wasn't breathing. He had to do something. He started pumping her chest and counted to thirty twice. Then he gave her mouth-to-mouth, all the while shouting in his mind,
"Please, God. Please, God."
He repeated the procedure over and over again until he was exhausted. Then he did what he should have done in the first

instance. He called for help. But he knew in his heart it was too late. Margaret was gone.

When the paramedics arrived they took over, and before very long they confirmed Bob's worst fears. Everything, it seemed to Bob, slowed down, moved at a snail's pace. To all intents and purposes, he was out of it, as their systems and procedures took over. In the end, the post-mortem examination confirmed that Margaret had died from natural causes. An aneurysm. She had worked hard all her life looking after other people and had never been ill a day in her life when suddenly her life was snuffed out by an aneurysm, just as Bob would snuff out a candle he had no further use for. It was a bitter pill for Bob to swallow.

All sorts of thoughts cascaded around in Bob's mind. The most turbulent thought that distressed him was: if he had called for help sooner than he did, he might have saved Margaret.

Lost in his rampaging thoughts, he nibbled at his lunch, until eventually he noticed his knife in one hand and his fork in the other performing a kind of slow dance over his empty plate. Confused, he watched the dancing cutlery make patterns in the air as if they had a life of their own. Then, realising he was talking to himself, he loosened his grip on the knife and fork and let them clatter on to his empty plate. He placed his hands palms down, pressing hard against the breakfast bar and breathing deeply held that position until the tension in his mind and body eased.

What Bob didn't know at the time was that, following her annual check-up, Margaret had been assigned less demanding nursing duties by her employers. She didn't tell Bob, but she retired a year later, to be with him. Patricia knew. Margaret had confided in her best friend, asking her to look out for Bob if anything happened to her.

Patricia and Bob's platonic friendship developed and matured until it seemed perfectly sensible that they share the rest of their lives together. And that's what they happily did. Then Patricia was taken suddenly too, in her sleep. When Bob woke up she was cold to his touch, gone. There was nothing he could do except pray, gather himself together, and make the necessary phone calls.

*Life is just a loan. You've got to make the most of it and try to move on*, he told himself.

The other salmon darne was untouched. It wouldn't go to waste. He would have it later, cold, in a sandwich or a salad, with a glass of dry white wine, perhaps. Bob always cooked the two pieces of salmon on Saturdays, as he had done for Patricia. It was second nature. He felt her closeness. But it was more than a habit. It had become a ritual of love and thanksgiving. He missed Patricia. He knew she was always with him, but he missed her in a very physical kind of way.

Bob wasn't a loner. He was well known locally and had many acquaintances, but had outlived almost all his childhood friends. In many ways, he was a very private person. His youthful appearance, physicality, and seemingly endless energy belied his ninety-one years. Sometimes he couldn't quite believe his age himself, and when doubt flickered across his mind he would check his birth certificate for confirmation.

"You're a lucky bugger," he would congratulate himself. "There's nothing wrong with you, even at your age. You've got nothing to complain about, thank God."

Content now in his mind, he washed up his lunch plate and the other bits and pieces, dried them off, and put everything away as Patricia would have liked. Then he sat down to consider what he might do with the rest of his day. Bob played golf on Saturday afternoons when the weather was inviting. 'Play', he knew, was a gross exaggeration. He went out for a bit of banter, encouraged by the offer of a ride on an acquaintance's buggy and the occasional swipe at a ball when he felt he could summon up enough energy to swing a club. This Saturday afternoon his acquaintance was indisposed. At a loose end, the notion of an afternoon spent binge-viewing television, bolstered by a few of his favourite Belgian beers, was too tempting.

Settled in his comfortable reclining chair, with the beers close to hand, Bob trawled through the TV channels searching for some live sport. Cricket, soccer, rugby, athletics … anything that would raise his pulse rate a little would be acceptable. Sipping his beer, he flicked through over three hundred channels and found nothing he wanted to watch. He couldn't believe it. Convinced he must have missed something he searched again, with the same result. Vexed and exasperated, he switched the TV off, downed his beer, and decided he would go for a walk and cool off.

After banging the door shut behind him Bob strode determinedly away, his mind flooded with thoughts of his experience trawling the TV channels.

*Three hundred-plus bloody TV channels but nothing worth watching. Where has all the sport gone?*

"It is Saturday afternoon, isn't it?" he asked himself, just to be sure. "Saturday's still the nation's day set aside for sport, isn't it? Or is it?" he wondered. "Everything's changing, and not for the best."

He walked on, talking to himself as he went. Eventually, he found himself walking through a park. A cricket match was in progress. He stopped, looked around, found a bench, sat down, settled, relaxed, and enjoyed the rest of his afternoon. The sunny Saturday afternoon slipped quietly away, apart from the occasional sound of leather on willow as the bowlers in their white cricket gear toiled through their allotted overs. When the match ended at around five-thirty, Bob strolled home enjoying the late afternoon sunshine.

About an hour later, crossing the threshold he stepped on the mail littering the floor. Gathering it up he made his way to his favourite chair, settled, and began sorting it. The mail offering cruise holidays he binned unopened. A couple of envelopes containing alumni stuff from universities were binned too. He continued sorting, sifting, and binning until he had only one piece of mail left to deal with. Holding the very official-looking envelope, he thumbed it open and extracted a thick embossed sheet of paper. It looked and felt expensive. He was intrigued.

As he unfolded the sheet of paper he discovered that it was a letter from the BBC. Slightly bemused, he read it paused and set it aside. He thought about it for a little while, then picked it up and read it again.

The gist of the letter was that the BBC, in its wisdom, was scrapping the universal free TV licence for the over seventy-five's. Ninety-one-year-old Bob sat quietly for a while imbibing his beer as he absorbed and digested what he had read. Earlier in the day he had twice scrolled through over three hundred channels but couldn't find anything he wanted to watch.

The BBC, he had heard somewhere, could afford to pay presenters and entertainers huge sums of money but couldn't afford a concession on the TV licence for people over seventy-five, never mind over ninety. In the golf club, he heard talk about someone getting paid nearly two million pounds for presenting a late-night highlights programme on football matches. Then he thought about their Lordships slumbering in the House of Lords receiving three hundred pounds a day, plus expenses. They knew a gravy train all right.

He had left his home that afternoon because there was nothing he wanted to watch, nothing to attract his interest, nothing he considered worth wasting his time watching. In retrospect he was glad. He had got out of the house, had some exercise, enjoyed a breath of fresh air, and was delighted to see younger folk on the cricket pitch enjoying a bit of sport.

Then his thoughts darkened and turned negative again. The sport he once watched was no longer available on the BBC. It had all been siphoned off, while the uncompetitive BBC squandered licence-payers' money on overpaid mediocre presenters and entertainers.

*A bit like the church. They get their money too easily*, he thought.

Bob loved watching the Test match cricket but couldn't afford Sky. He'd been careful with his money all his life and had been even more careful since retirement because he'd had only his pension to live on for the last twenty-five years. The FA Cup Final had gone the same way as Test match cricket. They and other national sporting events, some might say institutions, were no longer available to the masses on the BBC. He couldn't watch the Champions League football final between Liverpool and Spurs on the BBC, and him a lifelong

Liverpool supporter. He was livid about that. The Europa Cup Final was not available on terrestrial TV either.

But the biggest insult of all – oh, yes, make no mistake, Bob was starting to take all this stuff personally – was the British Open Golf Championship hosted at the Royal Portrush Golf Club. Bob lived only forty miles from Portrush, but at his age, he couldn't risk being in among the huge crowds. It was the first time in sixty-eight years that the Open Championship had returned to Northern Ireland. Was it live on the BBC? Not in Northern Ireland. Not in the UK. No way, José. People dependent on the BBC like Bob had to make do with late-night edited highlights, which amounted in essence watching, if you could stay awake long enough, players putting.

"There's a bit more to golf than putting," he moaned to himself. But boy, oh boy, didn't the local BBC go to town with their build-up coverage of it? It was all over the local news and current affairs programmes. They covered everything about it in microscopic detail, except of course live golf.

"Bloody disgrace," Bob said aloud to himself and anyone within hearing distance, as he got up and went into the kitchen to prepare his salmon salad. "Any sport worth watching is all pay-per-view now, and on top of that, you'll have to pay for a BBC licence to watch it and even though it's not on the BBC. Do they think people are stupid?" he ranted aloud to himself. With everything readied, he sat down at the breakfast bar with a bottle of dry white wine. He was disgusted with the BBC.

*It isn't worth it*, he thought, as he picked at his salad. Sipping the wine, his thoughts turned to Patricia and he mellowed. He was taking it all too seriously. He missed her.

Later, once the kitchen was tidied up, he thought about corking the wine bottle then thought better of it. He'd only taken a small glass with his food and thought another wouldn't do him any harm, so with the bottle and the glass in his hands he settled down to watch a bit of television – if he could find anything that interested him, that was. He didn't even bother to look at the BBC channels. From previous experience, he knew that on Saturday evenings it was a complete waste of time.

With his wine glass refreshed in one hand and the remote in the other, he began the ritual of the masses: channel surfing.

First up was a repeat of guess what? *One Foot in the Grave*. Before Victor Meldrew could utter his catchphrase Bob exclaimed,

"I don't believe it. That's all I need. A reminder that I have one foot in the grave. Thank you very much, whatever TV channel you are. That cheered me up no end."

He carried on flicking through the channels and found an advertisement. Somebody was rabbiting on about a prepaid funeral plan that encouraged people to protect their families against rising funeral costs. The idea was to plan ahead and save money. Bob laughed at the idea of someone spending a lot of money on an advert to entice him to protect a family he didn't have.

*Bloody daft*, he thought.

He took a long pull on his dry white wine and continued flicking, but nothing he wanted to watch surfaced. After a further set of flicks, he hit on an episode of *Rising Damp*. He remembered it, and Rigsby's remark to Alan:

"He's one of them." He thought,

*You wouldn't get away with that now. We're much too politically correct now.* After flicking on he came upon a crippled donkey laden with bricks, labouring its way up several flights of concrete stairs.

*Is this for real?* he thought, before realising it was a charity appeal. *But surely it's not real. They wouldn't do that to an animal, even if it was for charity, would they?*

Then he found an advert for Elite Singles.

"Too late for me, thank you very much," he said, thinking,

*I was never that desperate anyway.*

Eventually, he found something that perhaps he could stomach watching again: a repeat of *Tomorrow's World* while moaning,

"I'd prefer to know what tomorrow holds for me now, rather than what somebody thought the future was going to be forty-odd years ago."

As he reflected on the *Tomorrow's World* programme of forty years ago he concluded that much of what was envisaged impacted on him very little. His needs were few. Disgruntled, aggravated, he refilled his glass. Patricia wouldn't like him doing that, but she wasn't here right now. If she had been it would be very different. He wouldn't be wasting his time trawling bloody TV channels, for a start. Unintentionally his index finger hit the search button again. He found himself staring into the eyes of a dark-eyed child drinking polluted water. It was another tear-jerking charity appeal, but it was so realistic.

*Surely they're not filming a child drinking polluted water, are they? It can't get any worse, can it?* he thought.

Bob was very charitable. He maintained the direct debit contributions to the charities he and Patricia had chosen to support. He couldn't support every charitable appeal, much as he would like to, but he could do without the constant reminder of all the injustices in the world every time he put the television on. He felt targeted from every point on the compass. He searched for something to lighten his mood. He hit on a repeat of a Billy Connolly special, the one where he did the Glaswegian drunk incontinence pants routine.

"I'm not quite there just yet. Enough is enough," he shouted at the TV. The wine was doing its work.

More was to follow. A young woman clad in black underwear appeared on the screen. Instinctively Bob averted his eyes. Well, one eye. He had to see what it was all about. He didn't get it until she said,

"A little bit of wee is not going to stop me."

"Good God. She's advertising ladies' incontinence knickers," he exclaimed.

It was all a revelation for Bob.

"I've had to endure adverts for stairlifts and in the process almost convinced myself to get one, before I remembered I live in a bungalow. What are they trying to do to me? I'm confused enough." Flicking on in desperation, he happened on a selection of cookery programmes, ranging from how to open a tin of beans to ultra-fine dining.

*I know what I want and, what's more, what sustains me. Am I not living proof? They make it look easy, though, opening a tin of beans, don't they?* he thought, looking at his arthritic fingers. There were days when it was like a day's work for him. In the end, he had given up buying tinned stuff, preferring the frozen packs because they were easier to work with.

Then it was the gardening repeats. But that was not the end of it. He found channel after channel offering pointless quiz programmes, one after another, as entertainment.

"What do I know or want to know about Thin Lizzy albums, in whatever bloody decade they were? Does anyone really care?" Then Bob reminded himself,

"No one grows old by living. Folk age rapidly by losing interest in living. Whenever the government has to balance their books after squandering what was in the public purse, who pays the price? The poor, the disadvantaged, the vulnerable, the people who can't fight back, of course. Not the ones who caused the problems in the first place: the bankers, the MPs over claiming expenses, the sleepers in the House of Lords. Oh, no, not them.

The BBC, awash with money, overpaying presenters and entertainers, does it slim down its overstuffed organisation? Certainly not. Who needs repeat news ad nauseam 24/7, with hordes of staff circulating the world doing what? How many local BBC radio and TV channels does a small country like ours need? How much of their news is local, anyway? The BBC, like every organisation, takes on a life of its own. It's a survivor. And if the over seventy-five's have to pay for its survival, so be it. The BBC doesn't care," Bob ranted.

Enough was enough for Bob. While sipping his dry white wine he decided there and then that he would not be buying a TV licence from the BBC. He resolved never to buy a TV licence again. The wine bottle now emptied, his resolve intact, fortified, and emboldened, he decided to inform the BBC in writing of his intent.

This is what he wrote.

*Dear Mr BBC,*

With regard to your recent decision to scrap the free TV licence for the over seventy-fives, this is to inform you that I, a person over ninety, will not under any circumstances be obtaining a TV licence. I do intend, however, if ever I find something of interest to watch, which on the BBC channels is rare, to coax my ancient black-and-white TV back into life.

Giving you this advance warning is my way of inviting you to try, by whatever means at your disposal, to compel me to squander my meagre pension in support of the BBC. You may employ whatever means you must to compel me to get your licence, but I will not surrender. Never. Never. Never.

For your information, I have instructed my solicitor if I have to endure a court appearance, to advise the magistrate that I am adamant that I will not under any circumstances purchase a TV licence and I will not allow some well-meaning, interfering do-gooder to buy one for me.

I have also instructed my solicitor to inform the magistrate that I do not want a community service sentence because at my age I am not fit for it. It would probably be the end of me. But then I would no longer be a problem for you, would I?

Isn't it ironic that you give me another compelling reason to go on living? Thank you for that, at least. I do need to be incentivised now and then to be able to endure living, after being bombarded with all the demoralising rubbish spewing from my television. Not that I'm in any particular hurry to vacate this valley of tears, by the way.

I want the longest custodial sentence that my heinous crime merits, in one of the nice new prisons so often promised but yet to be delivered.

In prison, I will be sure of three good meals a day, every day, and I won't have to do the shopping, cooking, or washing-up. I'll be nice and warm and dry, and I won't have to light the fire and bring in the coal when it's raining or when the yard's icy in winter.

What a great relief it will be for me to have someone do my laundry for me. It was getting a bit awkward to manage the clothesline in the yard with my arthritis, and I never was much good at the ironing anyway.

115

*The housekeeping is becoming a bit of a bind, so I'll be delighted to relinquish that too.*

*Now, I would be up for some gardening therapy in the summer but would need raised beds if possible. I look forward to being able to exercise a little when I can. I understand that prison facilities are first-class. What size are their swimming pools? Another plus, by the way, is that I won't have to brave the elements to visit the library. Books will be brought by trolley to my cell daily, for private browsing.*

*I will also be able to take up crafts and other hobbies, and learn how to become an accomplished silver surfer on the Internet. I wouldn't need your TV licence. A coloured TV will be provided in my room. I believe we don't use the word cell any longer. Apparently, it's politically incorrect, sends the wrong message. And I would be able to watch Sky Sports. On my meagre pension I can't afford Sky or avail myself of Netflix and all the new streaming platforms I don't have at home. In addition, I will have my smartphone with Wi-Fi available en suite.*

*In Her Majesty's care – we're both of a similar age, you know – I'm sure all my health and welfare needs will be promptly attended to. I've been on the waiting list for thirty-six months for a hip replacement, and my arthritis is getting worse. I know you wouldn't want me to fall downstairs while in Her Majesty's protective care, would you? The media would have a field day, wouldn't they? Well, ITV would, don't you think?*

*But I'm sure the prison governor will find me a ground-floor room with a view. The cataract in my left eye is worsening fast but I've only been on the waiting list for treatment on the NHS for two years. I can't afford to go private. In prison, I think I will have a good chance of being seen to. Don't you? Pardon the pun.*

*I don't mind sharing. It would be nice to have company of an evening, something I don't have much of at present. Perhaps I might even pick up a useful trick or two for later in life. Also, mingling with and getting to know a cross-section of society enjoying Her Majesty's pleasure will be something especially informative, but I doubt I'll meet any bankers, BBC executives,*

116

*MPs, or lords of the realm. They're the class apart who always seem to escape the peoples' wrath – with a golden handshake, of course.*

*If I had a choice of cellmate – sorry, roommate – for one night I would invite the guy who burgled my home and took everything of value I had. It wasn't much, I might add. But it won't happen. He was never apprehended.*

*Your repetitive, 24/7, so-called news, with the rest of the rubbish your BBC excretes, has made my home a lonely place. Who wants to watch* Murder She Wrote *repeats at 7 a.m. on a Friday morning, I ask you? Unless you're a coal miner coming off shift, but we don't have coal miners any more. They dug themselves out of a job, and what did they get in return?*

*There are plenty enough repeat broadcasting channels without the BBC joining in. But then, if your BBC stripped out its repeats, it would have a threadbare schedule to offer. Go back to basics, if you must, but don't ask me to pay for what you're broadcasting now and your continuing excesses.*

*No, thank you. Get stuffed. You're a BBC all right: a Bloody Bloodsucking Charlatan.*

*Yours, looking forward to prison as soon as possible,*
*Bob*

*PS If you are thinking of visiting me in gaol don't worry, I won't be out. Please don't bring me black grapes. I dislike them as much as I dislike your BBC. Bring some lemons or limes, something to take the smile off my face as I enjoy Her Majesty's pleasure free of all care.*

*It wouldn't do to look too happy there. But I'll survive.*
*Wish you were here. You deserve it more than me.*
*R B Fitzgerald, OBE*

Well, Bob, true to his word, sent his letter to the BBC and copied it to his MP. To date he has not had a response from either. He wasn't expecting one. Bob, a nonagenarian, knows precisely where he stands, in the consciousness of society.

If and when there are any developments I'll let you know.

# Two Grumpy Neighbours

Jimmy, a sprightly seventy-five-year-old on his way to the corner shop, was in bad humour. As he opened his gate heading out, his neighbour Martin, an energetic sixty-year-old, swung his adjacent garden gate open, heading home. Jimmy, whose head was down, and whose eyes were scowling at the ground, didn't notice Martin.

"How're you doing, Jimmy? Haven't seen you for a while," Martin said. Jimmy raised his head to see, through sullen eyes, Martin quizzically observing him. As he reshaped his face, Martin continued.

"Jimmy, what's bothering you? You're looking vexed. What's annoying you?"

The reservoir in Jimmy's head burst.

"Annoying me. Annoying me." Dancing on his toes, he ranted, "You've no idea. Annoying doesn't describe it. I'm fed up, browned off, had enough. You've no idea."

"Jimmy, calm yourself down, man. Take it easy. Mind your blood pressure. It can't be all that bad. Whatever's got up your nose?" The placating sounds oozed from Martin's lips like a hot iron slithering over a damp cloth.

"It's the bloody painters, that's who's annoying me. They've been in the house these two weeks and, boy, I'm sorry I got them in," Jimmy retorted.

"Why did you get them in?" Martin queried, thinking to quell Jimmy's irritation.

"Because the whole house needed a lift inside. It was tired-looking. The white gloss paint on the doors was going yellow. It took me nearly two years to try and talk Madge into doing the place up. In the end, I decided to go ahead anyway. She wouldn't let me do it myself, you see. I wouldn't leave a neat enough job for her, and all that stuff."

"There's nothing wrong with the doors," says she. "They're not yellow. It's the way the sun's catching them."

"She can't see the yellowing doors, even with her glasses on. Bloody vanity. That's her problem if you ask me, but she can see all my faults easily enough without glasses."

"You'll be glad when it's all over, then. It'll be like living in a different house," Martin replied, with words slipping off his tongue like raindrops sliding down a windowpane.

"But, you've no idea, Martin. No idea, man." Jimmy, clinging to Martin like a drowning man, ranted on. "You see, if I was doing it, I would do one room at a time. You know. Finish one room before moving to the next one. But I wouldn't be moving quickly enough for Madge. She'd be poking her nose around the door, asking,

"How long are you going to be in there?" All the time casting her eagle eye in search of an errant drop of paint."

"Madge isn't that bad, Jimmy. Come on, man, everybody thinks the world of her," Martin continued, mollifying Jimmy, while the twinkle in his eyes suggested a well-rehearsed routine.

"Here's the way of it with these boys. They got me to prepare the living room for them. You know. Remove stuff, take down curtains, blinds, and all the rest of it. Then in they came with their dust sheets and spread them all around. Boy, did they make a big job of that?

Then Madge had to get in on the act. They arrived at nine o'clock and she gave them tea at ten o'clock. Aye, and the craic was good, Madge likes a yarn. Eventually, they started to paint the ceiling, but instead of carrying on working in that room, they got me to clear the other rooms so that they could do all the ceilings.

I'm nearly round the bloody bend. There's stuff everywhere. There's not a chair to sit on. I can't watch TV. All I hear, day in day out, is their transistor radios blaring. They have one each.

Wait till I tell you this," he continued excitedly. "Do you know I had to go into the bathroom the other day and sit on the toilet to get peace and privacy to read my mail? In my own house, for God's sake, man. It's driving me nuts."

119

"Auch, come on, Jimmy, you know you're exaggerating," Martin offered, changing tack from pacifying Jimmy to winding him up.

"Do you think so? Wait till I tell you. Madge gives them tea at ten o'clock and lunch at twelve o'clock. Can you believe it? And they'll sit there and talk and yarn. I get up and fidget around, hoping to encourage them back to work. And I'll tell you something else. They're not cheap. It's costing me a fortune, and Madge doesn't seem to understand."

"Well, why don't you put your foot down and tell them what you want done and how you want it done?" Martin suggested as he wound Jimmy's mental spring a little tighter.

"Put my foot down, put my foot down … Put my foot in it, you mean. Sure aren't the painters Madge's brother and nephew? I haven't a leg to stand on. And when they leave at the end of the day I'm the one that has to clean up after them. Madge doesn't see it. That's the amazing thing because if it was me I would be getting the rounds of the kitchen."

"Ah, sure, that explains it all," says Martin, frowning. "A storm in a teacup. You'll be as right as rain in no time. You're a lucky man you don't have my bother," he went on, inviting Jimmy's question.

"What bothers would that be?"

"We're getting in a new kitchen. There's been sparks, plumbers, and carpenters trailing in and out through the place for weeks, and boy, do they leave some mess. The sparks and plumbers knock holes in walls and floors and just leave it all for me to fix and clean up behind them as if I'm their mate or something."

"Don't be telling me," says Jimmy, eager for the honeyed, vicarious pleasure of tasting someone else's troubles. Music to his ears. He only just resisted running back into the house for his violin.

"Do you know," says Martin, "the carpenter is the worst."

"How can that be, Martin?" Jimmy queried, feigning ignorance of the process of carpentering.

"The trade's not like it used to be when hand tools were hand-powered and men's backs were stained with sweat. Now the hand tools are all electric-powered, you see. They have electric saws and planers and sanders, all sorts of electric-powered tools."

"That's only progress, technological advancement. You can't be against that. It increases productivity." Their roles now reversed, Jimmy was winding Martin up.

"Increased productivity, my foot. I'll tell you what's increased. The mess. He had to adjust some of the bedroom doors to ease them. He had all the doors off and room by room, door by door, he set to them with his electric planer thing. There was dust and shavings everywhere. Never occurred to him for a moment to take them outside and work. Oh, that would be too simple," Martin ranted.

"I'm sure Mabel had something to say about that, didn't she?" Jimmy innocently suggested, knowing full well that Mabel was very particular about that sort of thing. Martin rose to the bait like a trout to the fly.

When the inferno in his head calmed he leant over the garden wall conspiratorially, and, closer to Jimmy's ear, he whispered, looking furtively around,

"Wait till I tell you this. Last Friday I came home at lunchtime to discover that there was only one guy on the job. 'Where's the rest of them?' says I."

"They went up to Murphy's for lunch," says the guy.

"Oh, did they, indeed?" says I.

"Boys, oh boys, that's something else altogether. I never heard the like of that," muttered Jimmy, as sympathetically as a cat would purr to a mouse. He had Martin on a roll. No need to push. "Sure there's nothing you can do about that, Martin."

Martin, fit to be tied, continued.

"What? I tell you what I did. I jumped in the car and went up to Murphy's, went in, and there they were sitting with pints of beer and plates of grub in front o' them."

"You'll join us, Martin," says, the bright spark.

"I will not," says I, "for I can't afford to drink beer in the middle of the day. And if you can I must be paying you too much, and I'll tell you now you won't be paid for this half-day's work. And I turned on my heel and left them sitting."

121

"Boys, o' boys, Martin, it's changed times. In my day we worked six days a week from eight o'clock in the morning till six o'clock at night for little money. Nowadays you have to take money to tradesmen in wheelbarrows if you want to get anything done. It's changed times, right enough. They're the landed gentry now, all right."

"Anyway, what happened to the work? I suppose you had to get someone else to finish the job for you?"

"You know, Jimmy, I wasn't five minutes back at the house till they were back at their work and the job was finished in double quick time, I'm glad to say. But I can tell you, what I had to stand from Mabel was nothing ordinary. I've been on short rations this week or two."

"Is that a fact Martin," says Jimmy, just when Mabel, with her head out the front door, called out,

"I have your sirloin steak ready, Martin, love." Martin's face crimsoned.

"Good for you, Martin. It's beans on toast for me tonight," muttered Jimmy. "I was going down to the shop for a tin. We've run out. She only buys them a tin at a time now because of the sell-by date thing."

"No wonder, Jimmy," says Martin laughing as he walked away. "Sure you're nearly past yours. Take care now."

Jimmy laughed too as he went to fetch the tin of beans.

# The Plum Tree Fairy

If you were to step outside and look around, what you would see wasn't there when my great-grandfather was alive. There were trees, all right – native trees, the oak, the ash, and the hawthorn – but there weren't any streets or houses. It was all farmland. If you knew which direction to look in you would see a big plantation house with its enclosed south-facing garden, not a stone's throw away from here.

The place is run-down now, but it was once a well-doing farm of sizeable acreage, producing many a good cow and pig. It was a time long before the advent of the Massey Ferguson tractor and all the expensive farm machinery you see about the countryside these days. Nowadays you'll see farmers driving about, sitting up high and bouncing around on their sprung seats in their big machine, earplugs in listening to the radio or country music or something.

All the farm work way back then was done by hand. It was hard work. Ploughing the land for planting was done with horses and oxen. When you've walked behind a pair of big horses with the reins looped over your shoulders and held in your hands as you steer the plough, believe you me, son, you're working. You'd go home at night and have no bother sleeping. That's how tired you'd be.

The farmer and his wife who lived up in the big house had five children. They worked hard and were doing well enough. But tragedy struck. The farmer's wife died giving birth to their youngest child, a son. The widowed farmer, who was left with five young children, two boys and three girls, never married again. He thought so much of his dear departed wife that he wouldn't have another woman about the place. He reared the children himself.

In those times a farm couldn't support a big family. It wasn't intensive farming, as we know it today. It was subsistence farming. As the children grew up, one by one they had to leave

123

home and find work, if they could. The eldest child, John, was the first to go. The daughters, fine-looking girls, married well, as they say, and left home too. That left the father, with his youngest child Peter, to work the farm. Now, as time passed, John, a hard-working chap, had been working away in foreign lands for so long that his father had almost forgotten all about him.

Understandably, you might think, the father doted on his youngest son. He was petted, spoiled rotten, and, in his father's eyes, there was no fault in him. But the more Peter had, the more he wanted. He was greedy. Sadly, his father was blind to the greed that was in him. The neighbours didn't take to him at all. They respected the father, but they had little time for the son.

When the old man died, the farm and everything that went with it went to Peter. After the father's funeral, his children gathered together up in the big house. Instead of inviting his siblings to choose some memento of their father to have for themselves, irrespective of value, the young son doled out bits and pieces of bric-a-brac and things that were of no use or value to him. He wasn't giving anything away. He was getting rid of stuff he didn't want. His sisters passed no remarks. If they didn't want what he gave them it would be recycled quietly, one way or another.

His older brother John had never married. He had no family or home to call his own. He had travelled from far away across the seas to be at his father's funeral. It cost him every penny he possessed to be there, to pay his respects. All he owned was the clothes on his back.

When it came to his turn for the handout from his brother, he was given a lame donkey and an emaciated old cow. God only knows what age the cow was. The bones were sticking out of her. John had nowhere to live. His younger brother, charitable that he was, rented him the bothy at the foot of the garden to live in, on condition that he fixed it up and paid his rent on time. The bothy was a small hut used when needed for housing a hired farmhand.

John didn't grumble, kept a tight lip, and, having nowhere to live, humbly accepted his brother's offer. He led the donkey and cow down into the walled garden, made them a shelter for the night, then watered and fed them as best he could. The bothy was little more than a shack. It was in a bad state, but it was dry. He cleared a space, made a makeshift bed, and tried to sleep.

Next morning he set to work with a will, to make the best of his lot. He was a hard worker who could turn his hand to anything. He took the cow and the donkey out and tethered them on the side of the road so that they could graze the sweet grass on the long acre while he busied himself with other things.

The garden was overgrown. He started clearing it to give light to the few remaining ancient, uncared-for plum trees. Slowly, after careful pruning, they came back to life. He worked at the vegetable plot until he had it in good shape, and did the same with the herb garden. The overgrown berry bushes were pruned, reshaped and encouraged to produce fruit. It was hard, constant work, but he persevered and made good headway.

He gathered the fresh, lush grass for fodder for the donkey and the cow. Their fodder he supplemented with restorative herb mixes and massaged their aching hides and weary muscles with herb oils. Herb poultices wrapped in dock leaves applied to the donkey's legs cured its lameness. He also pared back and reshaped the donkey's hooves so that it could walk comfortably again.

When they were fit and ready, he turned the donkey and cow out, among the plum trees, to graze and fertilise the ground. Everything in the garden was healthy and happy. As well as doing all this, he also set about making the gardener's bothy habitable. Everything looked rosy.

But it wasn't.

John was working hard to stand still – scraping to get by. He didn't know where he was going to get the money to pay his rent from one day to the next. He was good with his hands at fixing things and managed to get odd jobs from neighbours. It was tough going, but then there was some good news. The donkey was fit to do a little bit of work, and the old cow started to produce a dribble of milk.

In the countryside around the big plantation house, it had long been rumoured that gold was hidden in the walled garden. It was also said that on special nights the animals in the garden talked, and if you asked them they would tell you where the gold was hidden. Peter knew of the rumour about the gold and, the greedier he became, the more he wanted to get his hands on it.

Time passed. The special time of the year, the time of the Winter Child was nearing. On the morning before Christmas Eve Peter came down into the garden. His brother John was working as always. He was never idle. It was the first time Peter had set foot in the garden since his father had gone to ground. He spoke to his brother disrespectfully.

"Tomorrow's Christmas Eve, and on the stroke of midnight hour the animals talk. That's what they say. There's treasure hidden somewhere in this garden. My father told me that. It's mine. I want it. I'm going to have it.

Tonight I'm going to pin the donkey's and the old cow's ears back and make them tell me where it is. You'll come and get me before the midnight hour. Do you hear me? Do that, and I might ease your rent." With that, he turned on his heel and went back up to the big house. His brother carried on with his work, saw to the donkey and cow, and at the end of the day went back to the bothy. He thought no more about the incident with his brother.

On Christmas Eve morning John had risen early to make ready everything for the Christmas celebration. He made his bothy look like a wee palace, brought in the birch Yule log, and put sprigs of holly in the stalls for the donkey and cow so that they would not feel left out. He doubled their feed of hay and herbs in the mangers and gave them plenty of water to drink.

126

Then he warmed up his last drop of plum poteen in a tin mug over a candle. As he put the mug to his mouth to sip his drink he remembered the day he made the poteen from the juice of the plums he'd harvested in the garden. He paused and thought,

*I'll share it with the plum trees. They yielded the plums. I'll give them a little drink.* He cut a leafed twig from the holly tree in the garden, dipped it into the poteen, and walked around the plum trees like a priest sprinkling them with holy water. When he had finished there was only a dribble of poteen left in his mug. He was about to drink it when he thought,

*No, the plum trees gave me their fruit. I'll give all of it back to them.*

John raised his mug high up over the roots of the oldest plum tree in the garden and let the poteen fall drop by drop on to its gnarled roots. Job done, he was about to go to the well to fetch some water when he heard a soft, motherly voice from inside the plum tree speak to him.

"Young man, please go and get your spade and dig down to my old rotten root. Sever it but don't throw it away. Put it with your Yule log and your bothy will never be without heat again. Hurry back with your spade when you've done that. Don't delay."

For a moment John was confused. He wondered who had spoken to him. He thought he was hearing things. Although he had heard of a fairy living in the garden he couldn't bring himself to believe that it was her.

Then something pushed, prodded him in the back. John didn't look behind him. He did as he was bid. He went and fetched his spade, severed the rotten root, put it with the Yule log in the bothy, and hurried back to the old plum tree.

"Thank you. I'm glad to be rid of that. It was like a bad tooth. Dig further down and see what you can find. What you find is yours, only yours. No one else's, do you understand?" the plum tree fairy said.

Not fully understanding what the voice was saying, John, did as he was told. His spade hit something solid. Scraping the soil away with his bare hands, he unearthed a small chest. He

127

lifted it out on to the ground, opened it and found, to his amazement, that it was full of gold coins.

"Take it, hide it, and don't tell anyone about it. Make haste. Time is pressing. Hurry back and cover over where you have been digging with some grass," the plum tree fairy commanded.

That's exactly what John did. With the treasure hidden and the digging covered up, the plum tree fairy spoke again.

"Go and fetch your brother. 'Tis close on midnight," she instructed him.

John went up to the big house and banged on the door. Out came his brother and without a word, ran past him as fast as his short legs could carry him down into the walled garden. John followed, eager to see what would happen. It was a dark, moonless night, but strangely there was a pure bright light coming from the stable window. Peter was drawn to it like a moth to a candle. He crept stealthily up to the window. The donkey and the cow were talking.

"Do you see that greedy young fellow," the donkey hee-hawed, "with his ear to the window listening to us? He thinks we're going to tell him where the treasure is."

"Sure it's where he'll never find it now," the cow mooed back. "For sure he's too late, the greedy wee miser. Someone else has got it already."

Well, the hee-hawing and the mooing that went on that night was something folk talked about for a long time. Sure half the country heard it. Peter, so angry that he was fit to be tied, plodded his way back up to the house. He was one sorry boy. It is said that he was never the same again. His brother watched him go from the shadows, then went over to say goodnight to the donkey and cow. They were still roaring their hee-haws and moos. John couldn't help himself. He laughed too.

On Christmas morning, the fire in the inglenook burnt the brightest and cheeriest John had ever seen it burn. The little table he had made himself was set for his breakfast of the two boiled eggs his hens had provided and porridge sweetened with warm milk from his cow. After breakfast, he saw to the

128

livestock and everything that needed attention before he made ready for the feast that was Christmas lunch.

Bread was baking in the Dutch oven and the vegetables from the garden were bubbling away contentedly in a large pot slung above the fire. The bothy was filled with the aromas of home cooking. John placed the home-made butter, churned from the old cow's rich yield of creamy milk, on the table beside the jug of buttermilk. It was a feast indeed. Generously buttered warm, fresh-baked bread with home-made vegetable broth, a bounteous salad from the garden with herbs of his choice, washed down with fresh buttermilk. What more could anyone ask for?

There was more. John had made a plum crumble pie that he served to himself with a large dollop of fresh cream that the old rejuvenated cow had yielded. What a Christmas they all had.

From that day on John was always able to pay his rent on demand, but he never changed his ways. He went about his business quietly, helping others in need.

The big plantation house and the garden are still there. The gold was never found after John hid it. It's still there somewhere in the garden. So if you fancy going up there at midnight on Christmas Eve and listening to the animals talking … it might be a rabbit and a hedgehog this time. Who knows? It doesn't matter. It might be your lucky Christmas.

Let me know how you get on.

I remember my grandfather telling me that story when I was a boy. It was told to him by his grandfather, and now I'm telling it to you.

# Letting Go

As the hall clock showed 0500 hours he left home, stepped outside into a windswept street, turned the collar of his coat up around his neck, and headed for his car. March had replaced February but there was no welcome in it, no early morning birdsong yet. He wanted to be in his office at 0600 hours to dispose of all the admin stuff he knew was necessary, but didn't relish doing, before the real working day started – which to him meant being amid the action on the factory floor.

Jack McLarnon was a self-made man, which was true. But he often thought that the people who made that comment about him more than once couldn't make a decent cup of tea for themselves or anybody else.

When that thought reared up he would remind himself that arrogance was no measure of any man, and those rich in genuine humility would without doubt profit more. But in truth, he was self-made if pulling oneself up by one's bootstraps was anything to go by. Not that any man in the street would notice it from his demeanour or behaviour. Jack didn't stand out in a crowd. He chose to live quietly, as best he could, far below the radar of celebrity.

He was the only child of a working-class family born in 1942 during the Second World War when decent people knew their place and had little encouragement to leave it. He never made it to grammar school, not that it mattered much to him. He was more interested in other pursuits, like football. Jack would look back years later and be thankful he hadn't gone to college or university otherwise, he might never have become a self-made millionaire.

*Too much education might have blunted, if not stunted, my curiosity, not stimulated it as it should*, he thought. His secondary education was experienced at a technical school for the academically impoverished, sometimes labelled late developers. What little latent ambition he might have had was being slowly eroded until, in a hands-on engineering workshop,

130

a teacher succeeded in making the mundane interesting. And, in the process of encouraging curiosity, an idea formed in Jack's young head. That moment of curiosity took an irresistible hold that shaped the rest of Jack's life. He thought about his idea, researched it, and started putting flesh on to its fragile frame.

His father, a quiet man, was a fitter in a local engineering works. Good with his hands, he was forever in his little backyard shed working at something. One evening after dinner Jack told his father about his idea. His father listened as he sucked on his pipe.

"I'll think a bit about it, son," he said, asked a few pertinent questions, and that was that. He *did* think about it, and a couple of nights later presented what he thought was Jack's idea in blueprint form.

"Is this something like you were talking about, son?"

Thus Jack's progress to becoming a self-made man had begun. From just a glimmer of an idea, a chat with his dad, the development of a prototype, and the start-up of a one-man manufacturing operation from a backyard shed, he became a self-made man, turning a zero-pound turnover into a multi-million-pound annual turnover, and in the process made a lot of people better off too.

But this story isn't about that. It's about something else, as you'll find out if you hang about and let me tell you.

It wasn't long before he was passing through the security gates into the McLarnon Industries complex. The backyard shed operation had grown over time to occupy a site of two hundred acres, in addition to several other smaller satellite sites strategically dotted around the country. The design and layout of the complex had Jack's fingerprints all over it. It was unusual in that there was no central administration building. He didn't believe in centralisation. He took the view that it stifled innovation and that the people responsible for each part of the business should be close to where the action was. Rank earned no privileges, such as designated car parking spaces or dining areas.

131

"We're all workers here. What's good for one is good for all," Jack would say. It didn't at times go down well, particularly with managers of departments returning from off-site meetings when they couldn't find a parking place close to their workplace. When they moaned about it Jack would just shrug and say,

"Sure the walk will do you good. It's good thinking time. Don't be wasting it." As he drove in through the gates that day he thought,

*That's all right in the summer but not on a cold wet windswept March morning like this.* Nevertheless, he did as he did every day: parked in a different place, thus forcing himself to walk to his room. He never called it an office. It was much more than that. It was, to all intents and purposes, the nerve centre of McLarnon Industries.

As soon as he was seated at his table he quickly disposed of all the routine bits and pieces leftover from yesterday and what had come in overnight. Then he moved on to the stuff that required some thinking and perhaps a discussion with colleagues, made his decisions, and cleared his desk. All the while in the back of his mind he was conscious of his off-site afternoon meeting. By coming in early and clearing his desk what he was doing was making time to get out of his room on to the shop floor so he could listen to the buzz of production and chat with people as he wandered around.

He didn't interfere in anything, get in anybody's way, or tread on any toes. He needed the fix that production gave him. He was that kind of person. But all the while he was trekking towards his favourite place, the research unit, to keep abreast of what they were doing, how they were progressing, and what was new. Most of all, he would be encouraging the new ideas and innovation in everything that McLarnon Industries was about. He avidly read the progress reports on all aspects of the business, but it wasn't the same as being there, seeing and experiencing all of it. It was, in essence, his natural habitat.

The morning sped away. He was so engrossed in what was going on around him that he didn't notice the time slipping past until people around him started going for lunch.

"Lunch. What time is it?" he asked himself, glancing at his watch to discover it had just gone 1300 hours, and he was to be at a meeting across town at 1400 hours. If he hurried and the traffic was kind he could just about make it. He speed-walked back to his room, hoping his haste would not attract attention, in case it suggested there was some kind of emergency.

Back in his room he put on his overcoat, grabbed his shoulder bag, swept from the room, ignoring the lift took to the stairs, running down three flights emerging into a cold bleak March afternoon. That's when his anxiety sored. He couldn't remember where he had parked his car. It had happened before at the airport when he had returned late at night after an early morning flight. He had parked in an empty car park, only to find it full beyond recognition on his return. He stopped abruptly and stood stock-still, like a pointer directing its master towards unsuspecting prey.

"What do I do when I've misplaced my car keys? Retrace my steps, actions, whatever," he told himself. The problem was that for a few moments, which seemed like an eternity, he didn't have a clue where to start. He couldn't remember where he had parked his car, even when he visualised driving in through the security gates earlier in the morning. The longer he stood there would lessen his chances of making his meeting on time. It was a very important meeting, the outcome of which would affect a lot of people.

Months earlier he had been sounded out on behalf of an American investment company expressing an interest in purchasing McLarnon Industries. The mooted offer was, in layman's terms, enormous, in the hundreds of millions of dollars, but he knew that his business was worth a lot more and was in no doubt that when it came to hard bargaining their offer would increase if they were serious. Part of the deal would be that he would stay on and manage the business.

It was a kind of inducement, he knew that. But they didn't know him. He didn't want to be a puppet on their string, doing their bidding as they went about reorganising the business he had built up to get the best bang for their buck by transferring the manufacturing capability to cheaper locations overseas, after his people, once they had trained others, had trained themselves out of a job.

He had other options to consider, including listing on the stock market, but that might mean giving up a huge amount of control, and that didn't lie well with Jack. His problem was that he cared about the people who had worked with him in building up the business, as well as the people working on the factory floor. They had families, mortgages, and futures to consider too.

Then it started raining again, a sleet-edged cutting rain, but only slowly at first. Overhead the black low-level nimbus clouds packed closer together, and gradually the drops of sleety rain grew bigger, lumpier, and heavier. Vengeful hailstones cascaded down on him, forcing his retreat to the shelter of the building he had left a little while ago. The dark and oppressive overcast, smothering sky mirrored the thoughts worming through the crevices in his mind, at the bottom of which was the remorseless, nascent notion that he might be losing his grip on reality.

He had no idea where he had parked his car and, as hard as he tried, he could not remember. As the air warmed, the hailstones lost mass and fell as rain. The nimbus clouds slackened their bindings and parted a little, enough for Jack to go looking for his car again. By then he had already missed the meeting. It was relegated in his order of priorities.

He frequently parked at his favourite place, the research labs, and that's where he headed first. It was a bit of a walk. He didn't mind. Inwardly he was glad of it. The cold air freshened his face, clearing away the mind fog. Jack didn't meet anyone en route and was soon searching the car park, activating his car keys occasionally to hopefully inject a moment of life into his wayward vehicle. Intent on his search he happened to glance up at the building in front of him, and spotted someone looking out of a window.

*Is he looking at me?* he wondered, quickly busying himself searching. But he couldn't stop himself from looking up again. This time there were two people at the window looking out.

*Are they looking at me? Are they talking about me?* The last thing he wanted was to be attracting attention.

*They'll think I'm nuts.*

He moved closer to the building, out of their line of sight, then stepped up on to a raised area, and surveyed the car park. His car wasn't there. He would have to look elsewhere, but where?

The main production unit was two hundred metres long and forty-five metres wide, orientated north to south lengthways and flanked by car parks on each side. That's where Jack decided he would go car hunting next. First, he searched the long west side, meeting people coming and going. Inwardly he was fuming at how ridiculous he felt and was conscious of his exposure to speculation and ridicule. When he realised that his search was fruitless he proceeded to search the smaller north car park, which yielded a similar result. Next, he tackled the east car park, which was the most used one for this particular facility. Here his anxiety crescendoed as he encountered quite a few people he knew, including one or two of his line managers. Inwardly he felt like the little lamb that had gone astray, hopelessly lost, desperate to be found. It was then that he realised that not only was he having difficulties locating his car, but he was also having difficulties holding on to himself. The afternoon was fading fast, never to be relived.

"Little lamb," he told himself, "don't be afraid. It'll be all right."

Jack was lost in his thoughts when a car door was suddenly flung open in front of him. Another step and he would have walked into it. A man emerged from the car apologising for his carelessness, and in a moment of recognition realised that he had almost bashed his boss. Jack's mind fog cleared. They knew each other well and chatted amiably as they walked towards the building's main entrance, all the while Jack pretending that this was where he was going.

135

Inside they went their separate ways. Jack headed to the south car park, his overcoat collar up around his neck as far as it could go in a feeble attempt at concealment. They had had a few incidents in the past of car theft and the last thing he needed was to be confronted by security personnel, as he now, somewhat furtively, plodded heavy-footed around, looking for his car. It wasn't there. The afternoon had lengthened and darkness had descended. He hadn't noticed the car park lights coming on, and the rain started pelting down like the wrath of God again. Jack was getting soaked but he didn't care.

*Being wet through is just like being in the swimming pool, only on this occasion I am not wearing the right gear for it*, he thought. That's when his mind lit up and he remembered where he had parked his car.

Last night he had put his swim bag in the car with the intention of swimming before his meeting today. The meeting that never happened because he had been so engrossed in the research lab he had forgotten all about it.

*Water under the bridge now*, he thought, laughing at his folly, as he made his way to the on-site fitness unit and found his car where he had parked it. After putting his sodden overcoat into the boot Jack sat in the driver's seat, mightily relieved, before heading home.

Driving home he was on autopilot. He was greatly worried because the memory lapse he had just experienced was, it seemed, occurring more frequently. It wasn't just forgetting where he had parked the car on this occasion. That had never happened at work before or in the afternoon. It had happened on other occasions, though. He had thought little of it at the time and had put it down to forgetfulness. Now it started to niggle at him. He recalled when he at first seemed to occasionally misplace things, like his reading glasses or his car keys. He found his car keys once in a wellington boot in the garden shed.

"They must have fallen in there," he managed to convince himself. But all the while the nagging thought was that he was slowly slipping into the twilight world of dementia, from which there was no escape. He had denied it, of course, consoling himself with the thought,

*That's what any sensible person would do.* He was angry and frustrated that these things were somehow sent to try him. But, after his initial emotional response, he reset himself and acknowledged the possibility of dementia. His anxiety grew faster than a spruce sapling in spring. He would have to tell his wife Vera. That was a must, but how could he inflict that on her after all she had been through already? Jack was a pragmatist.

"Deal with whatever comes your way and get on with it," was one of his mantras. But this wasn't about him, it was about her.

Vera's father, a widower, lived alone in a substantial property on the other side of town. His wife had died suddenly some twenty years previously. Her father had been devastated but managed to carry on with his life as best he could, keeping himself fit physically and mentally by walking, swimming, golfing, and playing bridge, albeit with a new partner. The latter took a bit of getting used to, but eventually, they became a formidable couple at the bridge table.

It was about five years after his wife had passed over that her father's memory loss had started. It was only trivial at first – misplaced keys and things – but gradually, incrementally, it worsened. On one occasion her father managed to lock himself out of the house. Trying to gain entry by way of a downstairs toilet window, he fell back onto the paved path, where he was found lying by his next-door neighbour. To add to their concern neighbours reported seeing unsavoury-looking characters calling at the house, apparently looking for Vera's father.

Other occurrences, together with Vera's need to hide her father's car keys to prevent him from driving, added to their concerns for his safety. After considering all their options it was decided that the best solution was for Vera's father to move in with them. It wasn't easy, selling the proposal to him: independently minded people value their independence highly and dislike intensely the notion of anyone telling them what to do. Slowly, gently, they managed to persuade him that it was best for him. He settled in quickly and life assumed a sort of normality. Vera's father went about his business, with the occasional foible, like putting salt in his tea instead of sugar, but with time his behaviour became more idiosyncratic and at times funny.

He was out walking with Vera one day when they met an old friend she hadn't seen for a while.

"Dad, this is my old friend, Demetri. I haven't seen him in such a long time," Vera said by way of introduction.

"Nice to meet you. I'm Dimensionless," her father, always the gentleman, responded. There were many such happenings as the links in his memory network loosened. Often they were hilariously funny. He went missing one day when Jack was at work, causing Vera great worry and concern. After searching his known haunts she found him where his friends had reported seeing him before, standing at the cenotaph in the centre of town asking the sculpted figure of a First World War soldier if he had seen his son. Vera's father didn't have a son. He was an only son. Perhaps he was, in his mind, searching for himself. Who knows? Once at Sunday lunch Jack was already seated at the table when Vera's father asked very politely,

"Do you mind if I join you? It's very busy in here today." When Jack said,

"Please do," "What's good on the menu today?" he continued the conversation as if he didn't know Jack. In the same vein, when he couldn't finish a meal he would ask for a doggy bag as if he was eating out in a restaurant. They started keeping plastic boxes for him to use and just got on as best they could. They could tell, however, that over time he was retreating into himself more and more.

He was a remarkable man in many ways, and never went to bed without saying his prayers. Never. He would say the Hail Mary prayer many times, but he always changed the ending from,

"Pray for us sinners, etc.," to, "Pray for me and Jimmy Todd," whoever in his mind Jimmy Todd was. Later they discovered when they met Jimmy Todd that he and Vera's father were childhood friends, neighbours it turned out.

Caring for her father was not without cost. It was taking its toll on Vera. It came to a head one day when her father mistook the linen cupboard for the toilet. Jack made a cardinal error by laughing and trying to explain to her that in his mind her father's behaviour was perfectly rational.

"If you think it is funny, Jack, you can bloody well clean it up," she said, putting on her coat and storming out.

That settled it in Jack's mind. They would have to get it sorted. Jack and Vera considered their options, which, in the end, only amounted to two: find a suitable residential care facility for her father or employ respite care to ease the burden at home. Their exploratory visits to various care facilities were not uplifting or encouraging. To their dismay, they saw residents parked around the periphery of rooms with televisions blaring at them. They were wallflowers waiting in vain for a glimmer of the sun to brighten their day. There was no conversation, no privacy, no stimulation. Even without the ever-present unappealing odour, it was depressing.

In the end, because their home was big and roomy enough to accommodate overnight respite carers, that was what they opted for. It was expensive but no more expensive than residential care, and it didn't really matter as Vera's father's pension more than covered it anyway. Not that it would have mattered if it hadn't. They could well afford it.

Vera's father was well looked after, and with the new arrangement, Jack and Vera got something of their lives back. As time passed her father's grip on reality continued to slip away. His funny little mishaps, ramblings, and mispronunciations gradually gave way to glimpses of a darker nature. At night in bed, his recitations of nursery rhymes and snatches of poems were increasingly supplemented with guttural incoherent mutterings arising from some deep-seated aggravation and suppressed anger. As the linkages in his mind deteriorated and were severed one by one he would cry out from the depths of his soul as if in terror, in a dense and hoarse tortured voice screaming for salvation. Jack knew that Vera's father's passing was not far away, and prepared her as best he could to face it.

That was all a long time ago now. He was on his way home. The black sky emptied drizzling snow on to the windscreen of the car, which was whisked away in waltz time by the soothing motion of the wipers. The traffic was heavy and moving fast, too fast for Jack. Everybody seemed to be in a hurry. The headlights of the oncoming traffic, some on full beam, dazzled his eyes, and some idiot, driving too close behind, filled his rear-view mirror. The falling snow was thicker and heavier now, forcing the wipers into quickstep to clear it.

He would have to tell Vera everything that had happened to him today. All of it. He owed her that much, at least. He didn't want to, but he was afraid to. He was afraid of the devil in his head, worming incessantly around, destroying him from within. Slowly, bit by bit, it was wearing him down, bullying him into submission, but he was fighting back.

If nothing else, Jack was a fighter. He would battle with all he could muster to save his sanity. Internally he was at war with himself, total war. No prisoners would be taken. A war he knew in his heart he couldn't win. He would never, ever submit, never give up.

Anger fuelled his fury. Grinding his teeth, he dug deep, summoned every ounce of will at his command, and wrestled with the devil in his mind head-on. Self-made he was, but he would not self-destruct. The duel in his head was fought out in frenzy all the way home.

Jack didn't want to end his life as a wallflower decorating an odious care facility.

"Not while I have breath in my body," he promised himself. No wonder folk call them God's waiting rooms. "No, not for me, thank you." But he knew in his heart of hearts that after all Vera had been through with her father he could not inflict a rerun of the same thing again on her. More of the same. No. He couldn't, he wouldn't. Self would be set aside and a wallflower he would become, knowing she would always be his sunshine, wherever in his mind he would be.

"To hell with me," he decided. "If that's what it takes, so be it."

140

Gripping the steering wheel, the fury within him undiminished, his mind played the ring-a-ring o' roses singing rhyme over and over and over all the way home.

He had been floundering, wallowing in self-pity. There was nothing heroic about it. Feelings of shame, helplessness, anxiety, dread, and inevitability had to be overcome and set aside with everything that screamed,

"Surrender, give up, let go."

His fear had grown so intense he could not contain it. He would not be silenced any longer. He had to tell Vera and prepare for the journey ahead. He would do it now.

His neural network activity increased. Red warning lights flashed at every one of the nodal interconnections. The network activity in his brain intensified. His system was surging, overloading. His mind was imploding. He couldn't cope. He was on the verge of self-destructing.

As the black, mutinous waves grew more mountainous his grip on the steering wheel tightened, vice-like, and his knuckles turned white.

His incoherent babbling mingled with his shouts of,

"Vera, Vera," roused her. She found him sitting wide-eyed and bolt upright in the bed beside her, rigid with fear, in a cold sweat. His arms were stretched forward, locked at the elbows, and his hands were clamped fiercely on to the imaginary steering wheel. Startled and alarmed, she reached out to him.

"What's wrong, Jack? What is it?" Gasping, comprehension and relief coloured his voice as he said,

"It was only a dream, thank God, but it seemed real."

Then slowly he described his dream in minute detail to Vera. When he had finished Vera said,

"In the name of God, Jack, are you right in the head? Sure you retired seven years ago. How long is it going take you to let go?"

"I have let go," Jack said, "but somewhere in the deep recesses of my mind a worm of reluctance persists."

They quietly mulled over the past. Memories flooded back, happy memories. Jack had built the business from scratch, nurtured and managed its growth, and trained his successors.

And when he had accomplished all that he could, he knew in his heart that it was time to pass the baton and move on.

Vera and he planned his retirement. Jack had been offered and considered taking on another paid challenge. But after discussing it with Vera he decided against it. Instead, he and Vera volunteered to work in support of various charities. They read more, walked more, and enjoyed life more than ever before. Vera reminded Jack that the forgetfulness incidents he recalled were nothing at all, other than a mind too full of stuff. When Jack suggested otherwise, Vera reminded him that he had had major parts in the last two productions of their local drama club. He had been word-perfect in both and never missed a beat.

"Good memories build a sense of aliveness, Jack," Vera said. "Let's keep on doing what we do. You don't want to go back to work, do you?" she asked.

"No," Jack emphatically responded.

At ease with himself, happy and contented, Jack snuggled beside Vera, his cheek against her breast, and gently slipped back into sleep.

# Scent of Seasoned Hay

When the war ended in 1945 he had taken his first uncertain steps into a new world order, not that he remembered anything about it. His mother had told him. A teenager from the south, she had migrated north in search of employment. His mother enjoyed if that is how she would have described it, a ninety-five-year stretch of life. Her siblings lived to a ripe old age too.

"We came from good stock," she would often proudly say.

It was a courageous undertaking to uproot from a rural community in the Republic of Ireland and relocate in Northern Ireland, a different nation with a different culture on a shared island. But she did. She found employment, settled, met, and married a northerner. Later when her firstborn forsook the comfort of her womb to enter his new world, the magnetic lure of home was so compelling that very soon he was taken on a presentation journey southwards, to meet his maternal grandmother. Many more journeys southwards, now beyond the reaches of childish memory, followed. Going 'down south' is an expression particular to northerners, as going 'up north' is to southerners on this shared island home.

His first reliable recollection of going down south was in the late 1940s when he had apparently reached the acknowledged age of reason, that critical moment in a child's intellectual development when knowledge of right and wrong is deemed to have been acquired. The real difference between right and wrong, learned the hard way by parental chastisement, was that parents decided in their best judgement what was right or wrong. Often, when they disagreed, he didn't know who or what was right or wrong. Later, with a little more acquired knowledge, he would wrestle with many interpretations of what precisely constituted the right or wrong in any given set of circumstances. But now is not the time to get bogged down in philosophical gymnastics. This tale is rooted in the imperfect memory of a child deemed to have reached the age of reason, migrating through adolescence.

Home in the north was a terraced house on a road that climbed gable by gable up a hill with a one in ten gradient known affectionately by the folk living there as the Brae. He was the firstborn of four children. On his first remembered journey southwards his mother lugged him and all their baggage down the Brae, past the meeting house, through winding lanes past the mill, and across the river footbridge to the railway station.

His first sight of the huge steam engine was frightening. It stood trembling, hissing, and groaning, belching out thick black fiery smoke like an infuriated dragon ready to devour anything and everything in its path. He was terrified and rooted to the platform, but his mother, his little hand grasped in hers, made him feel safe. Despite this, his wary eyes never left the huge, angry beast lest it pounced and devoured him.

They found an empty carriage, bundled all their stuff on board, stowed it away, settled themselves in, and waited for the moment of departure. He itched with uncontained excitement. Perched on the edge of his seat by the window, he was determined to see, observe, and absorb, as children unconsciously and unashamedly do, everything he could on this, his first remembered train journey. Little did he know then, that it was a journey he would make many times by train, bus, taxi, and bicycle in summer sunshine and bleak midwinter, such was the irresistible lure of his mother's birthplace. Sat on the cushioned carriage seat his little feet dangled freely above the floor. The sliding window, set into the carriage door, tight shut to keep out the black smoke, was opened and closed using the biggest leather strap he had ever seen, bigger even in every way than the one his father stropped when shaving. Everything was new to him. He was in wonderland.

Suddenly a whistle shrilled. He tensed. A uniformed man on the platform waved a green flag. The big engine at the front of the carriages released its pent-up energy, hissed, groaned, and grunted with the effort, as its big iron wheels slowly turned, pulling the train forward. As it gathered speed it made music on the track in a clickety-clackety rhythmic way. There was a beat to it that started him counting and rhyming: one potato, two potatoes, three potatoes, four; four potatoes, five potatoes, six potatoes more ... faster and faster until a tempo was set. In wonderland, his dangling feet danced to and fro with the swaying motion of the train. They were on their way southwards to a foreign country. One island, two cultures, two nations.

Out the window on his left, they passed along the length of Islandmagee, which, he was later to learn, was not an island at all. It was a peninsula once occupied by druids and witches. He was on a journey of discovery. The train was not an express train.

"This thing will stop at every hole in the hedge," his impatient mother said, but that didn't matter to him. They journeyed through places with mystical names: Glynn, Magheramorne, Ballycarry, Whitehead, Carrickfergus, Clipperstown, and Trooperslane on their way to Belfast. Later he would discover something of the colourful history of these quaint, often underappreciated places.

Magheramorne was the birthplace of Saint Comgall, who founded the great Abbey of Bangor, a recognised seat of learning and a major influence in the spread of Christianity in Western Europe. Ballycarry was where the oldest established congregation in the Presbyterian Church in Ireland was founded by Rev. Edward Brice, the first Presbyterian minister in Ireland. The poet James Orr, known as the Bard of Ballycarry, was one of the Ulster Weavers, contemporary with Robert Burns, and a United Irishman. William of Orange landed at Carrickfergus before he engaged the forces of King James at the Battle of the Boyne.

He would learn that the route travelled that day on his first remembered train journey was littered with history, which had shaped the landscape of many lives and generations. But this is not a history travelogue. This story is about something else.

Everything seemed hurried and frantic when they arrived in Belfast, busy rebuilding itself after the war. He didn't know that. How could he? After heaving their baggage on and off

145

various trams, they made their way across the city to board the Dublin train. But their destination wasn't Dublin.

On the journey south, he read the many strange place names as they steamed past, trying in his childish way to figure out what they meant. It was a good game, like the game of I spy that he would later play with his children on long car journeys. When the train stopped at a place called Goraghwood it was boarded by uniformed men shouting,

"Customs. Anything to declare? Customs. Anything to declare?" His mother told him what they were about and to keep quiet, but he didn't understand any of it. When a little older, he became expert in the art of smuggling butter, cigarettes, and other commodities, all for personal use, of course, when travelling north to south and vice versa, depending on family needs.

Looking back on it, the whole smuggling thing was very amateurish, but he was always particularly careful with the butter secreted about his person, in case it melted and betrayed his exaggerated display of childish innocence. Apart from their encounter with the customs men before they reached the territorial border between the two nations, the actual crossing of 'the Border' for the first time in his life was a non-event. For some reason, he had anticipated more drama, but nothing happened. As they journeyed on, he realised that the only thing of note was that the colours of some things were different. That's all he could remember about it.

An hour after the train had crossed the border they alighted in Dundalk, where his mother's sister lived. With their cases and baggage in hand, they trudged quite a way to her house, to be enthusiastically welcomed by his aunt and cousins. He had met her before but had no memory of it. She was new to him, as were his younger cousins. Her fulsome greetings to the weary northern travellers then, and on many visits thereafter, never changed. There was, forever etched on the soul of his being, a warmth of lasting kinship.

In late afternoon, happy, fed and rested they said their goodbyes and boarded a Dublin-bound bus, but they weren't going to Dublin. Their destination was the village of

Castlebellingham. His granny didn't live in the village. She lived some way outside it.

On boarding the bus his mother spoke with the driver. They didn't get off the bus in the village, as he thought they would. They alighted some way short of it at a request stop (that explained his mother's word in the bus driver's ear). In former times it was custom and practice in rural areas for bus drivers to allow passengers to alight at places convenient for them, at non-designated halts. So it was with them. They got off the bus at his mother's request by the side of the road, some considerable distance from the village. Then they humped their bags and baggage and themselves over a stile set into a hedgerow and trekked their way in a north-easterly direction through a herd of cattle, across the biggest field he had ever set foot in. His mother warned him, belatedly, to avoid the cowpats underfoot. Unfortunately, he had trodden on a very fresh one and thereafter walked dragging his left foot, trying in vain to clean the mess off his new shoe and sock.

Daylight was beginning to fade when they scrambled over another stile in a hedgerow and stepped on to the road opposite his grandmother's house. She was standing expectantly, waiting at her gate, framed under the overarching sycamore trees, beaming them welcome. Uninhibited, unencumbered, he ran across the road into her welcoming arms to be lifted, held close to her bosom, and hugged for what seemed a very long time. At that moment, the seed of kinship was sown, a seed that would germinate and flourish. His little heart sang with joy.

His granny wasn't a tall woman but she was strong. He felt it in her hug. She had lifted him as effortlessly as she lifted stokes of corn and bags of spuds. When she put him down and turned to her daughter he was able in a boyish way to get a good look at her, as she was at that moment. It was an image forever lodged in his memory. On her head, she wore a black bonnet with a red ribbon on it tied in a bow. The bonnet was held in place by two black laces tied under her chin. Draped around her shoulders she had a big woollen shawl that covered all of her, from under which a patterned apron glimpsed.

147

What filled his eyes were the rubber boots on her feet, men's rubber boots with the tops turned down. She looked so comical, eccentric, funny, and engaging. He suppressed a childish giggle. But she was real, a countrywoman through and through, born and reared in the country, and she would never change. Her honest weather-beaten face couldn't hide her inner joy as she ushered them into her home. Inside a turf-fuelled fire blazed, and the aroma of bread baking in a Dutch oven bid them welcome once again. At the scrubbed pine, table readied for their coming they were sat down and fed. He felt cherished.

His first impression of Granny's house was that it was bigger than his. It was a farmhouse with many acres of land attached to it, lots of cattle, a big orchard, outhouses, byres, and loads of farm machinery. He was a child from an urban working-class environment who had been magically conveyed into another world, a world of enchanting rural simplicity, an idyll that temporarily obscured reality. From his experience of living in that wonder-filled world that children inhabit, his imagination, tinged by a growing awareness through his whole adolescence of everything around him, would sober and reform his perceptions.

His granny wasn't tall and slender. She was short and rather thickset. There was nothing elegant about her. She was blessed with strong shoulders and hands like sods of turf. Her face was not classically proportioned, as facial beauty is often depicted. It was square and powerful with clear piercing blue eyes sheltering under narrow jet-black eyebrows. Generous unpainted lips and weather-beaten wrinkled skin were the most notable features in a face set hard against adversity, which would lighten any heart close enough to be warmed by a radiant smile. She was all countrywoman, dressed for working the farm. She was not dressed to please anyone but herself.

She was a bit eccentric at times, like the morning she came flying down the yard, a cut-down wellington boot – her favourite home footwear – on one foot and a slipper on the other. That was her. Needs must and all that. She had a temper that would render a grown man a submissive lamb before its fury, but that in a moment would disappear forgotten, like

148

yesterday's shower of rain. She always called him by his familiar name and seldom sent a harsh or hurtful word in his direction. As he matured, his fondness for her grew into love.

She had twelve children. Five didn't survive beyond infancy. Those who did include his mother, her five sisters, and her brother, the youngest of them. All are gone to ground now. His mother, the last to go, passed away a decade ago, four years short of becoming a centenarian.

Growing up into and through his teenage years, with much time in the summer spent at Granny's, he was subsumed into an extended family of aunts, uncles, and cousins.

The sisters were very close, a closeness that defied explanation, and continued after they had married, left home, and were busy with their own families. They wrote to each other regularly, visited the Ponderosa (as his mother had affectionately christened Granny's homestead) frequently, and circulated the local newspapers among themselves to keep each other abreast of the goings-on in and around Castlebellingham and further afield but, more importantly, the business of the people they knew in the shared neighbourhood of adolescence.

Granny was a widow. Her husband, his grandfather, had gone to ground before he was born, which is why he hasn't featured in this story thus far. He was killed in a bizarre road traffic accident. Father and son had bicycled to some distant place to buy a cart. Eventually, after much haggling, the difference was split, the deal was done, and the cart was bought. They didn't have a horse to yoke into the cart, so the plan was to haul it home by pedal power. They took hold of a cart shaft each and bicycled off towards home. The son was about twelve years old at the time.

On the way home, they had to travel a road that eased its way down into a valley. The momentum of the cart increased as they descended. Instead of them pulling the cart, it pushed them, until they completely lost control and were overrun. The runaway cart crashed into a stone wall. His grandfather impaled on the end of a shaft against the wall was killed instantly. It was after that that the son's speech impediment surfaced.

His grandmother, widowed with a big family to rear, set her face hard to the world and all that it had to throw at her. Doggedly she persevered, fiercely, independently and single-handedly reared her family. She was of the land, it was in her blood. She was a survivor, a breed set apart, a determined woman. What else could she do? The more he got to know her the more he admired her.

Often he accompanied his granny on her excursions to Dundalk. On these occasions she would dress up in her Sunday best: a black bonnet on her head, a plain white blouse, over which she wore a knitted cardigan with a collar, a long black ankle-length skirt, and a pair of black leather boots. Not the cut-down rubber boots: proper Sunday boots, which were separated from her feet by a pair of knitted woollen socks. Over everything, she wore summer and winter, a knee-length black buttoned-up coat. Her only concession to colour, other than black, was a red and white diamond-patterned linen scarf wrapped around her neck.

What took him a long time to understand was that she would meet people on these occasions who knew her background, and how she presented herself in such company was important to her. Self-respect, some would say.

They would leave the house, scramble over the stile, and cross the field through the herd of grazing cattle. If any of them didn't make way for her she would rap their rump with the blackthorn stick she always carried. If they had any survival instincts at all, they gracefully yielded the right of way. He was glad that they walked among intelligent cattle.

Over the stile on the far side of the field, they would wait with the patience only rural people seem to possess for the bus. Any northbound bus would do. His grandmother would make some mysterious gesture, the bus would slow and stop, they would board, she would address the bus driver by name, pass the time of day, and when seated they would be on their way. It was all very civilised. Where they boarded was not a designated bus stop. It was a courtesy stop. It was a way of life he would come to understand and appreciate. People had time for each other. On the return journey, the whole process was reversed. Unfamiliar with his grandmother's secret signs and acquaintances with bus drivers he would, when old enough to travel unaccompanied, take the long way to and from her home, boarding and alighting the bus in the village.

The village, a quiet, docile place at peace with itself and its pace of life, is still much the same today as it was then. Motorway modernity bypassed it, leaving it like an unspoiled island, with its distinctive charm. There are those, no doubt, who would view it quite differently.

Getting off the bus in the village and veering left past the green led to the mouth of the Sea Road, which stretched past his granny's house to end where it met the sea, five miles away as the crow flies. It was a narrow hedge-bounded tar-stoned road that shouldered its way at first up a slight incline and dipped here and there on its journey until it slid slowly down to greet the sea. His leg muscle memory recalled that it was at least a two-mile walk to Granny's from the village. Along the way cosy cottages huddled here and there, displaying their rural charm. Farm gates breached the hedgerows in two or three places, offering access to the farmsteads beyond. One single-storey farm dwelling he remembered had whitewashed walls, a thatched roof, and small windows, with access to the interior by way of a half-door. There was something ancient about it that fired his imagination.

Every time he walked that road alone, a deep, respectful feeling settled on him. At first, he felt he was an intruder in a landscape that he didn't understand. He was an alien, out of place. He would hear the cattle in the fields scuffling and munching, yet he felt drawn to the place. The cattle and their herdsmen were in their domain, but he was still on the outside looking in, an outsider. A sense of place is difficult to explain, but something hooked him, held him captive, and refused to release its claim. Much later he was to learn that his grandfather had herded cattle in the fields he had crossed. He had literally and metaphorically walked in his grandfather's footsteps. There was a dip, a hollow in the road, half a mile from his grandmother's house that was said to be haunted. He was uncomfortable, to say the least, walking through the hollow alone at night. Perhaps he had listened too intently to the fireside ghost stories.

His first impression of Granny's farm and a big house was unsustainable. The big house was a brick-built roughcast single-storey cottage, capped with a red-tiled roof, set on the brow of a hill that gently sloped its way to the sea. The tang of the sea was ever-present, especially when the wind was easterly.

The cottage, surrounded by acres of fertile farmlands as far as the eye could see, was truly blessed in its aspect. The nearest neighbour was about a mile back up the road towards the village. It had three rooms: the main room, which stretched from the front to the back of the cottage, and two bedrooms. The lower end of the cottage was bolstered by a lean-to cowshed and a piggery. The orchard consisted of half a dozen uncared-for apple trees that were well past their best but which still managed somehow to yield the most delicious fruit he had ever eaten, and a few overgrown blackberry and redcurrant bushes. It had little else to commend it.

Between the orchard and the cottage was the haggard, an outdoor area where the winter fodder for the cattle was stored. The cottage didn't have a mains water supply or plumbing of any description, and the magic of electricity hadn't reached it either. The toilet was down the yard. On his first visit to it, he searched in vain for a flusher. There wasn't one. It didn't flush and never would. It was one of those. This was another learning experience that didn't rest comfortably with him, but that was rural life in the raw. To survive he had to suffer it like everyone else. What else could he do?

The water supply was from a well, hidden away at the foot of the orchard, and there was nothing to do with wishing about it. His first assigned chore, after being shown where it was, and how to prime the hand pump to get water flowing, was to fill four enamel buckets with clean water every morning and bring them into the cottage. Boy, did he feel tall and manly? When night descended, blue tin oil lamps provided light in the family room. Candles sufficed in the bedrooms. It was for him another world, a world of rural domesticity that would shape him forever.

The farm was, in essence, a triangular plot of land about an acre in size, on which the cottage was built, with its apex fenced off to accommodate a couple of goats. Hidden among the abundant hedgerows, gooseberry bushes produced summer fruits. That was it in all its wonderful glory: lock, stock, and barrel stripped bare of sentiment and nostalgic yearnings. But in the memory of a child growing up, it was pivotal. It wasn't the big farm that he had imagined in his childish innocence.

His granny, coming from farming stock, farmed in a desperate, subsistence kind of way, against all the odds and the prevailing winds. She didn't own land, she rented it. The term often used was conacre, the letting of land on an annual basis. By conacre, she had the use of about twenty acres, on which she reared beef cattle and kept two or three cows. In the piggery, there was a sow with piglets sucking. That was it, all of it. But for him at the tender age of reason, it was everything his fertile imagination wanted it to be.

The front door of the cottage, which was always kept wide open except in winter, framed a small entrance hall, to the right of which was his grandmother's bedroom. The door to that room was always closed. The door to the left, which was frequently wide open, led to the main room, the beating heart of the cottage and all within its compass. It was a big space. Several pine dressers stood proudly at attention against the long wall displaying the blue, blue-and-white, and brown-speckled delph to everyone who entered. These interesting pieces made an impression on anyone entering the room not already blinded by familiarity. In the far left-hand corner the butter churn, corralled by an assortment of crocks, was stored safely out of harm's way until called into productive service again.

Fixed securely halfway up on the back wall was a large storage cupboard where things, including the provisions he often fetched from the village, were kept. A small two-foot square window in the right-hand corner, adjacent to the door that led to the second bedroom, looked out over a wide expanse of rich farmland stretching down to the sea. Standing on a chair on tiptoe at the window with the sea visible, he was able to tell when the incoming tide beckoned him to come and swim. Soon in his growing, he didn't need the chair to see the sea. Many happy summers were tidal-orientated.

On the windowsill sat an acid battery-powered radio. The huge batteries periodically needed their energy replenished. He had on occasions to take them to a place way beyond the village to be re-energised. It necessitated two journeys. The batteries took time to recharge.

The wall that separated the big family room from the two bedrooms had an inglenook, a big recessed cavern that housed a hearth, on which the fire for cooking and heating was built. It had all the accoutrements: long tongs and pokers, side cheeks for setting kettles and pots on, and an iron swivel arm on which to hang cooking pots over the fire. It was the living, beating heart of the cottage, the living breathing essence of the whole family.

In the evenings, it was the gathering place. He loved it. The earthiness of peat fire smoke on a late summer's evening anywhere still kindles fond memories, even as these inked words shape this page. From the left side of the inglenook, a three-foot-long low pine bench angled into the room. Above the inglenook, a long shelf obediently bore things of no particular value, and to its right, a cupboard reached from floor to ceiling. Once, when he had the place to himself he rummaged in the cupboard and found a seldom-used sheathed set of fishing rods.

A threadbare armchair took pride of place on the right of the inglenook. He often occupied that armchair as darkness descended and the luminous flames of the burning peat cast dancing shadows all around on the walls, before the blue tin oil lamps, lit one by one, enhanced the choreographed shadows. A scrubbed pine table stood at the centre of the room, always readied for purpose. Often during the day fowl wandered in, pecked their superior way around the room, and cast a cocked eye before departing, satisfied that all was as it should be. It was that kind of place: harmony within and without, everything at peace.

The family parish church was at a place called Kilsaran on the Dublin Road, three miles south of Castlebellingham. Every Sunday and on holy days, they walked together, a gaggle of cousins and adults, five miles there and back, none the worse for it unless it was pelting down with rain. Then it was a different story. Other families in clusters walked the Mass path too, passing the time of day with friends and neighbours on the way. In memory, it seems a world away, a different culture altogether.

His granny didn't live alone. Her daughter, Kathleen, the eldest of his mother's siblings, lived at home with her. She was a twin, but sadly her brother didn't survive the birthing process. As a child, he took his aunt as he found her, but slowly it dawned on him that she was different in some indefinable way. It never occurred to him, in the beginning, to wonder why she always sat on the angled bench seat by the inglenook. It was her place. Every morning she would emerge from her bedroom with a cushion in her hand and place it carefully, ever so carefully, on the bench seat. It was a daily ritual.

As he advanced in his use of reason, he cottoned on to the fact that she had never reached the use of reason, as he understood it, and never would. He, a boy, had intellectually outgrown her and would continue to grow, while she remained a child trapped in an ageing body. His childish curiosity focused on the big red birthmark on the left side of her face. He thought she must have fallen into the fire and got burnt, but he never probed or asked anybody about it. He just discreetly kept his child's eye on it lest it changed shape and came after him.

His Aunt Kathleen had what could be described as a general learning disability or, more precisely, an intellectual disability, which could have been caused during the birthing process (which her twin brother did not survive). He didn't know. Her disability was never discussed in his hearing. She simply never matured intellectually and was one of those people who in former times would have been secreted away understairs, out of sight, to hide the family shame. But in his granny's humble cottage there weren't any stairs. His aunt was out in the open,

155

getting on like everyone else with grandmother's daily allotted chores. She was never left idle, always employed, able to converse in her inoffensive way and always generous. But above all, she loved to sing and tell stories of she had a full repertoire. Aunt Kathleen was perhaps the gentlest, most loving person he had ever met.

His mother's youngest sibling Peter lived with his mother too. Over time he formed the impression that Peter was never really there. He was somewhere else or would have preferred to have been somewhere else. He was a boy when his father was killed. Little was known then about trauma. Counselling wasn't even a notion for anyone left to cope with the psychological aftermath of a horrific experience. It's not easy for anyone, and even harder perhaps for the only male child in a family struggling to survive, to grow up under the wing of a strong and determined dominant mother, whose battle with adversity may have dulled her sensitivity.

On top of that, he had to cope, throughout his schooling, with a speech impediment that in former times was often treated harshly by those who should have known better. Children being children, he could imagine the sniggering behind hands when his uncle stood to answer a teacher's question in class. Outside the classroom, the mocking could have been more intense. Did his uncle as a boy ever run home crying to his grieving, overwrought mother, who was trying to keep a roof over their heads and feed her seven children? He could only imagine from a distance what it must have been like for all concerned. After his Aunt Kathleen went to ground his uncle married and left home.

Though three people lived in the cottage all year round the seasonal influx of Granny's extended family swelled the numbers significantly. His mother and her three children would be put up in the cottage. Her sisters, who lived closer to the ancestral home, would visit at weekends with their children, who sometimes did what today is called a sleepover in 'the country', as Granny's place was affectionately referred to. In

156

summer there were often ten or more people sleeping in the cottage.

Where did they all sleep those wonderful summers away? The first time, he remembered, when all the cousins were together and bedtime approached, the pine table was set to one side, a boxlike thing against the back wall of the big family room, which he hadn't noticed before, was opened, and a frame was pulled out and unfolded piece by piece to rest on the bare concrete floor. Old straw mattresses were unearthed from somewhere and positioned on top of the frame, and with the addition of blankets, overcoats, and God knows what, a big bed was created. It was a huge thing in which the children, boys and girls, slept together head to toe. It was his introduction to a settle bed or a version of it. The precise mix of the genders of the sleepers is beyond memory but many happy nights were spent in that bed fooling around, listening to the adults chatting by the fire in the shadowy light. They slept head to toe, but he didn't recall his face meeting any smelly feet. To date, no ill effects have been reported, but it has been mooted once or twice since then that it could be fun to do it again sometime. But common sense has prevailed.

He remembered the summer's morning with crystal clarity when his grandmother said to him in her usual brusque way,

"*Buachaill*, go down below like a good chap and graze the cattle on the long acre." For a moment he thought she was talking to someone else. But there was no one there. It was just the two of them. It wasn't a request. It was a command. But, being a northern townie, he hadn't a clue what she was talking about and daren't dare let his ignorance show. Later he would learn that '*buachaill*' in Irish meant 'boy'. She meant him.

Uncertain what exactly she wanted him to do, he decided that all he could do was feign understanding, go down the road to the field where the cattle were, and hope for the best. Fortunately, on the way down he met a lad he knew. Once he had disclosed his dilemma, he was told that all his grandmother wanted him to do was to let the cattle out of the field and look after them while they munched the sweet grass growing along the side of the road. That was what she meant by 'the long acre'.

Happy as a sandpiper, he ran down to the field and was surprised to find the cattle expectantly waiting at the gate. He slid back the bar of the big five-barred gate and stood on the lowest bar while it gently swung open to let the cattle filter out at their leisure, to partake in what was a familiar outing for them. It wasn't a difficult chore even if he didn't know what he was doing, but at least the cattle seemed to know what they were about. In those days a tractor on the road was a rare sight. Practically all the farmers about the place relied on the good old power of the horse.

He spent many happy hours on the long acre. They weren't wasted. Away from other childish pursuits and distractions, he noticed things happening around him: trees budding, wildflowers blooming, hares as big as dogs leaping about – no wonder they called them mad – rabbits grazing, birds nesting, edible berries ripening, and the hedgerows bursting with life. As his interest in things around him on the long acre burgeoned, he became able to name the birds he saw: robins, blackbirds, thrushes (song and mistle), yellowhammers, linnets, finches, larks, and many more, and also to recognise them by their plumage, song, flight, habitat, diet, and more. He was a budding naturalist, all because he herded his grandmother's cattle on the long acre. His grandmother had words about the long acre she would recite when the humour was on her, and folk had gathered in the cottage, as they often did in the evening.

"The lark rises on the wind,

Along the lane, the cattle trod before me,

I am home again, and this soft rain that smothers me is my rain.

Here I stand, as my ancestors did before me,

I feel their lives surging through me,

They are everywhere, in all that grows and comes new again.

I know now, their memory will not fade,

The ground I stand upon holds their memory."

158

Herding cattle alone on the long acre was a journey of discovery, hidden worlds rooted in the hedgerows of life.

Other tasks were assigned and subsumed into the day-to-day life of the homestead. He learned on the job how to milk the cows by hand. It wasn't easy, as he hardly knew one end of a cow from the other. His uncle showed him how to sit on the milking stool with the pail clenched between his knees, keeping his right leg in tight against the cow lest she kicked out, how to relax the cow by stroking her udder, and how to pinch and squeeze her teats to release her creamy white milk.

When he first tried to milk a cow he clumsily tugged on her teats to no effect, while the poor bored animal munched away on her fodder. But when he mastered the pinch and squeeze technique it became easy, rhythmic, and strangely therapeutic. The pinch pressurised the teat and the squeeze released the milk. Then, in harmony with the cow, he milked to a clickety-clackety, pinch and squeeze slow beat of the steam engine pulling the train. Everything was a symphony for him in rural life.

It was but a short step from the byre with the fresh milk up the yard into the cottage, where another chore awaited his youthful enthusiasm: making butter. Pailfuls of fresh milk were emptied into earthenware crocks, covered, and allowed to sit until the cream formed. When the cream was ready to be skimmed off, the churn was readied for the making of butter. The churn itself was a small barrel mounted in a frame so that it could be rotated by turning a handle. When half-filled with the cream the lid of the barrel was secured, and at that point, it became his job to turn the handle to excite the cream in the rotating churn into releasing its stored butter. He found music in churning too. Like marathon runners finding their rhythm, he found his rhythm under Granny's watchful eye.

"Here I go, making butter today, butter today, butter today. Here I go, making butter today, all in the month of May," he would sing.

Through the spyglass in the lid of the churn, he could see the butter forming as the cream separated into butter and buttermilk. At the end of the churning process, the butter was skimmed off, placed on a board, and kneaded to remove as much moisture as possible, then salted to taste and made into pats using wooden bats and stored in the butter rack on the north-facing wall of the cottage. Sometimes in really warm weather the butter pats were lowered down and stored in the coolness of the well.

Butter needs bread, and his granny was good at providing that too. On the big pine table, she would set out her mixing bowl and ingredients: flour, butter, buttermilk, salt, sugar, and baking soda. Then she would load up the mixing bowl: flour by the handful, buttermilk by the mugful, butter by chunks, salt, plenty of it, and a country pinch of sugar. She would mix it all together by hand until it felt and looked right. There was no subtlety about it. Experience guided the whole process.

When content with her bread mix, she loaded it into a Dutch oven, incised it with a deep cross, lidded it, and placed it centre stage in the peat fire in the inglenook. On top of the Dutch oven, she piled burning turves so that the oven was heated from all sides. Somehow she knew when the bread was ready. He never figured how, but the bread was always perfectly cooked.

When taken out of the Dutch oven the warm bread was covered with a cloth and allowed to cool, but not always. A most memorable childhood moment was eating baked bread just out of the Dutch oven, generously buttered with home-made butter, and drinking a mug full of fresh buttermilk in his granny's cottage home. There was nothing like it. It captured for him the very essence of the place, together with the aromas of moments in time spent at his granny's, moments when he had her all to himself.

In summer thoughts turned to haymaking, to provide winter fodder for the animals. It was one of his favourite summertime activities, always filled with hectic endeavour. When ready to cut, the grass was mown by horse-drawn mowing machines. He remembered walking behind the mowers at a safe distance and coming upon the nests of beautiful little brown bees on the ground that had survived the cutting and feeling sad when happening on those that hadn't.

When the grass was cut all hands fell to with forks, tossing it to get it dried, a process that took several days, depending on the weather. That was a morning job after the rising sun had burnt off the dew deposited during the night. Then, with the weather holding, everyone would set to, frantically raking the hay into piles for cocking: the process of building the hay into large cone-shaped bundles ready for carting away to storage.

This was the part of the whole process associated with haymaking that he most looked forward to because he got to drive the horses transporting the hay. The cocks of hay in the field were manually winched up on to a horse-drawn slide, fixed securely in place, and taken away to storage with him, unaccompanied, holding the reins, in control of the horses. Or so he thought. Did he feel proud, or what?

But what he didn't realise at the time was that the horses knew the way to their destination as surely as he did. Their destination was the haggard in front of Granny's cottage. The cocks of hay were unloaded, to then be built upon a raised stone bed into a huge stack sufficient to feed all the livestock through winter and beyond, if necessary.

The stack was built very high, with slightly tapered sides and a pitched top to run the rain off. As the height of the stack increased the hay was forked up on to platforms at different levels until the stack was built. Once he found himself at the very top of the stack, king of the castle. It was scary. When the building of the stack was finished, weighted hay ropes were slung over the top of it, to secure the harvested fodder from the wrath of the winter gales to come.

There were occasions when the children at Granny's let their imaginations take flight, like the day they decided to take themselves to the fair and do a bit of trading. There was an old cart parked over in a corner of the haggard with its shafts resting on the ground. Why it was there is beyond memory because there wasn't a horse about the place to yoke into it, but that didn't matter to them.

With serious matters in mind, they commandeered it to transport their merchandise to the fair. They set about their work with serious intent, and soon crates, buckets, and boxes were gathered up, along with anything that could hold whatever their imagination construed as worth trading. Focusing on the poultry first, they set about rounding up chickens, ducks, geese, and turkeys, which were put into the crates then loaded on to the cart. They made an awful racket as they chased the fowl all over the place but, totally engrossed in their work, they didn't foresee the consequences of their endeavours.

With the supply of poultry exhausted, they hurried on like a plague of locusts to eggs: hens' eggs, ducks' eggs … It didn't matter. They collected and boxed them up by the dozen, brown and white. A man called every week at Granny's to buy them from her, so they knew they had a cash crop that would sell at the fair. Next, they raided the orchard, crating the cooking and eating apples stripped from the trees separately.

They had just loaded up the pats of butter, which they had taken from the food safe on the north wall of the cottage when all hell broke loose. Awoken from her afternoon nap by the clamorous fowl outside, Granny burst out of the cottage door like a whirling dervish, her arms thrashing about everywhere like windmills that had lost their bearings in a gale. Her hair was flying straight out behind her and whatever she had tried to pull on over what she was wearing in bed was neither half-on nor half-off. She was foaming at the mouth, screaming something about hens never laying again, disaster, ruination, and something like a prayer or an incantation. But she yelled it over and over again. When interpreted it was a promise to herself about what she was going to do when she got her hands on them. She was like a demented bat out of hell.

They ran from her as fast as they could, scared out of their wits, and thanks be to God that she didn't catch any of them that day. It was a long time before things quietened down enough around the haggard for them to get up enough courage to creep back towards the cottage. He was fortunate that his mother was there and that Granny's fury had subsided sufficiently to allow her to administer only a severe tongue-lashing. He got it full blast because, being the eldest, she deemed him the leader. There was no fooling about in the settle bed that night. They were like wee timid mice cowering under their blankets – caught, but not vanquished.

One of the things he enjoyed most about being in the country was the early morning walks when the sun was rising and all around seemed still and hushed. He learned that silenced birdsong often heralded the presence of predators hunting for breakfast. As his awareness of everything that was going on around him developed he walked quietly and observed hawks and buzzards circling and hovering, searching for prey. He saw a falcon take a pigeon in flight right in front of him, surprised hares as big as greyhounds in cornfields, and once even happened on a vixen and her cubs.

His favourite place to walk was a big field where a neighbour grazed horses, point-to-point racehorses and hunters. In that field, he found and harvested mushrooms, which he took back to his granny, who, needless to say, always put them to good use. It was close to that field where he first heard and saw a cuckoo and a corncrake, both secretive birds with distinctive sounds that have lingered in his memory. They were hard to spot. He was always surprised when a lark rose at his feet to lure him away from its nest on the ground. Something of a novice in the country, he eventually realised that although you may feel alone walking in fields in the early morning, or any other time for that matter, you are never completely alone in the country. Countryfolk watch over their land jealously. They keep an ever-ready watchful eye on it, and the novice wouldn't know they'd been observed until the day someone deliberately passed an oblique remark to let them know where and when they were spotted. Sometimes it's a warning.

When his granny got to know about his liking for long walks on his lonesome through the fields she took him aside one day, he thought to give him a talking-to. It was nothing like that, as it turned out. She wanted to warn him about the hungry grass, and to never go out walking in the field without some bread in his pocket.

The hungry grass, he was told, was a kind of rough grass that sprang up in tufts and that induced in anyone unfortunate to step on it an overwhelming feeling of hunger, leading to collapse and death unless something was immediately consumed. Hence the ready remedy: bread in your pocket. He was fortunate never to step on the hungry grass. The only things the bread in his pocket ever fed were the birds.

Evenings at Granny's at times were special. As the sky outside darkened and the curlew made its lonesome way home, the outside door was closed and silence crept around the cottage. The sea hushed, and the lit oil lamps with the bright fire in the inglenook banished the gathering gloom.

Occasionally folk would call, pull up a chair, and settle around the inglenook, and, with refreshments in hand, talk and tell stories long into the night. Two callers, bachelor brothers who were getting on a bit in years, who together farmed a couple of hundred acres further down the road, were frequent visitors. Granny often referred to them as hard martyrs, which he took to mean hard workers, but it could also have meant hard to put up with. So he learned to listen with a keen ear to what was said because often the tone of something said was the clue to its meaning. His granny had many sayings, too many to mention, but she would often say,

"That's a day would rear you," and it made no difference what sort of a day weather-wise it was. Or,

"Her face held a winter's rain," meaning someone grieving.

There's a link between the bachelor brothers and his childhood unease when walking through the hollow up the road alone at night. One night he listened, captivated when one of them told the story of a young lad who didn't have a 'full thatch on his roof', as they described his disability, and who came to a sorry end.

The lad was out on his wanderings one day, hungry, with not a farthing in his pocket. As chance would have it, he happened on a widow's cottage. The kitchen window was open to cool some freshly baked bread and a few cakes. Alongside them were a few farthings. The hungry lad couldn't resist the temptation. He lifted a cake, pocketed the farthings, and fled.

He didn't get far. He had nowhere to go. He was caught, tried, convicted, and hanged on a gibbet raised in the hollow up the road. It was said that if you listened carefully in the dead of night you could hear the squeaking of the ropes as he swung to and fro, especially if there was an offshore wind. Is it any wonder, after hearing that story, that he didn't like walking through the hollow alone at night?

The journey down south was one he would make many times by different means. An occasion worthy of mention that he couldn't recall was when as a boy he travelled south without his mother. The local scout troop had decided, for whatever reason, to hold their annual summer camp close to Castlebellingham. Ever the opportunist, on learning of the scout's summer camp destination his mother persuaded the scoutmaster to take him with them and deliver him to his granny. And that's what happened after he had enrolled as a temporary member of the scout troop.

In Dundalk, the troop changed trains to connect with one that served Castlebellingham. The local train they took that day had one carriage and ran on rubber wheels. On arrival at the village station, he was sat on the bar of a bicycle with his gear on the parcel rack at the rear and was pedalled away by the scoutmaster to his granny's. Sadly the branch line and village station are no longer in service. Of the journey, he remembers nothing. He was too young. But the scoutmaster has often reminded him of that journey, and so, like all good yarns, if it's repeated often enough it must be true. But it was true. His mother confirmed it.

The last time he walked the Sea Road was many years ago. It was a planned walk back through the memory and experiences of childhood. The Sea Road had more bungalows than huddled cottages. The atmosphere was different, and his sense of place was challenged as he trod warily along. The landscape had changed. Now he truly was an intruder. But he walked on resolutely to his granny's cottage. It hadn't changed. It was still there, unoccupied but cared for, and he was glad. He paused but didn't venture in, then walked on down to acknowledge the sea.

Bungalows and houses built and occupied by the sons and daughters of local farmers, people he knew, adorned the seafront now, and why not? They put in the hard yards and flourished. Good luck to them. It had changed a lot, but then nothing stays the same. That day he thought he would never walk the Sea Road again.

He stood at the end of the Sea Road gazing out over an incoming tide that seemed to have lost its welcoming voice. In former times a glimpse of it from the cottage window was sufficient invitation to take to its salty water. The sun behind him seeking its rest coloured the Cooley Mountains in clusters of blues and purples, inviting his mind's eye beyond to the majestic Mountains of Mourne and his home place in the hidden Glens of Antrim. As he turned to walk back up the long acre he heard again loud and clear the melancholy call of the curlew winging its way back too. He smiled.

*Some things are slower to change*, he thought, *but the wildlife senses change and will survive it if it can.*

A curlew knows that better than most. He had found a sense of peace in this place that only Mother Nature could give, and his heart sang with joy as he quickened his step up the road. Then the wedged gables of the cottage hove into sight, reaching heavenwards as if in prayer. He paused for a last look.

*My mornings were golden here, my afternoons azure blue, and my evenings crimson-tinged*, he thought, smiling to himself. The stile in the hedgerow on the other side of the road was still there, even if it looked lonely. Images of Grandmother clambering over that stile flashed joyfully across the monitor in his mind.

She was a hard martyr all right. There could be no doubt about that. A young widow with a big family to rear in hard times, but she didn't flinch. She gave everything she had, and more. Hard times make hard people, including women and hard women, lose something of their feminine gloss but nothing of their substance. She was an old, worn-out woman when laid to rest.

166

His feelings then were forever captured in Joseph Campbell's poem 'The Old Woman':

As a white candle
In a holy place,
So is the beauty
Of an aged face.

In a landscape of natural beauty, his granny eked out an existence. She had a hard life of service, of giving and loving in the stern face of unyielding adversity, but she never wilted. Often when things were really tough she would say,

"At least you can call the air you breathe your own."

When he cast a last sideways glance at the cottage he noticed for the first time the clumps of primroses stretching either side of the path from the gate to the front door.

*How appropriate*, he thought, as happy tears of childhood memories formed in his eyes.

In the beginning, his childish imagination took flight and created images of a big house, a big farm, and all that went with it. Viewed through a different prism it was a humble abode on a small plot of land, where people scraped out a living day by day without losing their humanity. There was a welcome for anyone at any time at their fireside.

As trees in autumn shed their leaves in preparation for new growth, in spring he cast off his childish romantic imaginative perceptions. The evening was closing in. It would be dark soon, and he wanted to be through the hollow up the road before darkness shrouded it.

Some things are not so easily shed.

# The Hungry Grass

He had been away so long he was now almost forgotten in the townland, where he had spent many happy summer holidays with his parents. Jackie Magill had, for his part, lost touch with the culture that had spawned him.

After years of harvesting oil in the beige-patterned deserts of Asia, he surrendered to the magnetic pull of home and returned to his roots, settling in the townland of Saint Cunning. The mottled green landscape, spread out far below, reached up in a welcoming embrace as his flight home pierced the cotton wool clouds and descended gracefully towards Belfast International Airport.

He an only child had spent many glorious summer holidays with his parents under the rim of Sallagh Braes, near the village of Cairncastle, in a cottage, they rented every year. Out of the city, he had the freedom to explore his surroundings, which he did to the full. Rural life, he quickly realised, was very different from city life. It was slower, more even-paced. The days seemed longer, the sun always shone, and he was never at a loss for something to do. People spoke differently too. It took a little while for him to become familiar with strange new words, the rhythm of speech and accents, but his ear soon tuned to the local idiom. At first, it seemed to Jackie that he was in a different world. But he settled quickly, made friends, adapted to rural life, and was reluctant to leave when it was time to return to the city.

Their summer holidays in Cairncastle ended abruptly when Jackie was tragically orphaned in a road traffic accident. Strapped securely in the back seat of the car, he survived the head-on collision with a vehicle driven by a person under the influence of alcohol. But his parents didn't. After a short time in hospital, he was discharged into the care of relatives in England to pick up the threads of life again. He was only twelve years old.

Although caring and loving, as his relatives were, they could never fill the emptiness in Jackie's heart no matter how hard they tried. He missed his parents and their summers together in Cairncastle. The burning ache in his young heart took many years to dull, but it never left him. It was always there, buried deep within the marrow of his being.

Fast-forwarding through a lifetime spent harvesting oil from the deserts and the seabeds of the world, retirement beckoned. The lure of his summer childhood experiences in Cairncastle was irresistible. He searched the Internet in the hope that he would find the cottage he had summered in with his parents, but it had been demolished to make way for a much larger, modern family dwelling. Disappointed, he continued searching the area from a distance, for somewhere to settle and plant roots. His search proved fruitless and frustrating.

Eventually, he concluded that the sensible thing to do would be to spend some time on the ground and reconnoitre the area. That's what he did. Two years previously he spent his summer vacation searching all around Cairncastle, for a suitable property without success. One day on the point of abandoning his search, driving north along the Drumnagreagh Road, he stopped the car, parked at the side of the road, and sat listening to the silence all around him. Relaxing, he let it enwrap him. Completely at ease, he left the car and strolled northwards with no object or destination in mind.

It was a beautiful summer's afternoon. Not searching for anything, he was just being in the moment. How far he walked he didn't know when across the road, looking seawards, he saw the mouth of a track, half-concealed by tangled brambles, loaded with blackberries. His curiosity instantly piqued he went to have a look. It felt like he was back in his childhood summertime again, exploring the byways and the hedgerows of bramble and whitethorn of Cairncastle. About three-quarters of a mile or so along the partially overgrown abandoned track, he saw it − a cottage, half-hidden in among the undergrowth and trees.

It was completely isolated. As far as Jackie could tell, there was no other dwelling of any description in sight for miles around. He had to check it out. It wasn't much more than a ruin. The doors and windows were all boarded up. There was no sign of anyone having been anywhere near it. The ring of malignant nettles standing three feet high had not been breached by man or beast. There and then he fell in love with it. He had found what he was searching for.

Back in the car he headed to town and began the search to find the owner of the derelict cottage. Months later, Jackie paid the asking price, bought it and the acre or two that went with it. He employed a local architect to obtain the necessary planning permission to renovate the cottage and make it habitable again. What Jackie didn't realise when he acquired the cottage was that it was located in the townland of Saint Cunning conjoined at its south-west boundary to the townlands of Ballygawn and Ballyruther. Oblivious, he just happily set about modernising the cottage. He couldn't move in quickly enough.

All this had happened long before the previous Christmas. Now, with winter on the wane and spring fast approaching, he had begun exploring his surrounds. His first foray was to walk the semicircular Sallagh Braes that caressed the village of Ballygalley, snuggled comfortably below its majestic cliff face. He fondly remembered walking with his father from Cairncastle to the standing stone at Killyglen, leaving the Mullaghsandall Road, climbing the wooden stile, and proceeding back to Cairncastle by way of Sallagh Braes on a sunny Sunday afternoon one summer. It was many years ago. A lifetime ago, it seemed.

As he walked the route it slowly dawned on him that there was no trace, no sign, to mark their passing, and felt saddened by the thought. Looking down beyond acute rim of Sallagh Braes he could see the village of Ballygalley nestling contentedly. In the old language Bailegallaidhe meant 'the townland of the flatterer', but Jackie didn't know that and it's doubtful if many of its current inhabitants did.

170

All Jackie saw was the cluster of Lego-size dwellings far away below him, lazily emitting wisps of chimney smoke into the crisp Saturday morning air. He walked slowly, savouring the moment, his walking boots carelessly brushing aside the heather and grasses scenting the air as he went. He didn't notice the little beaten tracks through the heathers, ferns, and grasses, bending lazily in the gentle breeze. His eyes were not yet attuned, nor were his antennae rurally calibrated. He heard larks singing but seldom saw them rising, and he didn't spot the peregrines or look behind him. Jackie was just walking happily in the landscape of memory.

Wandering on, he passed over Robin Young's Hill. Then he descended towards the Headless Cross car park, unaware of the promontory fort and the circular prehistoric earthworks he passed. Nor was he aware of the abundance of wildlife that took close notice of his passing. At the Headless Cross, after deciding that he had had enough for a first day's excursion, he turned and headed down towards Cairncastle and home.

On Sunday, his legs a bit stiff from Saturday's trek, Jackie settled for some reading and relaxation. His plan for Monday, weather permitting, was to walk over the hills from the Headless Cross to and back from Glenarm.

On Monday morning Jackie was up and about early. He breakfasted as usual on porridge, supplemented with blueberries and grapes, toasted wheaten bread, and coffee. With his rucksack on his shoulders, he was on his way before the wag-at-the-wall clock in the kitchen showed nine o'clock.

It was another bright, crisp, dry morning. After climbing over the stile on the Ballycoose Road he made his way up a fairly steep but short rutted climb until Scawt Hill hove into sight. There he paused and took in the view. Eastwards, he could see the crown of Ballygalley Head, with its distinctive golf course topography.

Irregular-shaped fields wrapped in hedges of whitethorn and bramble filled his eyes with shades of pastures green, as did the dark hues of the ploughed meadows that stretched seawards to the wet sands of Ballygalley beach. Panning southwards,

171

scanning over rough ground fit only for the hardiest of sheep, he could see in the far distance beyond the Inver Valley to the mouth of Larne Lough. To the west, Slemish Mountain a constant reminder of the Christianisation of the indigenous people in former times. Northwards Scawt Hill beckoned him towards Glenarm. Had the peculiar name excited his curiosity he would have discovered, that the origin of the name was rooted in the Ulster-Scots, the word 'scawd' meaning 'rugged' or 'scruffy'. An apt description.

But Jackie was strangely incurious about this and more. He had been living in the area for some months, settling in, getting to know his neighbours and the lie of the land. But, even though he had holidayed in the area as a child and now lived close to Cairncastle, he didn't know much about it. He didn't know that according to papal records in the year 1306 it was named Karkastell. Over time the name changed to Carncastle ('carn' is from the Gaelic, meaning 'mound'), and then later became Cairncastle.

But he must have heard about the Armada Tree, the souterrains, the mottes, and the folklore of the area. He was in a landscape ancient in history. Everyone knew about the majestic Spanish chestnut tree growing in the precincts of Saint Patrick's Church in Cairncastle. Legend has it that when the Spanish Armada foundered off the coast of North Antrim in 1588 a sailor from one of the stricken ships was washed ashore near Cairncastle. Locals took the body and buried it in the graveyard of Saint Patrick's Church. As time passed a sapling grew out of the unmarked sailor's grave. It was a Spanish Chestnut sapling believed to have grown from seeds in the sailor's pocket when he was buried. The old twisted and knarled tree has been around for hundreds of years. Jackie must have heard of it.

But as he stood wide-eyed, capturing the awesome panoramic view in front of him, he began to feel alienated. He was missing something. He could feel it but didn't know what. Had he looked down he would have seen that he was standing in among pockets of stone, limestone, and granite that had been formed aeons before the ancients populated the land. He would have observed the grasses bending in the breeze – tufted,

172

scraggy, thin, broad-bladed, thin-bladed, wiry – all sorts of grasses, of different shades of green. In among the grasses, weathered bracken, leaning towards spring, faced the breeze curled and unafraid. Heathers straining to purple, carelessly spread, decorated the undulating landscape above the patterned cultured farmlands way below.

He didn't notice the whitethorn hedgerows with their curling adornments of honeysuckle, nor the clusters of trees. He couldn't distinguish the native trees from the non-indigenous species. Looking down on the gardened houses far below, he was blind to the presence of the majestic yew trees that in the myths, legends, and culture of the land where he now lived symbolised resurrection and rebirth.

In the realm of ancient culture, the longevity of the yew tree brought into sharp focus the brief span of human life and all things held dear. He didn't notice the little copses of birch trees sprinkled throughout the landscape below, or the lone birch rising like a bride on her wedding morning from the hedgerow of whitethorn and dark red honeysuckle towards a new beginning in the springtime of its life. The birch a symbol of young love, like the heather waiting to bloom although appearing fragile is very hardy. It taught the ancients that in apparent weakness there is a great strength. The Yule log of choice of the ancients it was burnt in midwinter to welcome the coming of the new year.

Turning towards to Scawt Hill, he paid little attention to the solitary tree standing proudly on the hill's southward-facing side that had been shaped by the prevailing winds. The ancients had various names for it, including the delight of the eye and the lady of the mountain. In Celtic mythology, the rowan tree is associated with Bridget, the daughter of the Dagda, the lord and guardian of nature. Rowan trees were planted around ancient places for protection.

Jackie, oblivious of the lore of the land, traditions and customs that shaped the locals' way of life, comprehended little of what he saw.

Slowly he made his way towards Scawt Hill along a well-trodden path, unaware of the ancient pathways known as fairy

173

paths that ran in straight lines between prominent areas of high ground used by the ancients and the fairies. The shifting motions in the grasses he assumed were wind-induced. He didn't see the little beaten routes of rodents, rabbits, and fairy folk.

At the foot of Scawt Hill, he paused looked down on the townland of Saint Cunning and searched for his cottage, sheltered in the middle of a copse of birch trees. It was hard to spot but, knowing where to look, he found it. What he didn't spot was the coalescence of the townlands of Ballyruther and Ballygawn with Saint Cunning. And what he didn't know was that fairy holes existed where such fusion occurred.

Jackie's purpose in trekking from the Headless Cross over the hill country down to Glenarm was not in pursuit of the lore of the land. He was in search of something quite different, and this was just the first phase of his quest. But it would force him to reconcile, as best he could, the beliefs in and the experiences of folklore that had shaped the culture of the folk who lived in these ancient townlands.

A germ of a thought was planted in Jackie's head one day when he was in the middle of a desert oilfield. He had picked up a discarded magazine. Idly thumbing through it, he happened on an article that transported him back in time, to when he was a boy holidaying in Cairncastle. He was hooked. It wasn't a travelogue extolling the natural beauty of the Glens of Antrim, though for Jackie, sitting in a granular beige landscape of endless dunes, that would have been welcome enough.

The article was about the very popular TV series *Game of Thrones*, the first episode of which was filmed in the townland of Ballygawn, not a stone's throw from Cairncastle village. Jackie carefully removed the article from the magazine, kept it safe, and read it many times by torchlight in his desert bunk at night. His resolve to return to Cairncastle and find Winterfell Castle, and all the other sites where *Game of Thrones* was filmed in Season 1, over time intensified.

He had read that Ned Stark, the Warden of the North, had decapitated a soldier guilty of desertion somewhere on the seaward lea of Scawt Hill, and determined there and to find the precise location. His engineering background dictated that research and preparation, always essential companions, would be the keys to success, although serendipity sometimes lent a welcome hand. He trawled the Internet, obtained Ordnance Survey maps of the area, found many pertinent photographs, studied the DVDs of the first episode of *Game of Thrones*, searched the local newspapers for relevant information, and appealed by way of social media to anyone with photographs of the execution site or of the locale where it had occurred.

Now standing atop the dome of Scawt Hill, with all the data distilled from his researches, he sought by triangulation to pinpoint the location of the execution site. Refining his search, and gravitating towards a particular area, he noticed something that at first he had paid no heed to. It was the curious behaviour of the sheep. While grazing their way towards water, as they always did, they avoided an area that was of particular interest to him. It looked like a small patch of brownish bracken with a few clods of grass dotted about in it.

As the sheep approached it they stopped grazing and diverging around it with what seemed like purpose, gave it a wide berth. There was something about that particular patch that made them wary, uneasy, skittish, something unpleasant, something they sensed. Instinct coupled with industrious endeavour convinced him that he had found what he was searching for. Now all he had to do was claim his prize and take a selfie.

Jackie, full of himself, was about to head down the well-trodden path towards the brownish patch of rough-looking bracken mingled with grass when he noticed someone, a man, he thought, sitting a little way beyond it under the shade of a birch tree. He gave little thought to the lonesome figure and proceeded down Scawt Hill with a spring in his step towards what he believed was the spot where the decapitation had been enacted.

To reach the patch of ground he had to leave the beaten path. Recklessly he brushed aside the rough grasses and heathers with his boots and hurried towards his prize. The site looked fairly rounded in shape. The few clods of grass in it were rough, rushlike, lank, mottled, and coloured a dirty greyish-white. He didn't notice. He was excited, exuberant.

Feeling buoyant, Jackie stepped into the bracken circle. Moving into its centre he trod on one of the clods of dirty greyish-white lank grass that the sheep had so assiduously avoided. Suddenly, without warning, he felt a sharp pain, a sting, a bite, something in his right foot. A horrible sensation overwhelmed him. His stomach cramped with the most awful feeling of desperate hunger, a hunger he could not still. His knees buckled, he almost collapsed, and his vision blurred. He was lathered in sweat so cold he thought he was freezing to death. When he fell to the ground he knew he was dying and that there was nothing he could do about it. He was helpless.

Then all of a sudden he felt himself being roughly handled. His mouth was prised open and a lump of bread was forced into it. The bread was followed by a glug of milk from a bottle, which was shoved into his mouth. It was hard for Jackie to swallow, but with his mouth clamped shut he had little choice. With the bread and milk swallowed, the life force flowed through him again and in no time at all, he was back on his feet.

"That was the hungry grass you trod on," said the wee man he had looked down on from Scawt Hill. "Since that mock execution was filmed, nobody but a fool treks these hills without a morsel of bread and a drop of milk in their pocket. I'm here to make sure nobody dies for the want of it. The hungry grass kills cattle and sheep and all life that treads on it. That's why beasts have the wit to avoid it," he continued.

The wee man looking up at Jackie was no more than three feet tall. He was broad-shouldered, stout, and strong-looking. He was in many ways a mighty-looking little man. He was clothed in an emerald green jerkin with a belted back over a blue checked shirt, he wore a neckerchief at his neck, and his dark blue trousers were tucked into green socks visible above his brown laced boots. He stood bareheaded. His shoulder-length white hair framed his beardless face, out of which sparkled bright blue eyes. He had a wild wistful sort of dreamy, childlike look and a witching air about him, Jackie would learn

176

later, when he shared his experience with others knowledgeable in folklore, that he had encountered a grogach, one of the fairy folk, endowed with a generous disposition towards humans, especially those in need.

Back under the birch tree, they sat deep in conversation, with the grogach doing most of the talking.

"You're down below in the old cottage in Saint Cunning," he declared. Jackie nodded assent. "Do you know much about the place?"

"Not much," Jackie signalled with a shake of his head.

"Well, don't ever interfere with the fairy hole at the far end of your place, where the three townlands meet," the grogach advised.

Then, seeing that Jackie had no idea what he was talking about, he went on to explain that if ever illness or bad luck came about the place he should toss a quartz pebble, after spitting on it, into the fairy hole in the hope that the spirit world would take his illness or bad luck from him. The fairy hole, he elaborated further, lay on a fairy path between two fairy forts and that the path must never be disturbed, otherwise dire consequences would follow.

"Have you had any bother since you renovated the cottage?" He enquired. Jackie responded with a shake of his head. "Good. You're well set, then. All the fairies want from humans is respect. That's something else you need to know. But first, what do you know about Saint Cunning?"

"Nothing," Jackie confessed. The grogach smiled mischievously.

"Nobody does. But a holy man, a follower of Saint Patrick, lived here in the fifth century. The local chieftain was a very cruel man to his clan, so much so that the holy man spoke out against him many times, imploring him to change his ways, but he was obstinate. At one of his drunken feastings, he was heard to wish that someone would rid him of the holy man, and some of his henchmen did. The holy man was dragged across the fairy hole to the very spot where you were standing just now and decapitated.

177

The fairies were angered. They would not suffer their revered place to be violated with impunity. So they cursed the place and caused the hungry grass to grow there for a thousand years. Then, when a mock decapitation was re-enacted there, the fairies were again so angered that they brought the hungry grass back again. I'm here to save innocent folk like you," the grogach continued.

Jackie, who was listening, awestruck, had removed his boot and sock to massage the sole of his right foot. The grogach noticed.

"What you must do with your foot when you get home, is go down to the hermit in Ballyvaddy. Tell him I sent you. He will know what to give you. Take it, leave him some provisions, go home and rub what he gives you into your foot, cover the sole of your foot with the soft bark of the birch tree, and bandage it up with dock leaves. Do that three times a day for three days and you will have no more discomfort. Burn your sock as soon as you get home. Not in the house, though. Outside, beside the fairy hole," he instructed.

They talked at length until the darkening sky overhead threatened rain. A profound silence settled as night clothed the hills. It was time for Jackie to make his way home. He took great care where he put his feet walking back.

Jackie did as the grogach advised. As he applied the poteen-based lotion to the sole of his foot, a cool, soothing, healing sensation crept slowly up his leg, infusing his whole being. When he fitted the shaped soft birch bark to his foot like an insole it suddenly brought upon him a sensation of surprise. It was akin to delight but deeper: a gradual sensation of familiarity, of comprehension. Bandaging his birch-shod foot with the dock leaves, Jackie sensed a growing awareness impressing upon him. He experienced the same set of sensations each time he dressed his foot, but with increasing intensity. After three days dressing his foot as the grogach advised Jackie felt re-energised.

He resumed his quest for the *Game of Thrones* locations filmed in the Glens of Antrim and beyond, but never walked the hills again without a morsel of bread and a sup of milk on his person. Hills hold their secrets dear and deep. Jackie never saw the grogach again or met anyone who had.

It is said that you have to be born and reared in a place to know it. But it is possible to get to know and appreciate a culture by immersing in it. Jackie's encounter with the hungry grass and the grogach was his cultural baptism by the Glens.

Jackie's story is only one of many in the folklore annals of the townland of Saint Cunning.

Footnote: a Saint Cunning church is noted in Felix McKillop's book *Glenarm: A Local History*.

'Today the four cornerstones of the church are barely visible in a field called the Church Park.'

In his research, Felix discovered the location of the 'Church Park' field. He told me,

"A farmer in the area took me to the field ... he started scraping the grass with his foot... his foot was scraping the top of a flat stone. He moved to other areas, where he approximated the other three cornerstones would be ... to reveal the other stones. I was amazed to see this. Later I went back to measure the distances between the cornerstones. The measurements I made aligned with recorded measurements of the old church."

# Splintered Grief Unified

Christmas in Edinburgh with their daughter and family was a welcome, stress-free interlude for Frank and his wife Bridget. It had been a hectic year, coping with the prevailing winds of life that often stretched the boundaries of faith. They could let go, breathe deeply, relax, take time out, and focus on being in the moment. Their eldest grandchild, one of five, had just turned seventeen, with the expectation of university next year. It was a moment of serenity, removed from the everyday business of life when they wondered with incredulity how time had sprouted wings and flown swiftly away without them noticing. They didn't linger on the thought. It was enough to realise that their past was getting longer, while their future was resolutely heading in the opposite direction.

Always when visiting Edinburgh they trekked the Pentland Hills and the Braid Hills. On this visit, with the weather being refreshingly kind, they made the most of it. The morning air was fresh and crisp. It felt great to be alive. In the evenings everything softened and mellowed. Even the raucous rooks lost their voice. Slowly, since their arrival, their pressing cares and anxieties had eased quietly away.

On Christmas Eve, with their daughter's family, they made their way down through Braidburn Valley Park for midnight Mass in Saint Mark's Church in Oxgangs. Their Mass-going feet crunched the frosted grass under a starlit sky that rendered pocketed torches redundant. It was a familiar route past the library, down through roads lined with terraced houses to the little inconsequential church, tucked neatly away out of sight off the main thoroughfare. They always went to Saint Mark's when in Edinburgh. Frank had worshipped there when he was a student. He liked it. There was nothing pretentious about it, and they were always made welcome.

Once midnight Mass was over and happy Christmas greetings had been exchanged with strangers they made their way back home, with torches lighting their way beneath a darkened sky. Inside, with refreshments to hand, they settled. The seasonal wrapped gifts they had brought like the Magi for the babe in the manger, nestled comfortably in a pile under the Christmas tree.

Then the Christmas tradition of gift-giving got underway, as one by one all was revealed. There was never a hint of disappointment if a gift was unwanted or duplicated. But it wasn't just about giving. It was more about exchanging gifts.

The Magi received something in return for their long pursuit of an unusual star: the privilege of being present at a pivotal moment in the history of creation. For a moment, on the dawning of Christmas Day, they were the Magi, in receipt of something that couldn't be boxed and packaged: love.

All too soon, the Christmas season of goodwill to all men yielded to the necessities of everyday affairs, and it was time for them to return home and re-engage with the currents of life. They never stayed in Edinburgh to see in the new year. They preferred to be at home, away from all the exuberant celebrations, happy, after a good night's rest, to greet New Year's Day, like every other day and all that came with it, counting their blessings.

The short flight across the Irish Sea was uneventful. Back home on the North Antrim Coast, with Ayrshire clearly visible, they gathered up the mail accumulated behind the front door, checked the answering machine for messages, opened the windows to air the house, and settled to a nice cup of tea. With the nip that was in the air, it wasn't very long before the windows were closed and the central heating turned on. Frank was pouring Bridget a second cup of tea when she switched on the radio.

He realised then that the easy-going days in Edinburgh were over. Normality had returned. Bridget seldom listened to the radio. She used it as a suppressor, to subdue, to blank out sounds that irritated or annoyed her like Frank quietly sipping his tea. She was looking out the window at nothing in particular, anywhere but at him, a signal her anxieties had resurfaced much sooner than he had expected. Experience taught him it was best to say nothing because anything he

181

would say would only irritate her further. Bridget would open up and talk to him when she had made up her mind what to do, how to do it, and when to do it. That was how she was about some things. He was used to it.

About two years previously Bridget's eldest sibling Peter, feeling a bit under the weather with what he thought was a touch of flu, went to see his doctor. Following the initial consultation, blood tests and X-rays he was diagnosed with advanced lung cancer. Peter, at eighty-six years of age, was fit and active, had never been to see his doctor in his life before, had never smoked, and alcohol had never sullied his lips. It all seemed so unfair, the raw reality of life, beyond comprehension. It was something Bridget wrestled with.

His medical team tried to destroy the cancer with radiation therapy but the treatment failed. Then chemotherapy was tried and initially thought successful, but the cancer could not be tamed. It returned, emboldened, more aggressive than before. Surgery was mooted, but further investigation revealed that it was not an option. On a bright sunny morning, Peter's doctor apologetically uttered the words nobody ever wants to hear,

"I'm sorry. There's nothing more we can do."

For Bridget and Frank, from that moment their lives were on hold. To spend Christmas in Edinburgh was not an easy decision, but it was the right one. Their minds, especially Bridget's, were forced to focus elsewhere, if for only a short while. It was a necessary respite.

Peter shouldered his prognosis stoically, as he had done most things all his long life. He carried on working about the house and helping others as much as he could for as long as he could. Gradually he waned, stopped driving, working, and walking until he was receiving palliative care at home. But he was tough as old boots. He fought on. He wouldn't ever surrender his life. It would have to be wrenched from him.

Now back home, Bridget, desperate to know how her brother was, learned that his condition had not changed much. He tired easily and slept a lot. His family, and wider family circle, were reconciled to his passing. Watching and assisting

182

the slow passing of a person can be much more than wearisome and debilitating. Those in close attendance are forced to confront their mortality head-on.

For a little while, Bridget and Frank sat in silence. Suddenly the early evening stillness was shattered by the telephone's strident shrill. Startled, Bridget sprang to her feet, grabbed the phone, and, fearing the worst, gasped,

"Hello, hello." As she listened, her grip on the phone visibly tightened and her rigid body crumbled. Slowly she slumped down on to her seat, head bowed, shoulders rounded, mumbling,

"Oh, that's terrible. That's, awful." After listening some more Bridget said, "If there's anything we can do, don't hesitate," and with that, she cradled the phone. Knowing it was bad news Frank said nothing and waited. After an uneasy silence, Bridget abruptly said,

"Sheila's youngest child has been found dead at home." It wasn't what he expected to hear.

"What?" was all he could utter. Sheila was a close friend and neighbour. Her son Raymond, who was forty years of age, had been found dead at home that morning. Bridget sat stunned, disbelief registering on her ashen face. Frank knew that when Bridget had said,

"If there is anything we can do," she genuinely meant it, because her thoughts and concerns had immediately transferred to Sheila's family and lingered there. Frank had heard that phrase uttered so many times that it had lost its meaning. But, knowing Bridget, she meant what she said, and would find something useful to do without being asked.

Sheila and her family, deeply traumatised, couldn't cope with people calling to offer condolences. It was too much for them to bear. The funeral house was private. Raymond's funeral was a sad, sombre occasion. The sudden, untimely death of her neighbour's son had shifted Bridget's mind momentarily away from her brother Peter. But it was only a brief diversion. There was no hope for Peter in this life. Everyone, including Bridget, was reconciled to his passing. It

183

was only a matter of time, and time was ebbing quickly away from him. Hope for Peter was rooted firmly in the next life.

January eased into February. Peter slept through most hours of the day. His family bore silent witness. The driver in his arm drip-fed his medication as his breathing stretched, paused, slowed, and laboured. His ever-present family were by his side when he let go and quietly slipped away in his sleep. Even when death is expected, there is a finality when the last breath is expelled, and the skeletal frame that once supported life is redundant. For all silent bedside watchers there is a reality check, a, "Has he gone?" moment of disbelief, even though it was what they were expecting, hoping for – a happy release.

Everything about Bridget conveyed loss. It was as if a part of her had died. Her brother, the eldest of her fourteen siblings, had assumed a parental role with the passing of their parents in nurturing family cohesion, identity, and kinship. Being much younger than her brother, Bridget had looked up to him all her life and had turned to him when in need of advice. It was a sibling relationship that shaped, moulded, and reinforced her identity.

Over time, the unwelcome visitor, death, had nibbled Bridget's fourteen siblings down to six. With Peter's passing, as with the passing of eight of her other siblings, Bridget had little by little lost something of her self but found renewal, sustenance, and support in her own family. Peter's family given the nature of his illness had time to make all the necessary arrangements for his passing. In the end, all that needed doing was to prepare for when he would be returned home, readied in his coffin, in repose for mourners to pay their last respects.

He was laid out in his bedroom with the blinds half-closed. Flickering light from candles placed either side of the coffin created an atmosphere of prayerful serenity. Chairs arranged around the room facilitated those wishing to spend time in prayer and reflection. All was quiet and respectful. The family had selected some of the tools of his trade, symbols of his years spent providing for them, to go to the ground with him.

184

The church was packed for the funeral service. Family members read the chosen readings, grandchildren presented other symbols of their grandfather's trade, and the congregation had cause to laugh when the priest wondered aloud what the deceased, a joiner by trade, would say when he met the carpenter from Nazareth. It was a welcome moment of levity amid an ocean of grief. After the interment, many anecdotes were exchanged that added colour and dimension to Peter's eighty-six years of life.

Later, back home, Bridget and Frank reflected on past times shared with Peter. It was over forty years ago when they moved into their home. It was an old house that needed a lot of work doing to it, but, being young, they thought nothing of it. That is until they found themselves with the roof space conversion underway just before Christmas when snow fell non-stop for three days. They spent that Christmas with their young family under canvas. Not in a tent, although that might have been better. The canvas, a tarpaulin draped over the open roof, kept the snow at bay. Peter worked with Frank nights and weekends, helping to renovate and make their home habitable. In return Frank did the same for Peter, helping him to build his new house.

Two weeks after Peter's funeral, when some semblance of normality was returning, Peter's son Eamon called, looking for the addresses of family members living abroad to send them memorial cards marking his father's passing. Bridget was out at the time, but after a cup of tea and a chat with Frank and with the addresses in his hand, Eamon left and went about his business. He wasn't long out of the door when the phone rang and, thinking it was Bridget reminding him to attend to the casserole she had in the oven, Frank answered it.

It wasn't Bridget. It was her youngest sibling Norman, informing him rather bluntly that Bridget's younger brother Freddy had been found dead in bed that morning in Galway. The brother whose address he had just given to Eamon. Frank felt as if he had been hit by a four-by-two timber strut across the stomach. All the breath was knocked out of him. He

185

couldn't form a question, didn't know what to say. Eventually, he muttered,

"Are you sure? It can't be?" Crazy thoughts somersaulted through his head. "You must be joking." It wasn't a joke. He listened intently as Norman relayed the details of what had happened because he knew the interrogation he would be subjected to when he had to tell Bridget.

The details were sparse. His wife had brought him up a cup of tea and found him dead in bed where she'd left him half an hour before.

When the call ended he put the receiver down, slumped forward, and pressed his brow hard against the textured wallpaper. His arms dangled limply by his sides. How long he froze in that useless anguished gesture he didn't know. Bridget's two brothers and a neighbour's son had died within a few weeks of each other! Could it get any worse? Giving someone bad news by telephone from a distance was quite different from having to do it eyeball to eyeball. How was he going to tell Bridget when she came home? He didn't know.

He was sitting at the kitchen table with an untouched coffee when she walked in. She looked at him, and he knew from the look that she sensed something wasn't right.

"What's wrong, Frank?" she said. He tried to speak but no words left his mouth. "Are you alright?" she demanded, her frustration showing. He stuttered, telling Bridget that Peter's son had called to get the addresses to send out memorial cards. Then he just blurted out about the phone call from her brother Norman, telling him that her younger brother Freddy had been found dead in bed that morning.

Bridget looked at him as if he wasn't all there, then slowly her face registered disbelief and contorted. She reached for the back of a chair to steady herself and missed it, but he caught her before she hit the floor, managed her on to a chair, and made her some strong tea while she tried to take in everything he had said. After conducting a thorough interrogation, Bridget recovered sufficiently to start the process of phoning her remaining siblings to inform and be informed by them, if they knew more than she did, about what had happened. It was a long night. Nothing was certain, other than that her brother Freddy in Galway was dead.

Sleep eventually overcame them, but as the sun brightened the sky on Saturday morning, Bridget was up, not to greet the sun, welcome as it was, but to discover more about what had happened to Freddy. So began the relentless round of phone conversations with her siblings, each one energising the other. She was informed that Freddy's funeral was expected to be on the Monday coming. It all seemed surreal, confused, muddled, and too soon. He had just died yesterday, Friday, but for now, that was all the information there was to go on.

While Bridget was reacting and responding to the flow of information between her and her siblings, Frank was thinking about how they were going to get to Galway. Bridget wouldn't be able to cope with the long drive and the twenty-odd toll gates to be negotiated on the way. He couldn't drive because his left arm was in a sling. He had severely sprained his wrist two days before. As Saturday progressed from morning through afternoon towards evening, with Bridget still acting as an information conduit for relatives, Frank figured that the best way for them to get to Galway was by bus. They could be in Galway City early on Sunday evening, and accommodation close to the bus station was available. Making the journey by public transport would be good for them. It would remove all the stress of a very long drive, and they could use their bus passes there and back. They could travel for free.

*Every cloud has a sliver of silver in it,* Frank thought ironically.

As chance would have it, Bridget's phone calling yielded unexpected dividends. Bridget's other brother Ted and his wife Eileen were thinking along similar lines. In the end, they decided to make the long journey south-west to Galway as a foursome. A neighbour would drive them up to Belfast in good time to catch an early bus to Dublin that would connect with a Galway-bound bus. All was set fair as far as Frank was concerned.

It had gone long past ten o'clock on Saturday evening when Bridget eventually gave the telephone a rest. They hadn't even

187

thought about what they might need for what could be a longish stay in Galway. The hands-on the hall clock had long gone past midnight when they settled to sleep, content that all was readied for their early morning start.

On Sunday morning, after breakfasting early, they set about double-checking what they needed for their journey, especially their bus passes, euros, credit cards, mobile phones, and chargers, as well as all the other bits and pieces that women seem to be unable to do without. Content that they had everything, Bridget insisted that she take possession of the bus passes, cash, credit cards, and mobile phones for safekeeping, much to Frank's annoyance, but with only one useful arm there was little he could do to fend off her insistence. So, stripped of his manliness, for the first time in over fifty years of married life, he relaxed and waited for their ride to Belfast to arrive. Which it did ahead of time, announcing to their sleeping neighbours its arrival by sounding its horn. Bridget, anxiously waiting by the door, grabbed her weekend bag and rushed out to the waiting car. Frank followed less hurriedly behind, clutching his insignificant little bag.

The journey to Belfast was uneventful. When they gathered at the ticket booth to get their return bus tickets to Dublin and onward to Galway, the proverbial balloon went up. Bridget searched for her handbag but couldn't find it.

"Have you got my handbag, Frank?" she demanded, knowing full well he didn't. "I must have left it in the car." They hurriedly left the queue for bus tickets to search the car park, but their neighbour had long gone and with it, they thought, the handbag, containing their bus passes, cash, and credit cards, and everything else that needed safekeeping, including their mobile phones. Using her brother's phone, Bridget rang home in desperation to find out if the handbag was where she had left it, at the foot of the stairs beside the front door. It was. What a relief. But before ending the call she instructed her son to be sure to move the handbag and put it in a safe place.

The irony of the safe keeper misplacing the things to be kept safe hit her husband like a shower of bus passes. They were now stranded in Belfast without the means of getting back home to pick up the handbag that had been left behind. Even if they had been able to go back and collect it and resume their journey it would have meant that they would not arrive in Galway until late on Monday. It was a fiasco. Then Bridget's brother quietly said,

"Nothing to worry about. I've got plenty of money on my card. Let's go," and that was that.

The journey to Dublin was stress-free and surprisingly quick. They didn't have long to wait for their connection to Galway. However, they were blissfully unaware that they were not boarding an express bus for the long east-to-west journey across Ireland, through many towns that were shrouded in veils of history.

For a while, Frank read a little booklet, in essence, a collection of reminiscences lauding the simplicity of rural Irish life in former times. As they journeyed on, he observed the easy familiarity between the bus driver and the passengers as they boarded along the way. But it was more than mere familiarity. It oozed conviviality. This observation was confirmed when a lady boarded in Ballinasloe and asked to be dropped off in Loughrea, where she was going to visit her sister. The driver, gentleman that he was, asked where her sister lived, and, when told, said,

"It's no problem. I'll drop you off there," and with that assurance, the lady took a seat at the front of the bus. Then, mobile phone to her ear, she conversed with her sister in Loughrea.

"Mary, it's me," says she. "I'll be at your door in twenty minutes."

"How do you know?" asked Mary, on the other end of the phone. The lady answered,

"Because the bus driver just told me." The bus driver, true to his word, pulled up and stopped across the street from where Mary stood, arms folded, waiting outside her front door.

Once courtesies had been exchanged the lady alighted and the bus moved on, but not too far. A well-dressed gentleman, the sort of man who might have been to America, Bridget's mother might have said, moved up from the rear of the bus to take the seat the lady had warmed and asked if the driver would let him off a bit further along the next street. The bit further along was about a mile, but what's a mile or two to a bus driver keeping to a timetable in rural Ireland? Time there has stood still for aeons.

Needless to say, the driver cheerfully obliged, and also responded en route to other similar requests. It was an insight into a microcosm of rural Irish life that Frank had long thought extinct. Smiling inwardly, he tilted his seat back, relaxed, and pondered what he had witnessed. Letting it seep into his consciousness, he thought,

*There's hope for us yet.*

It was five o'clock in the evening when they reached Galway. They booked into their hotel, freshened up, and later met in the lobby to make their way to Freddy's home. At reception, they discovered his home was not, as they thought, just outside Galway. It was some thirty miles further south of it, and to get there they had to take a taxi. There was nothing else for it.

On nearing where Freddy lived they were surprised to be greeted by signs at the side of the road labelled *Funeral House*, directing mourners to a side road off to their left. Their taxi driver explained that it was something neighbours did for families in that part of the country. But even with the helpful sign, they doubted they would have easily found the funeral house by themselves. The taxi, following the directional sign, left the asphalt road and proceeded slowly along a maze of gravel-surfaced lanes, to arrive after many twists and turns at a house with vehicles randomly parked outside it. They knew then that they had arrived at the funeral house and, with arrangements made with their driver when to be collected for the return journey to Galway, they made their way tentatively towards the front of the house.

The front door was ajar and music filtered out. It didn't sound to them like a house in mourning. It sounded more like a celebration, and this caused them to think momentarily that

190

perhaps they were at the wrong house. Apprehensively, crossing the threshold, they encountered a woman laden with plates of food, who, on seeing them, casually said in a kind of soft brogue,

"Come on in. Sure you're very welcome," and with that, she disappeared, to quickly return empty-handed, smiling a question. "And who would you be, then?"

She was a bit disconcerted when the unannounced visitors introduced themselves as the deceased's sister, brother, and in-laws. But, fair play to her, quick as a flash she regained her composure and ushered them into the room where Bridget's brother was laid out. All the time this drama was unfolding at the door the music continued: traditional music, jigs, reels, and hornpipes, punctuated by an occasional lament.

The coffin rested lengthwise on a black-draped bier in the candlelit room of repose. Brass candlesticks, two at the head and two at the foot of the coffin, guttered in the draught caused by an open corner curtained window. The tall clock stood erect, silenced, just inside the door. Its motionless hands wouldn't orbit its passive enamelled face again until the waking of the deceased was done, and that would be in more than a day or two. The only uncovered pictures in the room were the picture of the Sacred Heart of Jesus above the deceased on the wall and the photographs of Freddy with his family on the mantelpiece. The delicate fragrance of flowers picked in the woods and hedgerows around the place, including bluebells, primroses, and wild garlic, perfumed the room in competition with the incense smoke rising in wisps from a tallboy huddled in a corner diagonally opposite the coffin in the room of repose.

All the windows were shrouded by curtains, which shut out the outside world and focused attention within. Things that Freddy's loving hands had brought to useful life bore silent witness on little side tables. The bodhrán with its tipper, eloquent, silent testaments to Freddie's skill as a master carpenter and an accomplished musician, would never now feel the beat of his heart again. Nor would the hammer and chisels laid at the foot of his coffin ever again sing in his hands to craft wood, hard and soft, to the designs of his mind.

Chairs were arranged around the room for mourners to spend quiet time in prayer and contemplation. Freddy's children and grandchildren kept a constant vigil. Respectful silence in the room demanded muted conversation, and filtering laments from an adjoining room added solemnity to the waking.

After entering the room of repose they took seats as family and friends moved slowly around the open coffin, viewing and touching Freddy. After settling and composing herself Bridget rose, and they followed in procession for the ritual of viewing the deceased. Freddie looked peaceful, at ease, his well-worked hands in a final clasp as they silently filed past to return to their seats. Then a woman, with rosary beads in her hands, entered the room and invited those present to join her in a decade of the rosary.

No one left the room. The choice of the Joyful Mysteries was a surprise. In any other context it would have been incongruous, but not at an Irish wake. The Hail Marys were said with meaning and import. They sat for a long time, unravelling their knotted thoughts, letting gathered memories of Freddy scroll across the meadows of their minds.

As a child, he was always singing around the house. A bit of an oddball, his siblings thought back then. He was very young when his father went to ground.

Over time and distance and changes in circumstances memories accrued are, by nature, fragmented, but none the less, especially at the time when a loved one has passed away, deeply cherished. The continuum of memory, in reality, is a continuous disordered and fragmented collection of shared experiences at particular points in time. In large families, the eldest siblings often have little memory of the youngest siblings, having moved through adolescence and left home before they were born. But they may well accumulate shared memories as time shrinks the gulf of age between them.

Slowly, gently, tentatively at first, conversations with Freddy's wife, son, and daughters began with hugs of commiseration and condolence and continued as love and kinship banished formality. Many memories were shared, huddled together in that room of repose, in Freddie's presence.

At midnight another decade of the rosary was recited, this time the Glorious Mysteries.

There was shock, intense grief, loss, and heartfelt sadness in the funeral house, but there was also an obvious heart-warming sense of celebration for the life of Freddie as they knew and loved him. In the adjoining room, the musicians played their music and traditional singers gave voice to their chosen words.

"Do you remember him singing this one?" a voice would ask before offering in a rendition of a song from Freddy's repertoire. It was a respectful musical celebration of a musician who was one of them, one of their own in many ways. In a little kitchen area at the back of the room, ladies busied themselves serving food and refreshments.

Everything that was happening around them was in many ways different from what they had experienced at Peter's and their neighbours' son's passing. It was celebratory. Frank could sense Bridget was more at home here, more comfortable. Or perhaps more at peace would be a better way of putting it. It was an entirely different, comforting experience. Culture and custom shape responses when grief is visited on families in different ways. It was an awakening in the west for Bridget and Frank.

They stayed much longer at the funeral house than intended, the craic was that good. When they had arrived they had braced themselves, expecting shock, grief, sorrow, anguish, and tears, which there were in abundance. But when leaving, grieving too, they felt strangely buoyant, uplifted, and inwardly at ease. In the taxi back to their hotel, they chatted about their first experience of waking the dead in the west of Ireland. The taxi driver, a middle-aged genial gentleman, added colour and flavour to their discourse.

It was long past midnight when they reached their hotel, bade each other goodnight, and retired, in the hope of a good night's sleep. Freddy's funeral Mass was set for noon, so they could, if they wished or needed, sleep in a while longer in the morning. But sleep didn't come easily for Bridget and Frank, as Bridget rewound in her head all that had happened when they were in the funeral house. It was something that neither of them

193

had experienced before. Frank tried as best he could to explain that the custom of waking the dead had its origins in Celtic culture, where mourners kept vigil with their dead until they went to ground.

"It's like when someone is terminally ill back home. The family sit with them. It's the same thing," he said. And he went on explaining that the viewing of the body was an important feature of death rituals in many cultures. The tradition of waking, except for the viewing of the body, had waned in urban areas of Ireland but it was still custom and practice in rural Ireland. They bandied about the notion of waking the dead far into the early hours of the morning agreeing that there was some logic to it. After all, Bridget said,

"We should be happy for a loved one to be going to the better place we call heaven. Sure isn't it the better place for us all, Frank?" Agreeing wholeheartedly with her deduction, Frank added,

"Sure isn't better to see the dead off with prayers, free of their cares, and to make music to lift the hearts of the ones in sorrow left behind? Sure that's what's waking the dead is all about." Quietly Bridget added,

"We were privileged to be there tonight." Contented, Bridget found sleep. Frank lay awake for a while thinking,

*When all's said and done there aren't too many folk in a rush to kiss goodbye to this valley of tears with all its pains and aches.* With much food for thought, he spent a restless night.

Monday morning dawned under a low, foreboding overcast sky, wet, cold, and miserable. Gone were the relaxed uplifting feelings of the night before. Anxiously they made their way to the village church for the funeral Mass. The disarming, unpretentious little church, built before the great famine in the 1800s, set well back from the road was strangely comforting. Modest and unassuming outside, there was nothing ornate about it inside. It was in every way in keeping with its setting and history. It was humbly functional.

They joined the folk gathered outside the church awaiting the arrival of the hearse, and when the coffin was shouldered

194

they joined the cortège as the musicians who played at the wake musically lamented the arrival of their friend. Once the preliminaries were over, they found a pew with the rest of the family. It was a simple but moving service, enriched by traditional music played with feeling plain for all to hear. Symbols of Freddy's life were placed on the altar by his grandchildren. Readings chosen by the family were read by his daughters. When Mass ended Freddy was taken to his place of rest lamented again by his musician friends.

After the interment, with the musicians playing happy music in another room, they quietly took their leave of the grieving family at Freddy's house and made their way to Galway bus station. They had done all they could to help ease the heavy burden of sudden loss suffered by Freddy's family. As the gravel crunched under their feet on the way to the gate the sound of music drifted after them, lightening their steps.

*That's probably what a wake's all about*, Frank thought, humming the lament. *To lighten your step going forward into an uncertain future.*

The journey home was uneventful. They had express buses all the way, with connections in their favour. There wasn't much conversation. They journeyed in silent contemplation, searching and adding to their respective archives of memory.

It was late in the evening when they sat down at home looking out of their big picture window. The moonlight was glittering on the dark, tranquil, murmuring sea in the North Channel below. The silhouetted Mull of Kintyre stretched out a welcome hand. As they pondered over their visit to Galway, snippets of memory ebbed and flowed. Frank said,

"I don't remember Freddy at our wedding."

"Ah, sure that was a long time ago. He would only have been a wee boy back then, and didn't we have a lot going on that day," Bridget said. Setting her tea down, she got up and left the room, to return with a bundle of photograph albums. Taking an album each, they searched for a photograph of Freddy. It took a while but they found one. It was a group photograph, with Freddy sitting cross-legged on the grass in front with his

195

longish, unruly curly blonde hair all over his face. They sat looking at the gangly boy and laughed.

Then Frank said,

"You know my one abiding memory of Freddy was at our daughter's wedding in Edinburgh. Do you remember?" Bridget started to laugh.

"Of course I do. I'll never forget it. Sure didn't him and his wife at the wedding reception get up and sing one of those old folk songs that went on and on forever? Wasn't I glad when it ended? Can you remember what it was called?"

"Aye, I remember it all right. Sure I'll never forget it. I'd never heard it before and I haven't heard it since thank God. It was called 'The Rattlin' Bog'. I think there were about twenty or more verses to the blessed thing. Freddy beat on the bodhrán and sang while his wife tooted on the tin whistle, singing alternate verses. Sure they nearly emptied the room," Frank said, laughing.

They sat and talked as the star-sprinkled sky and the moon's bright face faded behind gathering black clouds. Perhaps they would be spared rain tonight. The oily, languid Irish Sea slowly lost its glitter and became sullenly ominous. In the space of a few weeks after Christmas Bridget had lost two brothers and a young neighbour. Death, always the unwelcome visitor, had left its indelible imprint again.

*Everyone has to cope with death when it visits*, Frank mused. *There's no escaping. It shadows us from birth. It's all part of the mystery of being. One thing is for sure, there is nothing like a wake in the west of Ireland.*

Outside the darkness of night was giving way to a glimmer of dawning light in the east. They sat in silent contemplation, the sun on its eternal journey, forming a new day, filled them with hope.

"We emerge from the comforting darkness of the womb into the bright new light of an unfamiliar world to inhabit until in death we return to the welcoming darkness of Mother Earth," Frank said.

"Yes, but we grow in understanding, and our faith sustains us on our journey of discovery," Bridget responded. "Death is

196

the threshold we cross to enter the eternal world. I think of it now as going home. The body returns to clay. The soul is going home."

The wake in the west was an experience that Bridget and Frank would never forget. It was in every sense an awakening. In some inexplicable way, it unified the deaths of Freddy, Peter, and their neighbour's son Raymond. Although the three death scenarios they had experienced were distinctly different, each with its narrative satisfied the dramatic unities of occurrence, time, and place. Taken together, they were more than the sum of their parts. They were a holism that encouraged shared reflections on the multifaceted characteristics of each of the deceased.

In the comfort of faith, there is no need to grieve for the dead. They have gone to a better place, a place free of pain and suffering. In truth, the more they thought about it, the more energised and able they felt to embrace the day dawning before them, with all that would be in it.

In the tall ash tree at the back of the house, a blackbird cleared its throat and tried a song. They knew then that spring was in the offing. The larks would be rising in the clear air up on Sallagh Braes behind them, and the swallows too would soon be winging their way back to liven their skies. Comfortable and content, they nestled together to witness another sunrise.

Printed in Poland
by Amazon Fulfillment
Poland Sp. z o.o., Wrocław

61880642R00114